THE STORY OF YOU

Julie Myerson was born in Nottingham in 1960.
Her previous novels include *Sleepwalking*, *The Touch*,
Me and the Fat Man, *Laura Blundy* and *Something
Might Happen*. She lives in London.

JULIE MYERSON

The Story of You

VINTAGE BOOKS
London

Published by Vintage 2007

4 6 8 10 9 7 5

First published in Great Britain in 2006 by Jonathan Cape

Vintage
Random House, 20 Vauxhall Bridge Road,
London SW1V 2SA

www.vintage-books.co.uk

Addresses for companies within The Random House Group Limited can be
found at: www.randomhouse.co.uk/offices.htm

The Random House Group Limited Reg. No. 954009

A CIP catalogue record for this book
is available from the British Library

ISBN 9780099497097

Typeset in Bembo by Palimpsest Book Production Ltd,
Grangemouth, Stirlingshire

The Random House Group Limited supports The Forest Stewardship
Council® (FSC®), the leading international forest-certification organisation.
Our books carrying the FSC label are printed on FSC®-certified paper.
FSC is the only forest-certification scheme supported by the leading
environmental organisations, including Greenpeace. Our
paper procurement policy can be found at
www.randomhouse.co.uk/environment

MIX
Paper from
responsible sources
FSC® C016897

Printed and bound in Great Britain by Clays Ltd, St Ives plc

for Jono with big love

Someone should take this girl in his arms and hold her tight, I thought. Probably someone other than me. Someone qualified to give her something.

Haruki Murakami, *The Wind-Up Bird Chronicle*

PARIS

It begins with snow, the story of you. I've tried so many other beginnings. I've had it begin with heat, with light, in another country – wilder, dirtier, poorer – in another bed, not this one. But each time I come zooming back to that house in the most run-down part of the city and that freezing black night when we kissed for so many hours, you and me – a ferocious kind of kissing that took us both by surprise, coming as it did out of nowhere and going on until the sky grew pale and we both slept.

It begins with snow – and there we both are, frozen on the edge of that long-ago student room, horizontal, half-undressed, laughing, threaded together. I am just nineteen, you are almost twenty. Not so young but young enough to imagine we're already pretty old – right bang there in the middle of things. And the room is large, high-ceilinged and smelling of winter cold and damp, and the bed is a stained and sagging single mattress pushed right up against the wall. Next to it, a saucer full of ash, a pack of Rizlas (yours), a pair of unlaced trainers, an inside-out pink lurex sock (mine). Not much else in the room except, in the bed, the two of us, suddenly knitted together – tongue finding tongue, lip wet against lip, cool sweetness of saliva slipping from mouth to mouth.

They said it was too cold to snow, but flakes have been squeezing themselves out all night – at first tiny and pitiful, then grander, fatter, shaken hard and fast through the dark night sky. Several long hours from now we'll wake in that curtainless room to the perfect bright silence that is snow.

It begins with snow – and with a pearl. Not a real one, foolish boy, a fake pearl, made of plastic. Shiny and creamy, toy jewellery, a plastic pearl from a plastic necklace. Most likely it came out of a cracker – for it's the kind of thing I wear back then, along with the sparkly socks, old washed-out coloured vests and crumpled satin flowers in my hair.

My dungarees are pale yellow, baggy round the knees, with one clip always missing, my earrings are mauve plastic daisies. I am a disco girl, a boogie queen, a girl without past or future, who never eats enough and does her washing at the launderette and cries most Sundays just from pure, uncomplicated loneliness.

And I'm playing with the necklace – nervous as I lie there in the darkness whispering to you, not that close to you and certainly not touching you, and nervous but kind of burstingly happy as well, when suddenly I pull too hard on the string and – oh – the whole thing breaks.

The pearls spill everywhere.

They go spilling on the old brown nylon carpet which is full of crumbs and now, a scattering of plastic pearls. And you look straight at me and, leaning up on your elbow with your head propped on your hand, you reach out in the dark room, unlit except for the blue flame of the Calor gas heater and you pick one up and before I can say or do anything you put it in your mouth.

Hey, I say, give that back.

My face is surprised but I think I am laughing.

You shut your eyes and shake your head. Your skin is pale and sad from too many drugs and no sleep, your hair straggly white-blond, long enough to touch your collar. You look like an exhausted angel but inside you are most definitely a boy. Once you left a shirt on the back of a chair in the living room and I put it to my face and breathed in your smell and liked it so much, I felt ashamed.

Give it back, I say again, though I don't know if I mean it or not. We've pulled the fire up close, too close, and the left side of my cheek is burning.

Come and get it.

What?

Come and get it, you say, keeping your odd, light eyes on me. Sometimes, in those days, you frighten me just a little but it's a sweet damp fear that makes my heart turn over and over till I go soft inside.

So I move towards you and – well, it's a long time ago now but I like to think that as I put my hand out to touch your mouth with the pearl in it, you stop me. That instead you reach out with your long boy's hand and cup the back of my neck, my hair, and pull me gently to you, showing

3

me what you mean me to do – to take it with my mouth not my hand, to take it from you just like that.

My heart turns over, the way it has to. I am breathless with nerves.

Or maybe not. Maybe I just take a breath and move towards you anyway, made bolder by the daring of what you've just done. And maybe I touch your lips gently, shyly, with my almost open mouth and before I can go further you part my lips with your tongue and slide the pearl in, from your mouth to mine. Wet and warm, the hot shock of saliva. And once the little pearl is in my mouth – a hard, light bullet of plastic – maybe you press your face to mine and take it back again from my mouth, still holding my head in both your rough boy's hands and leaving your tongue there a good long time. Your hands pressing my hair to my ears so I am briefly invisible to the world. Your tongue sliding in and against mine – promise of a deeper touch. Oh, baby.

Or maybe not. Does it even matter now? What I know is we move that pearl between us for some moments, before we lose it in the bed, a poor forgotten small fake thing we have no need of any more – because by then it's real and no one in the world can stop us continuing what we've started.

I am just nineteen, you're almost twenty. Only months between us but they mean a lot of life, those months back then. You know things, but I don't know you, not really. You're an American. You come from New Jersey. You have a guitar in a battered black case with stickers on and you touch it all the time even when you're not playing. You never sleep, you just crash and now I think of it, that word's entirely apt: sleep can claim you at any time and anywhere, a violent and final thing.

And we make each other laugh. You are funny and so am I, though not as funny perhaps as we'd both like to think we are. Sometimes, though, I'm afraid of you. Sometimes I don't know what to think of the things you say and do. Once, on the landing, you start to yell at me about some small thing and for a few quick seconds I can't take my eyes away from your face. I can't resist you – I never could – you know that now. If you come into a room just as I am about to leave it, I have to change my plans and stay – always, just in case you do or say something interesting.

I really liked it, you know, that you weren't cool, that your face was so open, that it told me everything.

You liked it?

Yeah. Course I did. It was good. If you really want to know, it turned me on.

You'll say this to me one night in the very far future, lying close up against me and cupping my face in your hands all over again.

And I'll smile – with surprise but also because it's all so funny.

Easy to say that now, I'll reply as I gaze at the sweet, familiar curve of your upper lip, but you didn't want me, not back then, you know you didn't. Whatever you say now, you had other things on your mind.

What things, silly girl?

I don't know. Just things. And you know something? All I ever wanted back then was for you to want me.

You'll start to laugh.

Don't laugh, I'll say.

Oh, you'll go, laughing some more and shaking your head, oh foolish girl, it's just that you didn't understand a thing back then, you didn't know the half of it. It wasn't about wanting, not at all. Those games we all played, they were about something else entirely.

But what – what were they all about?

And I'll ask you this, not because I really need to know, but because I want to see, right now after all this time, how you'll answer. And you'll look at me and touch my face for a quick second but you'll say nothing and I'll think how after all you're just like the photo I still have of you somewhere – secretly stashed at the bottom of a box, smiling all the time beneath a pile of other photos, impossible to forget, flat and shiny and perfect, my old love. Telling me nothing but acting all the time as if you had the answers, as if you knew, as if you know.

All the same, whatever you might try to tell me one day, the kissing is a total surprise, something that comes out of that unexpected cold blue night, an extra.

You have on a grey jersey, frayed at the wrists and with holes in both elbows. You yawn a lot. Your face is white. It makes me ache, the sight of your shirt showing through the patched wool. I have on my dungarees. You smoke and cough too much, I giggle. I have to take my daisy earrings off because they dig into the lobes of my ears when you push me back on the pillow and roll your face against mine. You smell exactly as I knew you would, of boy but of cigarette too – a sweet, ashy, musky smell – and, faintly, of yesterday's onions.

I don't mind it. I would like any smell of yours and that's the truth. Your grandfather was from Dublin and loved the feel of pianos under his fingers and when you told me his name and the size of shoe he took, my eyes filled up with tears just because he belonged to you, because he did his best for the family, selling pianos, and because you were a part of him.

You look in my eyes and then you laugh.

What? I say, though I know you're only thinking what I'm thinking.

Nice, you say, this is nice.

Your voice is low and tight.

Don't you think, Rosy, that this is nice?

Mmm, I say, it is, it's definitely nice.

Neither of us have ever done anything, not really, but you are good at looking as if you have. We keep our clothes on the whole time, though I like to think maybe you have a go at taking mine off. Or maybe not. Anyway I can tell you now I would never have let you. Back then I am fantastically, crucially shy, a girl on the edge. All I've ever done is write poetry and think about the things I'll never dare do. So we kiss and keep our clothes on, and then we can't help it, we sleep. A big silence comes down as the snow falls.

I can see everything, feel everything, just as if it's now, today, five minutes ago. Your pale face smiling at me, the terrible blunt coldness of the air, the warm place on the sheets where finally you creep on top of me and stay there, breathing, pressing yourself on me gently till my thighs aren't there any more. Till I'm not there – the rest of me, dissolved.

And, beyond us, the rest – the room, the house, the big old house, where a bomb once exploded its way into the bricks and people, or so we've been told. Now rented to students who'll manage without a fridge – painted magnolia, awaiting developers.

Here it is, the house. The creak of the uncarpeted stairs, someone's philosophy books piled upside down on the third step up. The Average White Band poster peeling off the landing wall, the ugly brown stain in the bath down the passage where the plug doesn't fit and the hot water is never sufficient, the dirty wooden floor which gives you splinters, the soles of my feet grown grey from padding across it.

And then, the washing-up rota no one pays any attention to. The joints and spliffs and full-up ashtrays, the mugs with fag ends floating in them, the milk turned green, the used plates covered in a dried orange sauce and stacked on the record player. The perpetual smell of garlic and bolognese – the only thing you boys can ever cook – and the dealers, the animals in black and brown leather who sit at our kitchen table and stare at their knees and hardly ever speak.

Money piled for the payphone. Trainers piled on the windowsill, next to a bottle of milk. Nights of *Dark Side of the Moon*. The sour and overflowing kitchen bin which no one ever empties. The boys called Niall and Gerry and those whose names we never even know.

My mum worries. She doesn't know why I want to share a house with so many boys. I tell her there are two of us. Two girls and six boys. I tell her that it's safer, with boys. I tell her this as a picture flashes into my mind: our front door left swinging open into darkness when someone comes home too wrecked to close it. I don't tell her this. Instead, when she says it's cheaper in hall and there are washing machines, I reply that it's more fun here and there's a launderette on the corner.

Which isn't quite true. And anyway none of us wear clean clothes back then. We all smell the same – of tobacco, of warm skin and – sometimes, in my case – Charlie by Revlon, though the girl in the magazine ad has long blonde hair and a blue trouser suit and a lot of confidence and I have none of these things.

Baby?

I don't know if you're awake. You open your eyes – same colour now as the darkness – and look at me a moment but then you close them again. You don't need to see anything, don't need to know anything, this will do for now. I know how you feel – I feel it too, I feel exactly the same. Our futures are out there somewhere, beyond the bed, the ashtray and the sparkly sock, but we don't care, we're smiling, you're still smiling – we feel the same, we know that.

This has just happened to us and it might be anything or nothing, it might go either way. Strange things happen. They said it was too cold to snow but just a glance at the window tells us they're wrong.

There I am, moving in against you, carefully. Your hair touches my face and I feel your lips on the edge of my ear and I shiver and I feel the shiver everywhere, in places I've never shivered before.

I don't love you, not yet, not then. This is then,

remember? This is just the beginning. I think I know every-thing, but what I can have no idea of is this: that you're about to leave an imprint on me. A sensual, lasting imprint by which I'll end up measuring everything else, all my life, always – every man, every touch, every kiss, everything, pretty much for ever.

It begins with snow. It always does.

Snow was squeezing itself out of a frozen sky on the morning more than twenty years later when I finally called Tom's mobile and asked him to come home.

Now?

His voice was shaky and afraid as I knew it would be. Why? What is it? Are you all right?

I'm sorry, I told him, I can't talk. Please. Just come.

I heard him take a breath. He said nothing but I could hear him wondering what to do, what to ask me next.

Has something happened? he said finally.

Something had, oh yes it had, but I could not answer him, I could not speak. I felt that if I did, something worse might happen, something else. I'd never felt so out of control of my body, as if the whole of me might overflow at any moment.

I could feel my shirt's cool wetness on my chest, an hour of crying. I'd managed to get Finlay and Jack off to school before the tears started, but after that it had been quick. I'd fallen apart. Crawled up the stairs all undone on hands and knees. I am a bad person, said the voice in my head, and my life has reached a halt, called a halt, this halt, this terrible halt, and it is all of my own making.

Nicole? Tom was saying and I could hear so much

concern in his voice that it broke me up. Nicole, are you still there?

I'm still here, I whispered.

Outside, tiny flakes were drifting sideways past the lamp-post. It wouldn't settle, I knew that. As each one touched the pavement it dissolved to nothing, a frozen stain beneath a bleached-out sky.

It begins with snow and with a woman who must tell her husband the truth before she dissolves to nothing.

I don't do this lightly. She doesn't do it lightly. It took me a very long time to dial his number. Mobiles have long numbers. There are many chances to change your mind, to hang up. Several times I'd managed all but the last three digits and then stopped.

Why? Why do it? Wait. Wait and think.

And I'd hunched my knees up in that bed of ours and I'd rested my head on my hands and I'd sobbed. Because I knew that pressing the last three would be the thing that changed this family of ours, its shape, its history, for ever.

For a while I could not do it and then something snapped and my fingers worked faster than me and I remembered the last few weeks and then I could do it, I did it and I let him answer.

It's me.

Nicole. Sweetie. (An intake of breath.) Are you OK?

There was dread in his voice. He knew already, how could he not know? The one thing about Tom is he always knows.

No, I said. No, Tom. I'm sorry but I'm not OK.

Fifteen minutes later, his key in the door.

Nic?

He leaned his bike against the wall of the narrow hall and called up to me as I knew he would. He called me Nic. Nicole. Not my real name but what he'd always called me, since he first found it out, lying on top of me and laughing and kissing my eyes, his fist full of my hair, full of questions – in the days when he still wanted to know things.

It's my middle name, I said, in a voice of wonder as if I'd only just heard it myself.

Nicole? he said. Really? I like that. That's gorgeous.

I gazed at him with hope in my eyes. I wanted to be gorgeous.

Hello, Nicole, he said, and he never called me Rosy again. Rosy became someone else – Rosemary Nicole McArthur, published poet, OK just one small volume and three years ago now, but still. The first real poem I ever wrote – in that I allowed it to have a beginning, middle and end – I entered in a competition. I submitted it in disguise – R. N. McArthur.

But it's about babies, Tom laughed. You really imagine they're going to think it's by a man?

I didn't care. It won.

Nicole, Rosemary, Nic, Rosy. Sometimes you can step outside of a name. Just for a moment or two you can step outside of it and there's the name and there are you, stranded and clueless on the outside, and for a few unnerving moments it's possible to see it clearly for what it is. A name, a word you call someone – a brief flavour on the tongue, stronger or sweeter depending on what you think or know of that person. But how does that leave you, the person? Nameless and stranded, I think.

You're a chameleon, Tom used to say, in a slightly disappointed voice, as if that explained it all. Or, You're the most exciting person I know, he'd say, and that too would be in a sad voice, as if a part of him was already preparing to lose me.

Rosemary McArthur, my name on the spine of a book. Rosemary N. McArthur, except we took the N out at proof stage. Even Jack was impressed.

Hey, you're just like John Hegley, he said, when the package arrived and I ripped the brown paper off. I had sixteen copies lined up with perfect neatness on my shelf to the left of my desk and I looked at them still almost every day and I wondered, who does she think she is, this woman with her paper and her words?

Nic?

I knew what he'd be doing. I knew he'd be unclipping his cycle helmet, glancing worriedly up the stairs as he did it. I knew he'd dump his bag and lay his gloves, one on top of the other, on the second step of the stairs and unzip his jacket which, like his helmet, would be glistening with flakes of snow turning fast to wet. I knew he would hang the jacket over the banister knob, where it would later, eventually, be caught by a passing child and slip off to the floor. Then he'd take the stairs two at a time.

It begins with snow, always with snow. A freezing cold January, midway through the term, a winter like we've never known before, the light popping and crackling with cold, water frozen in the pipes, the electricity bill still unpaid.

The house is on the edge of the city, off the big grey

main road where the buses slide and grunt up and down towards the town. No central heating, in winter we all wear our coats and hats indoors. And we've run out of gas cylinders, the bright blue heavy ones you have to get delivered. Or let's just say that you and the others have – leaving the heaters on all night as you smoke till dawn.

Your room-mate is reading sociology and wears dark fingerless gloves even in bed. He has spots under his beard and you say he's a freak but he's not as bad as the boy upstairs who tapes bin bags to his windows and lives in darkness and once touched my bottom on the stairs. I try never to be alone with him. If I hear him put the kettle on, I skip coffee and go straight to lectures.

One night we see a ghost on the landing – a blurry shape, frozen for one second in the half-darkness.

It's the guy who got bombed, you all tease, come back to seek vengeance, and you laugh and make spook noises and everyone thinks it's really funny. Except for me, I don't, I'm afraid and I don't sleep for a week.

Another night the ceiling in your room starts to fall in – plaster dust spilling on your bed. By the next day the hole is bigger. You ask if you can come and sleep in my room, in the other bed, just for one night?

Why?

We are sitting at the big wooden table in the living room with our going-cold mugs of coffee. There are others in there. You don't look at me. You're concentrating on your Bic lighter, flicking and flicking it, trying to light a cigarette. All over the table is loose tobacco and Rizla papers, someone's stained woollen scarf discarded among the mess.

Because you have some gas left and because there's plaster

all over my bed, you say in a take-it-or-leave-it voice, keeping your eyes fixed on the lighter.

I hesitate. The girl I share my room with has gone home to Sussex for three days.

Go on, you say as a tiny flame appears, just tonight, Rosy, please. You don't understand how fucking cold I am.

You frown hard at the flame and the cigarette lights. I look at you. I can see it on your face and body, how cold you are. But then you're always cold. Your clothes are thin and threadbare, you have no warm things at all, not even a coat. In the winter you still wear a thin, grey pinstripe jacket, worn out at the elbows and with the hem all undone. We don't know if you're rich or poor, all we know is your dad was a clever man who died and that you're a student in a foreign place and you can't afford to go home much. At Christmas when we go back to our families, you stay on alone in the house and work in a bar.

Alone in the house. It takes another twenty years before that breaks my heart.

Go ahead, I say, I'm sure she won't mind.

You glance at me. Despite everything you look surprised.

You're sure? Smoke comes out of your nose and you pick a thread of tobacco off your lip.

I smile.

And so you slide under the blanket on her bed which is right next to mine and I turn out the light and you turn over, away from me. I look at the top of your head for a long time. It's very still but I know you're not asleep. The room is quiet. I can't hear your breath. I can't hear anything.

Hey, Rosy, you say after a while, d'you want to talk?

★   ★   ★

It was very cold that first morning in the hotel, colder even than the day before. One or two tiny flakes were floating down out of the darkness. I knew that even if the snow settled it would be slush by breakfast time.

The whole thing was Tom's idea – he arranged everything, two nights in Paris, first-class on the Eurostar. It was supposed to be a surprise but in the end he had to tell me because of planning what to do with the boys. We left Finlay with Tom's mother and Jack went to a friend's, an arrangement which delighted him. Ever since he was born, Jack liked to be anywhere at all but home. Nothing was more exciting to him than a travel cot in a strange house with new people.

Fin, though, was the exact opposite. Last time we did a long weekend away, he'd stayed with a friend from school, but was too homesick to have fun. He wouldn't say anything when I spoke to him on the phone but I could tell from the long pauses and the drooping tightness in his voice. They do everything differently from us, he told me when I finally picked him up. Two hours of homework and no TV on a school day. I don't mean to be nasty or anything but they're really awful people.

The hotel was the strangest place – white all over, everything white. White sofas, white walls, white beds, white corridors. Something of the lunatic asylum about it, though I wouldn't have said so to Tom. Large but intimate and chic, he'd said, reading from the brochure about where we were going – and fucking expensive, he added, sliding his hands down inside my jeans.

There was an entirely white foyer filled with strobes of pink and green light. A long white leather sofa, the kind which seats about a dozen people, and a huge gas fire made of pebbles which gave out no warmth when you stretched your hand towards it.

No warmth from the bar people either. The girl in a white shirt didn't allow even the smallest glimmer of a smile at Tom as she shovelled ice into a tall metal jug. We arrived at three in the afternoon and because they were still getting our room ready, we had a complimentary Grey Goose vodka on the sofa and Tom kissed my neck until I shuddered.

My Nic, he said. My beautiful Nic.

I smiled. It felt weird to have vodka at three in the afternoon but then this was our anniversary and we were child-free. My thighs felt like they were sticking to the leather even though I had tights on.

I hope Fin's all right, I said.

We're not going to talk about the kids, he told me sternly, and though I knew what he meant, my heart crinkled up as it always did when Mary came into my head.

The hotel was so chic that the rooms were opened not by key or card but by finger-sensor. This meant you stuck your finger in the hole and there'd be a click and then you could push the door open.

Mine didn't work at first so I was locked out and had to get Tom to do it and so Tom had to call the man to do my finger all over again. Not a man really but a boy – about eighteen years old and a beautiful wide-open face and so bilingual you'd think he was English but he wasn't. The hotel was pretty new and he said he was proud to have worked there ever since it opened. He was at the Ritz before. So many old people there, he said with a frown, I really had enough if you want to know. That place, it felt like a morgue.

The boy touched the sensor to see what was wrong. It seemed to be working for him.

That's funny, he said.

The corridor we all stood in was dark and hot and the carpet under our feet felt thick enough to trip us. I had this strange feeling – I kept wanting to look behind me and I didn't know why.

At home, Tom told the boy, this woman can fuse lights just by touching them. I'm not joking.

The boy held my wrist gently and placed my finger back in the slot.

You have to shut your eyes and concentrate incredibly hard, he said, or it won't work.

I shut my eyes and Tom laughed.

You can get her every time, he said, and the boy smiled but didn't laugh.

Try it now please, he said. I put my finger in and it clicked.

Da, da! he said.

Thanks a lot, said Tom, and as the boy walked away down the corridor, a thread of fear snuck around my heart.

As soon as we were in the room, Tom wanted sex.

Come here, he said, and pulled me on the bed which was white and washed with palest pink light just like downstairs. Like the corridor, the whole room was too hot – the sort of heavy hotness you get in hotels that makes you just want to give up and lie down. Next to the bed was a control panel. Fin would have adored it.

Look, I said, trying to sound lite, buttons!

I pressed one and the bed turned apple green. Then another and the room went dark like under water. Then another and half the window's curtains swished back with an electronic noise and the TV sputtered on. I looked outside and saw there was a courtyard, tall shutters, black iron railings, all so perfectly foreign it looked like a backdrop to a film or something. It was beginning to snow.

Look, I said, snow.

I felt faraway, as if I was in a film myself. The sad and fearful feeling was still with me, but receding. Tom was laughing.

Press another of those and the whole place might explode.

If we're lucky, I said.

Sexy, he said. Mmm. Love among the ruins.

He wasn't going to stop mentioning sex. The TV had an episode of *Friends* with subtitles. Monica was sitting on a sofa next to Phoebe. Tom zapped it off and pulled me onto him and somehow got my skirt up and my knickers off.

I do love you, he said. I love you when you're happy.

In the night I woke suddenly to hear the burr of the fan in the bathroom, as if someone had switched the light on, though I could see they hadn't as there was no sign of light, only the moon streaming coolly between the curtains.

I listened again.

Very quiet, beneath the sound of the fan, I thought I could hear a voice. It was a murmur – the indistinct murmur of a boy's voice, or a young man's – not saying anything that I could make out but muttering softly all the while, a bit like someone dropping something then picking it up again then dropping it again and cursing quietly to himself.

Straightaway, with my heart banging crazily, I sat up in the bed but as soon as I did the voice stopped – well, of course, I thought, because it's a dream, it has to be. It certainly wasn't Tom – and I turned my head just to check and saw that he was sleeping beside me with his mouth wide open and one leg and his bottom flung out of the sheet, somehow managing, as he always did, to keep all the covers over on his side.

The boy's voice came again and this time I could hear actual words – Oh fuck it, I thought I heard and, Oh god. God, god, god. And there was a slight tearing sound, a dense crackle, halfway between paper and cloth, which made my bones go stiff.

My eyes were wide open now and I could feel my blood slowing a little and it was strange but I remember thinking that although I was quite tense, still I wasn't scared, not really. And now there came a long sigh – such a long sad sigh, then nothing for a moment, then another sigh.

Who's there? I called softly but no answer came.

For a while I wondered what to do but in the end I didn't do anything. I didn't wake Tom. Instead I just lay back down and took some big breaths and felt myself fill up with an intense kind of happiness, as if someone had found a secret empty place inside me and poured something warm in there.

I felt a strange kind of click in my head, like a click of recognition, and then I was aware that I was relaxing for what felt like the first time in ages. It felt as if my heart had untangled. And as I let myself go, I kept my eyes on the window where a tiny portion of the curtain had been left drawn back and I wasn't at all surprised to see that out there, as well as the strong white moon, was a sky full of snow, falling thick and fast.

I slept easily then. And for the first time in almost twenty years, I dreamt of you.

In the morning when I wake it feels late. The room is light already and Tom's up. I can hear him in the bathroom. The curtains are half pulled back, sun floods in and the TV's on with the sound turned down. CNN news. Tom loves CNN in hotel bedrooms. He doesn't watch it but he has to have it on.

Background noise, he always says, it makes me feel on holiday.

Now he walks in to the room, naked, scratching his stomach, looks at me.

Hello gorgeous, he says, and I realise he hasn't called me that in a long time.

I feel funny, I tell him.

You look funny.

No, I mean it.

You think I don't?

What time is it? I need to phone Fin.

Not yet, he says, and he sits on the bed and puts his hand on my stomach and his voice goes low. In a minute.

I can smell hotel soap. I sigh and turn over, pull his hand under my arm and kiss his fingers, feel the bump of his knuckles, the wedding band I gave him even though we are not married. We are not married, and this anniversary, the only one we ever celebrate, is the anniversary of the day we decided – on purpose – to have a baby. He suggested it and I said yes. It was a good moment, the most romantic thing we ever did.

It's a beautiful day. The sky outside the window is the kind of bright blue that goes on for ever.

Did the snow settle? I ask him. Is it snowy out there?

Tom pulls his hand out from under my arm and kisses my shoulder.

What snow?

Last night. There was loads.

He frowns. I don't think it snowed, he says.

Yes it did, I tell him. In the night. I was woken by some-thing and I looked out and saw it. It was coming down really thickly.

He shrugs and goes to the window, lifts the net.

Well there's no snow out there, Nic, not even a trace of it.

He lets the net drop. The fabric takes a second to settle, as if I'm watching in slow motion.

Come on, woman, he says, I need to get out of here. I've got to have either coffee or sex, pronto. So you either let me get back into bed with you right now or else I run you a bath and we go and find a café.

The second one, I tell him, please.

And I settle back on the pillow in the sunshine and in my head I hear the bath running, the water crashing out of the pipes. I feel myself drifting back to sleep and hope Tom will wake me, call me, when it's ready. I think of the café where we'll have breakfast. But next time I open my eyes, Tom's asleep beside me, the sun's all gone, sucked from the room, in fact it's not even light, it's still the darkest part of the night and the snow is still falling.

You stand there in your sweater and tattered brown cords that you kept on all night and the gas has finally run out, our night of the pearl necklace has run out and now, in daylight, I can see you exactly as you always are – and the truth is there are pimples on your skin and the watery blue of your eyes shows just how tired you are. Furiously tired. You yawn and scratch at your neck.

I think you want to go from my room now but are too polite to say so. I think you'll never want to kiss me again, that from now on when we meet you won't look at me, and that this night will fade away so even I don't think it really ever happened. I think –

Hey, you say. What're you thinking?

Nothing, I say a little too quickly.

You are. I can see you, so much going on in your funny head, funny girl.

I smile and I watch you search in your pocket for a roll-up or half a one or whatever you might have left.

Stop it, you say in a commanding voice.

Stop what?

Stop thinking.

Why?

Why? Because I don't like it, I can't deal with it so early in the morning, I can't deal with what's going on in that head of yours.

It's eleven, I say, unnecessarily.

You look at the table, then, What's this?

Nothing.

23

I throw a slightly damp towel over my typewriter which has the one sheet of paper sticking out.

You're writing something?

No.

You won't talk to me about it?

No, I say and I see there are still pearls all over the floor and I feel suddenly sad. You've put your sneakers on but the laces are still undone.

What's the matter? you say, and I can't answer because I'm tired and so very afraid that you're about to leave that a part of me has already begun to say goodbye.

You shrug and go to the window and look out at the snow. You look either sad and hurt or cool and uninterested, I don't know which it is. Neither do you perhaps. The room is blinding white but the sky's quite grey still, loaded with cold.

Fuck, you say, look at that. There won't be any buses all frigging day.

For a while now I'd been waking several times a night, every single night. I'd even gone to see the doctor about it. She'd tucked her smooth blonde hair behind her ears and laid her pen on the desk and looked at me carefully. It was clear she'd read my notes because of all the questions she didn't ask me.

And you're eating properly?

Always, I lied in my brightest voice.

She was silent for a moment and then she said she'd be frank with me. That she could prescribe anything I wanted – antidepressants, sleeping tablets – but she felt quite strongly that I was the kind of person who might do better without. She said she personally thought I was doing well, that all I really needed was time.

Tom had two theories. He said I should exercise more – swimming or running. Something for your heart, he said. I almost laughed. He liked to run – he was always running, sometimes it seemed to me that he never stood still these days, not really, not if he could help it. He asked if I'd like to come out running with him and I said I'd think about it, but I was lying, I knew I wouldn't. You could run around the block for all you were worth but if your heart was breaking, what difference did it make how hard you worked it?

The other theory was that I should just get on and write something.

If you could have another little book of poems published, he said, and being Tom he meant it with complete generosity and kindness, it would make a differ-ence, Nic. You'd see, I mean it, darling. I know that writing makes you happy and I'm not just saying it. Please think about it.

I tried to see what he was saying but inside I wanted to laugh. He sounded like a person with faith when he spoke like that, but I'd seen him, for all his talk of exer-cise and poetry, just as bad as me, curled on the floor in his tracksuit on a Sunday afternoon and sobbing till the snot fell in strings onto the carpet. After a while, loss burns a hole inside you. And it's permanent. Somewhere inside you, however hard you try to behave normally, there will always be that hole.

To please him and also to be alone, I spent some hours in my study pretending. But two lines, this was all I had in my head so far. Or, to look at it another way, it seemed to be all I had left, those two fucking lines, no more than that, nothing else left to say. Maybe the palest suggestion of a third, if I didn't think too hard about it. But if I tried to get it down, it slipped away. So there I was, back to two.

The other thing I didn't dare tell Tom was, I didn't really want to be better – why should I? Why should I wish to get beyond this difficult place where I was now? I knew that after something like this happened you were meant to move on, but this made no sense to me. All I wanted was to stay right here where I was, close to her. Without that possibility, life felt pointless.

So many times I'd sit up quickly into blackness, that same heart just pumping out tears because I couldn't help it and Tom would say I was just in a habit of it now, which might well have been true but since when did realising it provide a cure?

But then again, as I finally admitted to the doctor, I'd never been a great sleeper, not even as a child. As soon as I could walk and was no longer trapped in a cot, I used to get up and do crazy things in the night – not quite sleepwalking but just frantic little half-awake things that made no particular sense to anyone but me.

I'd search for stuff – lost china ornaments, an old sock, a tiger sticker from the petrol station. I'd talk to my toys. I'd turn on the taps and flush the toilet even if I hadn't used it, just for something to do. It used to wake my parents and drive them wild. But I didn't mean harm by it. I think I was just enjoying the sound of all that water racing through the silent house.

★   ★   ★

Dawn in Paris — or the faint mud light before dawn. I stood at the window and watched the sky move through its different colours, and now and then I turned to check Tom was still sleeping. I had on one of his sweaters but nothing else and my naked bottom was freezing cold, cold and goose-pimpling. I knew that Tom would tell me to put something on. He'd turned the heating right down before we slept as he could never stand sleeping in hot rooms. He never felt the cold at all, not the way I did. Put something on, he always said if I tried to complain.

Because of the chicness of the hotel, the bed was on a kind of podium, a platform, and up there Tom was breathing lightly. I moved closer to the window and watched my breath on the glass for a few moments, and then I pulled back the two layers — one linen, the other sort of chiffon stuff — and moved myself so I was sandwiched in between. In there was nice — it reminded me of games that the boys might have played a few years ago, games to do with dens and sardines and the safeness of being small.

I thought it must have snowed quite heavily in the night, because there was a thick round crust on all the windowsills and the balcony opposite. I wondered if those were apartments over there — certainly I didn't think they could be part of the hotel. The room with the balcony still (or already?) had a light on, now at 5 a.m., and I could just make out the curve of a woman's cardiganed shoulder. Now and then it moved, swift and purposeful, a wide-awake kind of movement. I wondered if the owner of the shoulder had got up early or else had perhaps never even gone to bed.

If I moved my face up close to the window and looked straight down I could see right through the glass roof into the room with the big white leather sofa, where we'd had our vodka the afternoon before, though that already felt like more than a week ago. Time had messed itself up somehow and gone strange. And the room below looked as sad and empty as I felt at that moment. I could not see a single soul down there.

Tom's travel alarm on the table said 5.03. As I watched, the red, lit-up 3 clicked and somehow became a 4.

I pressed my hands over my face. I had a bunched-up wad of hotel tissues in my hand, but they were of such poor quality, so small and flimsy, that they dissolved too quickly under the weight and dampness of my tears. I cried as quietly as I could. I always tried hard not to wake Tom with my sobs.

One of the very first things that made me love Tom was how from the start there was no messing whatsoever about how much we should be together. All that careful stepping around each other that people do at the beginning of a relationship, the desperate attempts not to appear needy, well Tom never did that.

I don't play games, he said one morning when I got up and, crouched naked on the bedroom floor, tried once again to stuff my few poor things into a bag in an attempt to return to my bedsit. I know what I want and I just want to be with you, Nicole.

I looked at him, lying naked in bed licking the butter off his breakfast knife, and I was touched. But not touched enough. Maybe I should have realised that this was Tom's way of being romantic, that commitment came easily to him, he was never afraid of it. Maybe I should have valued that more. In fact, he'd been married very briefly and very young, to a friend from university, a woman three years younger than him. It was her idea, apparently, to get married, but I think he did love her deeply. Tom never did things he didn't mean.

In the wedding pictures, he looked so incredibly young, startled, dazed almost. Longish hair, round face, thin boy's body, sharp around the edges. You could imagine his mum straightening his tie, spitting on a handkerchief to wipe his face. The bride looked radiant, with the blonde poise and dark eyes of fairy stories, far more certain of herself. Something in the way she held herself said yes, I'm here, this is it, this is what I want. It was a big white wedding, swathes of fabric, ruffles everywhere.

From what Tom told me, the marriage came apart suddenly, quietly, quickly, easily, for no reason he'd ever managed to understand.

She kicked me out, he told me later with a directness which touched me. I wanted to try and make it work, but she wouldn't, so what could I do?

After the split, he'd taken about three months to recover. He slept on floors, then rented a flat from a friend. Finally his parents helped him buy a small run-down cottage on the edge of a well-kept council estate close to the city. Two small bedrooms, an outdoor toilet and a backyard. It took him six months to knock down walls and plaster and paint and make it lovely. He did a lot of it himself, in the evenings and at weekends. When I first saw it, there was a fire in the grate and a kitten sleeping on the shelf. Tom has a way of making places feel like home.

After that, almost as if he wanted to override the home

29

feeling, he had a succession of crazy girlfriends – each one a little stranger than the last. The Carolines, I called them, because at least one of them had been called Caroline and I could never be bothered to remember the rest. Besides, in my head they all rolled themselves into one ball of uneasiness. Even though all of these relationships had been short-lived, casual even, still I was always afraid that at any moment one or other of them would knock on the door and demand to be allowed back into Tom's clean new life. Hello, I'm Caroline and I'm back. His house, after all, was so calm and ordered, so obviously a good place to be. That was in the early days, when I still barely knew Tom, and wasn't at all sure of my place in his life.

At that time he was still waiting for his divorce to become final and absolute or whatever you call it, and I wondered if he'd ask me to marry him when it did. I wondered how long it would be before he told me he loved me.

You ask me, years later, whether I married for love. Tell me you did, Rosy, you say. I just really need to hear that, whatever else has happened, you at least did that.

And I am lost for words. I don't know what you expect me to say. Marry, and love – the words give me such a jolt. So I tell you the truth – that I never, in fact, married at all, that Tom never asked me, he never wanted to, not even once the divorce came through, not even once we had children.

And you didn't want to?

I think about this. When I think about those early days with Tom, I see sunshine, lightness, summer mornings filled with hope.

I did want to, yes.

Then why the fuck didn't he marry you? you demand to know, and for a moment or two I love you for how shocked you sound.

I explain what I know: that he thought he'd failed the first time and couldn't go through it all again. Not in front of all those people anyway. That it would have felt like a farce.

OK, but you could have done it quietly, just the two of you.

I hesitate.

All the same, I say, I think he still would have felt compromised somehow. I could almost understand it. He's very pure like that.

You make a noise of exasperation and plant a kiss on my forehead.

Great. But – what about you?

I don't think he thought very much about me, I say.

We are very quiet after that, you and I. You have on an old grey T-shirt and you're holding me tight, very tight, your arms around me, my hand on your dick which is quite soft because you're thinking so hard. And I'm wondering why I've never been held like that, not ever, not so tight that I feel I could not possibly slip and fall, not now, not ever.

I can hear your heart bumping and it's oddly fast, like a baby's.

I wiped my eyes and put the tissues in the bin and went to pee. In the dark bathroom, I sat on the loo with my head in my hands and only a little came out. There was a single orchid in a vase by the bath and I could smell its shadow in the thin dawn light – a drift of scent, expensive and white.

I could also smell my own knees and they smelled of sex and of Tom and of the semen that came out of him. We'd made love twice in the night because of it being our anniversary, though I wasn't there for much of it. He knew it and he didn't mind, not especially. There'd always been a largeness to Tom, a willingness to move beyond the moment, and I'd been grateful for it. Though sometimes I wasn't sure whether that was better or worse, that he always accommodated my absences so easily.

I wiped myself and sniffed at the tissue. Tom always laughed at the way I inspected every little thing that came out of me. It was the same with the children, too, when they were small. But I knew Tom's semen better than almost anything – its white wetness, the way it dried hard and shiny, the way it felt the wrong kind of slippery on your fingers in the shower. It had been in my life for years – so much of it, the stuff all our babies were made of, the stuff of life.

Soon after Mary was born, Tom had a vasectomy. He said he did it for me and for our sex life – and certainly I believed him about this – but also because he was through with babies, personally. I was surprised. I asked him how he could possibly be so sure, so final, and he smiled at me.

Come on, Nic, he said, we can't possibly have more kids. We can barely cope with the boys' homework as it is.

I looked down at the girl at my breast. Her eyes were closed and her white tuft of hair stuck up on her head. A strange criss-cross of violet veins on the side of her head. I'd showed it to the midwife, worried, but she'd reassured me it was perfectly normal in a baby with such fair skin.

You have an angel there, she said, a real beauty. Bet she'll give you some right old trouble when she's bigger.

For now she was pure, untainted by the demands of the world. But Tom was right of course – one day we'd have to get her through her times tables. She'd need PE kit, name tapes sewed on. Forms would have to be filled in for her, sandwiches made, sleepovers had. It wasn't that I didn't think three children was enough, I just hated the finality of saying so.

I didn't flush the toilet as I didn't want to wake him. I pulled on a sweater and jeans but no underwear, stuffed my feet into my warm boots, grabbed my coat and scarf and left the room as softly as I could. I had to hope that my finger would remember how to open the door again when I returned.

The foyer downstairs was empty, though the cold pebble fire still flickered. There was a smell of cleaning fluid. A dark-skinned man in a white jacket carried a hoover through to the bar area. He carried it with great care as though it were a small baby or else a precious thing made of glass and he bowed his head to me as I walked past, softly across the white marble floor, as if it were not at all an extraordinary thing to see guests creeping out at this time.

As I reached the great glass doors – hoping they'd automatically slide open so I didn't have to find anyone to help me – a woman dressed all in black slipped out from behind the counter at reception.

Madame?

Yes?

Here — it is for you.

Unsmiling, she reached into the pigeonholes behind her and, barely looking at my face, placed a note in my hand. I saw that her lashes were very thick and black, noticeably so, her face so smooth with powder it looked dusty in the halogen light. There was a bowl of lilies on the counter and the scent hung sickly in the air between us, almost blotting out the cleaning-fluid smell.

I stopped and gazed at the note. It was written on a small scrap of paper and not even folded. I knew the woman must have seen what it said and I felt myself flush.

Please, I asked her, do you know — when did this come?

She pressed her lips together and shook her head.

I am only just arrived here. In the night I guess, sometime?

Do you know who left it?

She took a step away from me.

I am sorry, Madame.

Out in the street, cold hit me. I walked three or four steps on the icy pavement to get away from the hotel before I stopped and looked properly at the piece of paper in my hand and felt a rush in my chest, the sharp feel of my breath tearing away. It was a piece of squared paper, very small faint blue squares, the sort a schoolchild might use. On it, in sloping blue biro, in a neat handwriting that I seemed to remember from another world, not here:

I'm waiting for you. X.

* * *

34

Her name was Mary but almost from the first day, we all called her Baby.

The first night we were home from the hospital, Fin was so overexcited about the whole idea of having a baby sister that he woke in the night extremely agitated. Though he seemed half asleep, he wouldn't settle, nothing would soothe him.

Baby, he kept on saying, Baby, Baby.

I sat on the edge of his bed and stroked his hair. My body, so recently opened, felt fragile as eggs. I didn't care. I was so madly happy. I leaned in towards him and kissed his nose. He put his arms out and held me in a hug and patted my shoulder, little rubbing circular pats, something he'd done since he was small. But he wasn't small any more, he was nine now. Nine years old and in Year 4 – something I used to have trouble remembering but not now, not any more, because a baby in the house made him seem suddenly huge and robust, and that's the way life goes. Things only grow big when smaller ones come along.

I keep thinking about Baby, he said with a sigh.

Baby's fine, I told him, she's fast asleep, lovely and peaceful.

Why sleeping?

Well, it's hard work being born. She's tired. Also it's the middle of the night, Fin sweetheart, and you should be asleep too.

He sighed again and looked right into my eyes. It was something he often did. Sometimes I thought he could see straight into the centre of me and out the other side.

Where is she though, where, Mummy? Where?

In our bed. With Daddy. You want to see her?

He went quiet for the first time and looked at me. His eyes were wet with uncried tears. He nodded and rubbed his nose. So I led him to our bed and let him see where she was sleeping, right in the middle, laid on her fleece, all six pounds thirteen ounces of her, an impossibly small individual next to the devastating largeness of Tom. Both were breathing noiselessly. You could see their chests going up and down, her tiny one and his big one. With her eyes shut she looked perfect. Each fist was curled up tight.

What's she holding? Fin whispered, tugging on my dressing gown.

Nothing. That's how babies' hands are when they first come out, all scrunched up like that.

Fin smiled.

There, I told him, Baby's fine. Will you go to sleep now? I settled him and that was that.

That was another cold January just like this one and a million others. Even on that night, Baby's first night in our home, there was snow just waiting to fall from a chill black sky. Back in our room I felt a layer of cold air settle over the bed and I turned the electric heater up.

It felt good to be cold and alone out in the street – it feels good – out of the overheated hotel and into the dim raw cold. It wasn't yet light, not properly, but there's the beginning of a frozen redness falling from behind the tall buildings, not quite a light and certainly not sunshine but all the same, the start of a different day.

The snow has settled, not much of it, but still – a pleasant crunch under my feet. Like walking on sugar, I thought, and I realised I liked it and I hadn't felt so optimistic in a long time. Everything looked bright and pleasing and clean in this light and I've no map with me and no idea where I am but that's OK, I thought. As long as I remember the way back to the hotel, that's fine. I'm not like Tom. I don't always need to know precisely where I've been.

My hands were shoved deep in my pockets but they still felt cold. In my left pocket between my fingers is the note. It's here, I think, it's safely here and I still have it, it's real and in my pocket.

I took the first right turning I came to, to get off the main boulevard, and saw a woman walking quickly past, carrying two baskets. It seemed like something out of a fairy story – the woman and the baskets, the strange earliness of the morning and the fact that I had no idea where I was going, no sense of what sort of a journey I was really on.

She nods at me, the woman, and I nod back. Behind her a small stout man is pulling up the security grille on his shop with a hook, bending and grunting with the effort. He did not look at me, it didn't matter. The metal grille made a loud rolling noise and I saw that the doorway above his head was carved with the fat and smiling face of a sun.

Another man is clearing the pavement outside his shop with a spade. The scrape rings out in the freezing air. There was some grit on the main street outside the hotel, but here the roads look icier. There is no traffic and ahead of me just one strange single lamp-post, again like something out of a story – magical, still lit, its light growing paler as the sky bursts quietly into dawn.

Behind the chimneys the moon is going down, sliding

away as the round red light of the sun appears and then disappears as I walk. Red flicking in and out of my sight line. I passed some people all dressed up in velvet as if going home from an all-night party and I laughed to myself because of how much it all felt like a game, even though it is almost dawn and my cheeks are numb with cold and I realise I don't really mind what happens next.

I smile and my breath spills right out in front of me into the blue freezing air. I'm happy for the first time in ages but my hands are so cold now I can barely feel them. On the edge of the street by some digging and roadworks I stop, delve in my bag for my lip balm. Someone has tied a bunch of flowers to a lamp-post, but they're dead and sad already. I use the tip of my finger to put some balm on my mouth, then I pull on my gloves.

I know you watch me come into the café. I know it and I am ready for it. Though remember, you have an advantage over me. You are already there and already seated so now it's easy for you. All you have to do is sit back and wait and look. That's the simple job, the waiting for it to happen. For me it's much harder as I have to do the whole thing of walking in and taking in every single person in there, wondering if any of them are you and if so, how it's going to feel – that first quick moment when my face meets yours.

It's been more than twenty years. How can it not be shocking?

Well it's so early there are only about four in the café, dotted about, all men as it turns out. Smoke rises in straight lines from the tables. Quick, I think, which one doesn't look French? Are any of them fair-haired?

But just when I'm afraid that you won't be here, that it isn't true, there you are, right in the furthest corner. A smoky corner, I am drawn to that corner. That corner has you in it, that corner is you. You do not move – you don't need to – but I think you raise your hand. The sensation I have – because I dare not look properly – is of a man, a solid, fair presence in brown or grey, and the certainty that he's been waiting for me. As if you've just called me, I walk right over and stand there in front of you.

I stand there and I just don't know where this moment can possibly go. You blink at me over your glasses. Little rimless glasses. You never had glasses before. From behind them, you smile and it's the old smile, definitely and it cracks my heart. I glance at you, then down at the floor again. It's not my fault that I can't look.

Your hair is pale blond still but streaked with grey. Short and brushed back where it used to be long. You're not skinny any more, no one could call you skinny. Not ragged either. Your clothes look expensive, well made in that American way. No frayed edges, no creases. If it wasn't you, if I didn't know this person was you, then I'm afraid I might just despise these clothes a little because in truth you look like just any solid, pale middle-aged man. Slightly off-putting. A businessman. You look like you know your place in the world and that's why I'm not sure I'd have recognised you. You didn't used to be like that. You were never a man with glasses in well-made clothes.

But then again. As I get closer, I see how blue your eyes are still. And that you're still smiling, smiling so much, far too much.

So.

That's it, that's what you say, after all these years, just that, a tiny non-committal word. So.

So?

I shut my eyes and try to listen to your voice – your voice which is, definitely, just the same. That one word.

So, you found me, you say.

I stand there and I don't know but it feels as if all my words have gone.

No, I say, you've got it wrong. It was you – you found me.

You smile.

Hey, you say, and your smile grows bigger.

But how? I say.

How what?

How did you do it? I don't know how you found me. This morning, I mean, did you come to the hotel? I don't understand what happened. I have no idea why I even came to this place.

I tell you this and it is true. I walked from my hotel and I got a note though the note didn't tell me what to do or where to go, but I came here and here you were, and that's all I know. I don't even know my way around Paris. It's like I sleepwalked my way here, every step perfect and purposeful, eyes tight shut, moving forwards through the ice or the snow to you, yet never knowing what I did or how I did it.

What's going on? I say.

You sit forward in your seat and look a little concerned. The frown you make shows the wrinkles on your face, a little patch of dry skin on your temples.

My note. You got the note?

Yes, I tell you, yes, I got it but – I don't understand.

Hush, silly girl, you say, relax. Sit down.

Is it really you? I say and you laugh again.

Yep, it's me. Look, all me. Way too much of me, I'm sorry to say.

You say this and you make a gesture that is a reference to the size of yourself. You're not fat but you're solid. You don't look like you go hungry any more. You look like you eat meals in restaurants these days.

I think all of this but I say nothing. Instead I stand on the spot and hug myself.

Hey, you say softly, you're thinking too much. Stop, wait. Sit. Come on, I mean it, coat off.

I try to sit on the bench next to you but you put out a hand and stop me. A short square hand, clean nails. With a jolt, I realise I remember your hands.

No, you say, no. Here, opposite, I need to look at you. It's been so long. Just do that for me, please?

We are silent for a moment, taking each other in.

Rosy, you say, as if that were the answer, as if that were all that's necessary to make everything fall into place. I swallow and then I laugh. No one's called me Rosy in a long time.

Yes, I reply, it's me, still the same old Rosy.

Your walk. It's exactly the same.

I blush. No!

Yes. Oh sure, oh yes.

How do I walk?

With a bit of a bounce. I could show you but I guess I shouldn't here in this place, it might bother the customers.

I make a face and you reach over and touch my gloved hand with yours, just in a friendly way.

Hey, it's nice, you say, I mean it. It's attractive.

I shake my head.

You have glasses, I say rather stupidly.

You sigh.

Oh Rosy, I'm so fucking blind these days. You wouldn't believe it.

Well, you look just the same, I tell you, but it's clear you don't quite buy it and you laugh at me.

Sweet girl, thank you. But no, don't lie to me, I don't. I'm not good. I'm fat, I'm old. I drink and smoke too much.

So am I, I tell you, I've had three kids. I'm – we're both of us middle-aged.

Never, you say, not you, not middle-aged. You look – well you look just perfect.

I can't think what to say to this so I peel off my gloves and ease off my coat and let it fall over the back of the chair. An old man is smoking and watching us. He pretends to read his paper but he keeps on looking at me.

You want some coffee?

My heart jolts when you say that. I used to love the way you said it – cwaffee. Back then I used to make you say it over and over again so I could smile at it.

Yes please, I say, noticing that you've already had one and that sugar packets are torn open all over the table. But only if you've got time for another.

You look at me with a serious face.

I've got time, you say. I've definitely got time.

I say nothing. I don't know what you mean by this.

It's so fucking early, you add, I need at least three more of those before I can even begin to think.

You call the waiter over and you order. You make no attempt to speak French or even to speak slowly. The waiter therefore ignores you and turns to me, so I have to reorder, in French.

You laugh.

They look right through you here if you're a dumb fat-assed Yank, you say.

I look at you and bite my lip.

You can't speak any French?

Not a word. Typical dumb American.

Hey, I begin, but you stop me.

Stop, you're doing it again.

Doing what?

Thinking. You're thinking too much. Save it for later.

I laugh out loud because you're right. I was thinking. You reach out and – very gently – touch the skin next to my eyes.

You're older, you say after a moment, but you look – fucking adorable.

Minutes pass. Or I think they are minutes. They could be whole hours or days. Time has crinkled up on itself again and gone strange. The waiter brings our coffees. Two half-full glasses of water as well. He has a pen in his mouth and a silver tray on the other arm and he slams everything down a little too hard, shoves the small white piece of paper that is the bill under my saucer. Three crumbs are there by the saucer. I notice those crumbs.

I put my cold fingers on the café table. I need to feel it, see if it is real. You're watching me. You know what I'm doing. It feels real enough – red Formica, chipped at the edges, a burn mark here and there, a scattering of white sugar. The metal ashtray has a cigarette stub in it – two stubs actually, both yours. You're lighting another. I watch you inhale with your head slightly on one side as you shake out the match, and in that second I remember you doing that, all those years ago, in exactly that way. That action of yours sucks me straight back to the past and I can't help it, I shiver.

Shouldn't be smoking, you say, even though I've made no comment about it. Only had one the whole of yesterday. Trying to stop. You don't believe me, do you?

I look at you and you return my gaze, steadily. You almost seem to be speaking to yourself. Certainly you don't seem to mind that I haven't replied. You just continue to talk.

Snow, you say. Have you seen? It snowed in the night?

Yes, I whisper and I stare at you and wonder if you're thinking what I'm thinking.

What? Rosy, what is it?

I take a breath and without knowing why, I feel my eyes fill up with tears.

It's this – it's you, finding you here like this. Please don't tell me to stop thinking because it's impossible, my head is just so full, I'm just so –

You shake your head and smile at me as if it all should be completely obvious. I put my hand behind my neck and squeeze it. I wonder if it will wake me up. I look at your eyes. Their greyness and their blueness, so many colours in there.

Just so what? you whisper.

You're not real are you, I say at last.

And you're looking at me now with a sad look, as if

you know what will happen next – a hint of the boy who used to be there. And my stomach hurts already, partly because I know what you're going to say.

No. No, baby, I'm not.

Baby. I feel so cold inside as you say this, as you call me baby.

I feel tears coming again.

What are you then?

You stub out the cigarette even though it's only halfway through. You look less happy now, as if none of this was your doing and you don't want to hurt me but you'll have to.

I'm whatever you want me to be.

I need –

Hush.

You won't look at me now. You're looking down at the table.

I need you to be real, I'm surprised to hear myself say.

And somehow me admitting it, me saying those six small words, that does it. Those words make the whole room, café, tables, chairs, come rushing in around me and I can't help it then. I put my head in my hands as the tears come. I am ashamed to be crying already, so early in the morning and before anything has happened.

I feel your warm hand on my wrist.

Hush, you say again. Hush, sweetheart, baby. It's OK.

We sit for a moment or two like that, my face in the salty darkness of my sleeve, your hand on me. Something warm flows then, from you to me, and as that connection happens – a feeling I remember so intensely from before – it was like everything else had disappeared and I felt quite calm, completely calm and oddly still. And when I looked up, the hand had gone and so had you. There was only one cup of coffee on the table. The three crumbs were gone. The ashtray was clean, the sugar intact, unspilled. For a second or two I was completely unsurprised. And then my heart just swerved.

I must have gasped aloud or something, because the waiter came over, money rattling in his big apron.

Madame?

I could not speak. Trembling, I took some coins from my purse and put them on the silver tray, hoping I'd left enough, and then I snatched up my coat and ran into the street, looking both ways, looking for you. But the street was empty. The snow had stopped falling but outside the café it was thick and deep on the ground, smooth and undisturbed, no footprints at all. Certainly no one had walked past this place in the last ten minutes or so, not on this side of the pavement anyway.

I ran back into the café and tried to ask in French if they'd seen the man.

L'homme?

The waiter looked confused and glanced at his friend who was sitting on a high stool at the bar, reading a newspaper.

L'homme qui était avec moi. The man I was with. *L'Américain.* Did you see where he went? Which way did he go? Please?

The waiter said something then, spoke quickly to his friend, I didn't understand any of the words. Then the friend put down his paper, folded it carefully and looked at me quite sympathetically. He gestured to the table, where the one coffee cup still sat.

46

I am very sorry, Madame, he said. We hear what you say. But I think it is just you alone – I think there is no man with you today.

As I walked out of the café the snow was falling hard and fast again. Tears were on my face. I felt in my pockets for the piece of paper, for your note, but there was nothing, just my gloves and a screwed-up receipt for a newspaper we had bought at Waterloo before we boarded the Eurostar.

Neither of our two boys were planned – though they weren't exactly accidents either. Tom and I knew we were going to spend our lives together, so we just decided to go right ahead and see what happened. And what happened was first – almost straightaway – Jack and then, four and a bit years later, Finlay.

Jack was always the sociable one. Right from when he was tiny, he wouldn't ever sleep for long – he drove us mad with his waking and crying. If, at three or four in the morning, dizzy with sleep, Tom sat up in bed and propped him on his knees and held him and looked at him, then he was happy. But if Tom's eyes began to droop and close, if his grip relaxed even for a second, then the wail that came from Jack was terrible to hear. It wasn't his fault. He needed company, he laughed a lot. He smiled long before the books say babies are meant to smile.

Fin was different from the start. The moment he came out of me, he gave me a long look, yawned, made a judgement and nestled in closer. My Fin. A placid, easy-going baby who slept when it was dark and fed when he was hungry. I thought we had it all sorted out, now, with our second one. Of course that wasn't it at all. That was just how he was, that was Fin. If I'd learned anything in all my time of being a mother, it was that babies came out exactly as the people they were, the people they were always going to be, ready-made and fully formed. You could do small things here and there to alter and influence them, but that was all. The imprint they made on the world in their first few hours – no, seconds – was, by and large, the imprint they would continue to make throughout their lives.

By the age of three or four, Fin was already doing it. He'd be playing happily with bricks or a truck or something, building and loading – and then he'd stop, pause, seem to listen for something, and sigh the biggest, longest sigh. We used to laugh and call it his world-weary sigh. But it got less funny as he got older. Sometimes his mouth would turn right down at the corners and a fat, quiet tear would roll down his cheek. For no reason at all that we could see. Or at least, if you went to comfort him, if you asked him what was the matter he couldn't say. He would just lay his head on your shoulder and suck furiously on his thumb or the piece of blue furry blanket that he carried everywhere with him.

Then one day, at the age of about seven or maybe it was eight, he came to me and said, Mummy, I can't bear it all.

I pulled him to me and looked at his face. I could see he was trembling on the verge of tears.

My darling, can't bear what? I said.

His mouth pulled down in a twitchy way as he tried not to cry. He moved his small hands around as if struggling to show me something inexplicable, indescribable.

All of this, he said.

All of what?

The world, he said. It's like – a little sob caught in his throat – it's like I'm just waiting for it all to end.

I stared at him. I didn't know what to do, what to say.

Is something making you sad? I asked him, very seriously now, because I was his mother and I needed to know.

He seemed to stop and think about this.

I haven't been sad since Lex died, he said. Lex was our tabby cat who had died of kidney failure. One morning she had just got up and toppled over again and that was that, she had to be put down that afternoon. I felt at the time it was a harsh, or at least dramatic, introduction to death for the boys. On the other hand, she was quite old and she hadn't really suffered and that had to be good.

But I remembered that death and the gusts of sobs that came from Fin all afternoon – a contrast to the awed and slightly excited silence from Jack, who just wanted to know how soon we could get a new kitten.

Then what is it, my darling? I need to know what's making you feel like this. What's going to end? Nothing's going to end.

He looked at me for a long time then – as if he was the adult, not I, and he was trying to decide how much truth I could cope with. I took his little hand and kissed it lots of times to change the mood, to make him laugh, the same way I used to blow raspberries on his naked tummy when I changed his nappy, just to hear him giggle. He let me do it but he didn't laugh.

Nothing's going to end, I said again.

He sighed.

The world is fine, we're all fine, I told him.

OK, he said. But the level and composed way in which he said it made me feel I was failing him somehow, that he'd decided to take responsibility for my mood, instead of the other way round, and there was nothing I as his mother could do to switch our roles.

It was months before I relived this conversation to myself in the light of something that had happened to me, long ago. I was eighteen, in my gap year and was in the Boboli Gardens in Florence on a hot June day. It was my afternoon off from being an au pair. I had bread and cheese, cherries, water, a novel to read. It was boiling hot and the air smelled of frangipani, mimosa. I could hear the bubble of the fountains, bees, distant laughter. On anybody's terms, this was heaven. I lay back on my rug and took a deep and satisfied breath — and then it happened.

The world went dark. The noise of people laughing and walking, the water falling, the hum of the bees, all receded and went deadly quiet. I sat up quickly. I felt that all light and life, every shred of goodness, was being sucked out of my particular space. The world went flat and thick and black and seemed to tilt and, for a few brief seconds, I saw into the abyss. The sensation didn't last long, though it left me trembling. I told no one at the time because I knew how crazy it would sound.

It never came again, that moment, not like that, but I carried the memory and the dark fact of it with me from then on. It was always with me, somewhere, beneath every small good thing that I thought or felt or did and it never really went, but remained lodged at the core of all I felt and experienced. I was always afraid the world would tilt again, that I would get another glimpse of the abyss.

You had a panic attack, Tom told me simply when, quite early on in our relationship, I tried to tell him about the Boboli Gardens moment. I didn't think of it often but when I did, it was, I realised, pivotal for me. Those few brief seconds had changed everything.

No, I told him, though I could see why he would say it, no, it wasn't that. I just know it wasn't. This was different.

But – no one else around you was affected? Life went on as normal?

Yes. I suppose so.

And it didn't last long?

No, thank god.

Tom looked at me and shook his head.

I rest my case. It was all in your head, sweetheart. I'm aware it doesn't make it any less real for you, but trust me, darling, it was a panic attack.

I didn't try any harder to convince him. What was the point? Here, I thought, was another reason why I loved Tom: he had never known the abyss. Unlike Fin. Unlike you.

I came back to find Tom propped up in the bed on about eight pillows, watching CNN. He didn't look at all happy. Keeping his eyes on the screen and talking with the blank voice he used when he was hurt, he asked me where I'd been.

I came and sat on the edge of the big double bed without taking off my coat. I folded my hands in my lap and I tried hard to think. In my head, I'd prepared nothing, I didn't know why. Even coming back through the streets – a journey I could barely remember – even coming up in the strange quick lift, no easy explanations or even lies had entered my head. I knew that my cheeks were pink from the cold, and the room was incredibly hot and smelled of a strange, heavy perfume and the curtains were half open. This was all I seemed to know.

There's snow out there, I told him, you should see. It's lovely – really snowy.

Tom turned to look at me then looked straight back at the screen. On the TV some soldiers were getting into a jeep somewhere. The screen was filled up with khaki.

I asked you a question, he said.

I went out, I told him, and I noticed with a wave of shock that I didn't care whether he believed me or not.

Out?

Yes. For a walk.

Do you mind if I ask why? He asked me this in a voice that was loaded with cold.

I hesitated a moment and tried reaching for his hand but he wouldn't give it.

Oh Tom, I said.

What? He sounded softer now. What is it, Nic?

I remained silent.

Tell me, he said.

I took a breath and tried to think what to say.

How can I help you if you won't tell me? he said then.

I don't know, I told him, but I'm fine, really I am. There's nothing wrong and I don't need you to help me.

As I said it, I realised it had come out meaner than I meant it to. Tom licked his lips and shut his eyes for a second.

Thanks a lot, he said.

I'm sorry. I didn't mean it like that.

52

What then? How did you mean it?

I don't know, I said. Just – not like that.

I wondered then for a few brief seconds whether I should tell him the truth. I didn't especially want to hide anything from him. I hadn't knowingly hidden anything from Tom – except maybe, slightly, the full cost of a new pair of shoes or a dress – in the whole of our time together. But I had no idea what it was that had just happened to me, so what could I possibly say? Or maybe I knew it wasn't just that. There was also a feeling in me right from the start that I had to hide this. I had to hide something about me and you.

Tom zapped off the TV and turned to me.

I panicked, he said in a small voice. I didn't know where you were. When I saw your coat was gone – well, anything could have happened. For fuck's sake, Nicole, why didn't you just tell me you were going out?

I didn't want to wake you. I couldn't sleep. I hardly slept all night. Anyway it wasn't some big plan, I promise you it wasn't. I didn't know I was going till – I went.

All of this was the truth, all of it, but it didn't help much. I watched as Tom's face went small and tight and as I watched I realised I'd seen this face a hundred times. And I knew, in a dull way, that I'd ruined everything now – our anniversary, this fun and carefree and romantic time we were supposed to be having.

Are you OK? I asked him and he stared at me.

Of course I'm not OK. I'm worried about you. Why couldn't you sleep? I slept.

It was ungrateful of me, that's what he was thinking. He brought me here to this expensive and absurdly luxurious hotel with the laser-door system and the bed on a podium and still, despite all that, I couldn't sleep. I pulled off my coat and reached across to the bedside table for a tissue to blow my nose.

I woke up in the night and, well, the snow – I began and then I stopped, unsure. The sky outside our window was now bright and blue but I felt confused. My stomach turned over. Was there snow on the ground or not?

I just felt bad, I told him as I balled up the tissue in my hand, in the night. I'm so sorry Tom, but that's what I felt.

Tom was silent again and I knew why. Me saying I felt bad was taking us back there, into an area where he'd rather not go.

Look, Nicole, he said instead, do anything you want, I don't mind what you do, but don't just walk out on me without saying anything.

All right, I told, him and felt relieved because I honestly thought I could agree to that. Then I just sat there and after a moment or two I took his hand and this time he let me.

Actually I ran into an old friend, I told him before I even knew I was saying it. Straightaway I flushed and I knew he clocked it because he turned again to stare at me.

What? Who?

Just – someone I used to know. Years ago.

But where, who? What do you mean ran into? You mean just now?

I tried to look him in the eye.

In a café, would you believe? I said, and I tried to laugh.

I mean, I just walked in and he was right there, just sitting there, I couldn't believe it.

I laughed again, to make it sound more OK, but Tom frowned.

Let me get this straight. You went into a café on your own?

What's wrong with that?

And who is this person? Male or female?

Just – an old friend. Male.

Of course, said Tom.

What do you mean of course?

He ignored me.

And – so you talked?

Of course. Of course we talked.

But who? he said again, as if searching for the right question to ask. What old friend?

Just – a boy I knew – ages ago, at university.

Tom folded his arms and glanced out of the window.

Just a boy you knew. A man now, I take it?

Yes, I said, remembering your sturdy clothes, your impossibly solid self, your glasses, a man.

And you were with him just now.

Well – it was so weird. He just disappeared.

He what?

He just went, he left – without saying goodbye.

This time it was Tom who tried to laugh.

What? Did you upset him or something?

I don't think so, no.

Did he know you were here with me?

Of course he did, I replied, but even as I said it I realised I had no idea whether this was true or not.

I could see Tom thinking about this. Outside our bedroom door someone rattled past with a trolley or a tray. I heard the burr as the lift was called, the ding as it reached our floor.

Tom pulled back the covers and got out of bed and went to the bathroom. I heard the seat of the toilet go up and I heard him wait a couple of seconds, then came the familiar dribble of his pee.

But – who was it? He carried on talking from the bathroom, Is it someone you've told me about? I mean do I know about this man? Was he a boyfriend?

I heard the seat go back down and I smiled.

No, he wasn't, not really, no.

Tom came back into the room and took my cold hand in his warm one and, to hide my embarrassment, I kissed his stomach, a nice flat stomach where the line of hair started wispy and thickened as it went lower. He pulled back from me and put his two hands on my shoulders and I laughed softly.

Nicole, he said with a sigh that seemed to mean he'd forgiven me, sometimes I just don't know what to say to you.

I know. I know you don't.

You're absolutely sure you didn't dream this?

No. Yes. I was there, Tom. It was real, I added but even as I said it, the words spliced a cold taste in my mouth.

But look, sweetheart, you have to admit it's one fuck of a huge coincidence.

I know. I know it is.

And then as I said that, I remembered the strange fact of your note and that I hadn't told him about that. It's gone now anyway, I thought, I've lost it. I wondered if the woman downstairs would mention it and I thought that it was unlikely, that they had to be discreet in these places, didn't they? Just as well I no longer have it, I thought, as I'd have had to hide it or throw it away. For some reason the idea of having to do this filled me up with loneliness.

What is it? Tom said. What's up?

I felt a mean and unexpected burst of anger towards him.

You know what's up, I told him, and I wondered if he did.

He turned away from me and sighed and I felt a part of him closing. He went over to the chair and started to put on his pants, his trousers. He picked up his watch, slipped it over his wrist.

This is our anniversary trip, he said at last. Can't we at least have some time off?

I looked at him.

Well, can't we?

You're always having time off, I told him finally.

What's that supposed to mean?

You know exactly what it means.

He was silent for a moment.

I'm trying, he said miserably and slowly, to do everything right. I'm giving you as much love as I possibly can. I'm being – well – incredibly patient. Any normal person would agree that I'm being a bloody fucking saint.

Great, I said, and I didn't bother to try and keep the bitterness out of my voice.

But – I just can't seem to give you what you want.

All I want, I whispered to him then in a voice so small

and angry that it shocked me, is for us to be able to talk about her.

I looked at Tom, head bowed, his long wrists hanging on his knees, and I waited to see what he'd say.

We've talked about her, he said. She's all we've talked about for so long, Nicole.

I said nothing.

Darling, we've talked. What's it all been if not talking?

I need to be able to mention her, I told him.

You do. You do mention her.

I mean every day, easily, without a fuss, without feeling – without –

Yes?

Without you doing that face.

What face?

That closed face that you do when – well, it's so cold, that face of yours.

He made an impatient noise and he sat on the bed and slumped so that the folds of flesh above his stomach showed. I thought he looked suddenly old, demolished. I thought how you could see the old man he would be – the thin, slack arms, the shrunken chest.

I mean it, Tom, I told him, and suddenly I didn't care what he thought of me. You can't even say her fucking name.

He shook his head, took a breath.

That's below the belt, he said quietly.

Well, you can't.

I know. I can't. It's not a rejection of her. Or of you. I just can't.

We both sat for a while then and watched the dead

blankness of the TV screen. Everything else had been forgotten, my encounter with you, the morning, the snow, it had all gone, it maybe never happened. Instead something strange was happening. She was right back there in the room with us.

Tom spoke slowly.

The only way I can hold myself together, he said, is by dividing things up. Quite literally. I divide things up and deal with them when I can. I can't justify it, I can't explain it, it's what I do. Does that make any sense to you at all?

I shrugged but really only to fend him off. The truth was I couldn't think any more about him because now I was alert to what was happening in the room, alert to her.

Sometimes, he said even more slowly, as if he was making up the thoughts as he went along, sometimes grief is about silence. It doesn't always have to be about speaking, Nic, about expressing every single little thing.

I said nothing.

It can be, he said, I mean it. Grief can be silent. We don't always have to talk. We have to go on with our lives, with the family we have. Sometimes just being together should be enough.

It should be, I heard myself agreeing, as she wrapped herself around me.

But it's not?

But I can hardly speak to him as I'm concentrating so hard on my little girl. Because the shape of the room has in these last few minutes been broken into, the air has been pierced with such a brightness and sweetness and suddenly she's so closely there, for a second or two, that I dare not breathe. My baby girl. I daren't even change my mind or the slightest bend of my thoughts, in case –

Baby?

She's gone, said Tom as if he could read my feelings.

No, I whispered, please no.

Yes, he said.

We ate lunch at a restaurant in a little cobbled backstreet behind Notre Dame. It was the third restaurant we went into but the first I actually agreed to eat at. This pickiness of mine was a long-standing joke between us. It wasn't to do with the food so much as the place. It had to feel right. Tom was incredibly patient. There's something real about this place, I told him, and when he asked me why, I confessed that it was mostly that I liked the old spidery vine clambering up the side and the way it looked like a sepia picture of itself.

Funny woman, he said. It's nothing like as swish as the other one.

Yes, I agreed, realising he'd entirely missed the point.

In fact it's quite scruffy.

But in the right way, I told him, and he laughed and kissed the side of my face.

Inside, there was a black wrought-iron spiral staircase twisting right up through the middle of the room and at first we thought it might be nice to eat upstairs, but once we squeezed ourselves up there, we discovered a room thick with smoke and old men in berets eating beef, with napkins tied around their necks like cartoon people. And, lying flat out on the floor, a large old collie dog entirely blind in both eyes.

Poor old thing, said Tom as she lifted her head and gazed at us with milky eyes. He bent to rub her head and I loved him for it for a moment or two.

We went back downstairs where it was almost as busy and we chose a table right at the back, where we were brought cracked plastic menus, a jug of water and some bread.

Full of French people, Tom remarked, taking off his coat and jacket and looking around him with pleasure. Always a good sign.

And he reached out and touched my hand – partly I think because he wanted to make up for our last conversation, but also because he was hungry and suddenly happy at the almost immediate prospect of wine and food. He smiled at me and it was almost a real smile.

No kids and no car, he said, perfect. We can get plastered.

I hope Fin got to school all right, I said before I could quite stop myself but, before Tom could make a face at me, I apologised, and this time I meant it.

He smiled and took a breath as if he was about to say something, then paused. He looked at me, moved the bread basket out of the way so he could take my hand again.

He's eleven years old, he said in a gentle voice but also as if he'd been thinking about this a lot and building up to saying it. And it's good for him, to have to manage a little. I think he actually enjoys it and it makes him behave better. He's got to stop always being the baby, Nic.

As he spoke he seemed to realise what he'd just said and I saw him flinch a little and I felt for him. This time it was me who put my hand out to him, brushed his knuckles with my fingertips.

You're right, I told him, I have to stop worrying. Actually, you know, I'm not even that worried. Your mother's so good and – well, I think it was just habit that made me say that.

Tom smiled.

He's got to pull away from you a little. It's what boys do.

I know that, I told him.

You're a good mother, a good woman and – he lowered his voice – a good fuck. Now where's that waiter? I need a drink and I need it now.

I picked up my bag and went to the loo. It was the same one for men and for women, a tiny brown room behind a rickety door. An air-freshener with a picture of lily of the valley on it, a saint or the Virgin on the wall. I squatted to pee because it wasn't all that clean, and then I rinsed my hands under the single cold tap and put on lipstick. In the tarnished old mirror I thought that my cheeks looked quite polished and rosy – maybe from the fresh cold air – and anyone who didn't know me would say I looked very well indeed.

I put a finger up and touched the small smile lines around my eyes – the ones you had touched only this morning, though already it seemed like a snatch of a moment from someone else's lifetime – and I wondered briefly what was happening to me. Then I picked up my mind and moved it away from those thoughts and I returned to the table and to real life and to Tom who was pulling the centre out of a piece of baguette and stuffing it in his mouth.

I heard this amazing programme on the radio, I told him. There was this woman and she was about sixty-five, or

– yes, that was it – it was her sixty-fifth birthday or something. And when she was fifteen she'd written this letter to herself and sealed it and it wasn't to be opened till she turned sixty-five. Fifty years, can you imagine?

The waiter put a carafe of wine down on the table and Tom poured me some.

And she still had it?

Yes. Not only that but she opened it right there and then on the radio and read it out, in front of all those people, those listeners.

Hmm. Bit risky perhaps? said Tom as he poured wine into his own tumbler. I took a sip and it was perfect, rough and red and it grazed my tongue and lips in exactly the right way. I decided to stop thinking about children, or even about anything, and I laughed.

Good wine, I told Tom.

You like it?

I do, yes. Well I don't think I could have done it, what the woman did. But you know – it was so strange – she didn't recognise a word of it, couldn't even remember writing it. Not a single word. She was quite taken aback. She said it was rather like having this stranger write to her – quite a bossy stranger in fact, telling her what she might be thinking and feeling now, telling her what their hopes and fears and concerns were back then –

What would it be, said Tom instantly thinking of the wider implications. Let me see – the fifties? Fear of Russians? World annihilation?

I nodded, though I wasn't thinking of those things at all.

But really what was strange, I told him, was that in some

63

ways the fifteen-year-old seemed more grown-up and contained than her older self. It was funny but it upset me a bit –

Did it? Tom said, and straightaway he looked nervous.

I was – I don't know – I was a little shaken by it.

Really? he said. But darling why?

I don't know. It was just – it seemed incredibly sad and I don't know why – that small urgent voice from the past, you know, the way it both was and wasn't her. It was like getting a message from a ghost.

But not a ghost. Because the old self was her, wasn't it?

It was a self that had long gone, I told him, and as I spoke I knew that my voice was wobbling a little even though I so wished it wouldn't. So it felt like a ghost, it might as well have been.

Sweetheart, Tom said, and he put his hand back on mine as he studied the menu, you always put such a dark gloss on things. Not everything's sad you know. It actually sounds rather amazing to me, rather a wonderful thing to bother to do – romantic even. Not to mention brave, to open it right there on the radio.

I looked at him and thoughts began to stack up in my head – thoughts along the lines of, yes, he's a perfectly normal good kind man, sitting with his wife in a foreign place and intent on choosing something good to eat. And though he is used to the wife being like this – so odd and unconnected – all the same he wonders why she can't just join in with his good moods and normal thoughts and why, when he's only trying to talk to her, she insists on feeling so – but I don't finish that thought because I'm interrupted by the memory of your face in the café, the shock of the solid shape of you, the glasses, the brushed-back hair, your mouth that once, long ago, contained a pearl. Your hand on my wrist. Baby? You're not real are you?

I was shaken, I told Tom again. It undid me completely, if you really want to know.

The thing is, Tom began to say, but already I wasn't listening.

Two tables away, a baby, maybe nine or ten months, with black curly hair and gold earrings, was busy throwing a blue plastic mouse on the floor. Each time she threw it, she laughed madly and her mother picked it up. Eventually, after the fourth or fifth pick-up, the father had had enough and he took it and tucked it away behind him. When the baby reached out for the mouse, he made a gesture as if to say he didn't know where it was, that it was gone. The baby opened her mouth in a wide O and screamed.

I've lost you, haven't I? said Tom.

We were in heaven with our boys, Tom and I. They seemed to make sense of everything, of life, of our love, of us. We couldn't imagine what we'd done before they came along – how we'd spent our time, energy, money even. We couldn't remember what had made us laugh before, or what we'd worried about.

I wasn't one of those mothers who hanker for a girl, just for the sake of pretty clothes and all that. I was never going to be totally against the idea of another baby – what mother ever says no to the possibility? – but I was very content with my boys. If this was it, then I was happy. I really believed back then that our family felt pretty complete. So the way Mary came along was eerily perfect – as if someone somewhere had other plans for us.

I woke one morning at exactly 6 a.m. and then fell back to sleep – straight into a dream, the way you sometimes do. We – Tom and the boys and I – were in a strange sort of hotel somewhere. A dark garden, white marble steps, a glinty bar, people dressed up. Maybe it was night, it was hard to tell. And I had a mobile phone and I was calling our friends in New York to make an arrangement as they were due to come over in a couple of weeks.

A tiny blonde child was following me around, a girl I'd never seen before. I didn't look right at her, I couldn't for some reason, but I gradually became aware of her, I knew she was there. Blue eyes, a pale face, stiff white hair. A fragile little girl. For some reason I handed her the phone and asked her to dial the number for me. I don't know why, it made no sense, she was only about four years old. It was a dream thing.

When she'd done it, she handed it back, but instead of our New York friends, the phone was answered by someone whose voice I sort of knew, a woman, not a friend, in fact barely an acquaintance really – someone I'd come across a couple of times in the past and had recently heard was very ill.

This woman had cancer and she was in the final stages. I knew this. She was dying. This was all I knew. And I was so flustered to find myself suddenly talking to her – she had a name like Rachel or Rebecca and I knew that I knew it but, just when I needed it, I couldn't find it anywhere in my head – for a moment I couldn't get my bearings. I was embarrassed, yes, but also confused. It

66

seemed terribly rude not to remember her name — as if the fact that she was dying had already wiped her off my memory — but anyway wasn't this supposed to be our friends' apartment? Was it possible that they'd moved without telling us? Or else perhaps they'd lent the apartment to this woman? But then again, wouldn't I know that by now?

In the dream I felt that I seemed to ask her these questions and she seemed to answer them whilst providing almost no information at all. All I could make out was that she was there in bed in that apartment all alone and with no one to talk to, and she'd been there some time. A very long time. Just waiting for someone to call.

I didn't know what to do. I knew I couldn't just apologise for my mistake and hang up on her. Though I barely knew her and had nothing to say to her, still that seemed too cold and unfriendly under the circumstances.

So I wandered through the hotel till I found a quiet, carpeted stairway away from the crowd and I sat down on the bottom step and I took some deep calm breaths and I tried to talk to her. But I was no good. I didn't know what to say. I was stuck, lost for words. I could hear myself being hopeless. What, after all, could I possibly say? Not only that, but it was hardly my business. And anyway I wasn't really a friend of hers, I was just a passing acquaintance, so to attempt any kind of deeper conversation seemed somehow false.

I knew also that this was all a fluke. That if the small blonde child (she'd followed me right through the hotel and was still standing there breathing at my elbow) hadn't somehow mistakenly dialled her number, then this poor woman's death would have been a thing I just heard of in passing – at a party, in the back of a newspaper. And I had to admit though I'd certainly have been sorry, still I wouldn't have spent much time thinking of her. I didn't know her or her family. So I felt myself to be in a doubly difficult position. I felt awful – for her, for me.

But I needn't have worried. It seemed we didn't need to talk much to each other. She seemed comfortable just to have me there at the end of the phone, even being silent. In fact whole minutes passed and we said almost nothing to each other and she didn't seem to mind that I felt helpless and useless, she seemed happy enough just to have someone on the other end of the line.

And though I now and then thought I detected anger in her voice, bitterness too, well I could understand that. She didn't care much for me, but then why on earth should she? If I could perform this one small service for her, of being there, then wasn't that enough for both of us? This was a dream, remember. Somehow in the dream it did seem to be enough – and quite logical – that I could do that.

Though I couldn't see her, I knew exactly how she looked, alone in her bed in that apartment. I knew she was thin and that her skin was drawn and pinched and yellow and she looked bad. I knew she was waiting to die and I knew she was ferociously lonely and – I don't remember what happened then. Maybe she hung up, or I did, because all I remember was that the small blonde child slipped her hand in mine and I looked in her eyes – the clearest, most trusting eyes – and it suddenly came to me that I knew her from somewhere.

Mary? I said. Is it you?

She kept on looking at me as the dream ended as swiftly as it had begun and I woke up beside Tom in the early bedroom light and I wept. I cried my heart out.

It was 6.03. The dream had seemed to last more than an hour but in fact had taken precisely three minutes.

I felt so helpless. I was shaking as I tried to explain the dream to Tom. I tried to tell him how desperately sad it was about the woman, how surprising and unbearable even though I didn't know her.

He rubbed my shoulders. It was only a dream, he said, and I could hear from his voice how much he wanted to go back to sleep. But then I tried to tell him also how I'd somehow known this Mary child, and my lurch of recognition for her had been so strong and startling, so over-powering that when the dream ended, I was just bereft. I'd already forgotten the poor woman. I felt I just wanted to dive back in there and find my little blonde girl, bring her back.

Poor love, muttered Tom but even as he spoke, his breath drifted back into the rhythms of sleep.

I sat on the bed and carried on weeping, monstrous, shuddering sobs that seemed to come from a place so deeply and strangely inside me that it might as well have belonged back in the dream. And even though he was half asleep, Tom went on rubbing my back, and his hands moved in ever more organised circles and then his fingers moved down to the crack of my bottom and he leaned in and started kissing me right there at the base of my spine. I turned to him and I let him hold me and he kissed and kissed me and pulled me back to bed and then he told me that, dream or no dream, I'd woken him now and he wanted me.

We made love that morning without me putting my diaphragm in. Tom knew that, in fact it was all down to him. I began to get up to go and get it but he grabbed my hand and pulled me back. Leave it, he whispered as his hands moved me closer and his leg came over mine, I mean it. It doesn't matter.

It's the green time, I warned him, because in those complicated days I used a kind of fertility machine to determine what days I needed to use protection.

He put his fingers on my mouth as he slid inside me.

Shhh. Let's make a baby. Let's make that little girl – let's make Mary.

Three weeks later I did a pregnancy test and it was positive. Thirty-six weeks after that, I held her in my arms. My blonde girlchild. I'd missed her so very much.

Hello, Mary, I said.

After lunch we walked around Notre Dame, Tom and me. It seemed like a bit of a touristy thing to do but we felt we should, being so close. The snow by then had dissolved to slush, brown and disappointing slush which slooshed through the tyres of all the vehicles that were beginning to make the tails of traffic which would form the slow and grinding rush hour through Paris.

We went into the cathedral. Inside it was echoey like a train station and everywhere there were cameras being pointed at the rose and blue and violet and blackish windows. They were quite overpowering to look at, these windows, like jewels on fire, the weak afternoon sun spilling through colour. But no one was looking at them except through a lens.

I pulled at Tom's coat sleeve.

But – are they allowed to take photographs?

He shrugged and pulled me close to him. I don't see anyone stopping them, he said.

Yes, but in a church?

He put his other arm around me and squeezed me hard. Come on, he said, I've had enough of this place. I feel a siesta coming on.

We walked out past a blaze of small candles and one woman, dressed all in black, holding onto the back of a wooden chair, weeping and crossing and crossing herself. I knew what Tom was thinking and I thought I felt him move me quickly past.

Outside, the air was bitterly cold and the wind hit you in the back of the neck. Pigeons were flapping up across the square and traffic horns bellowed around us. We stood on Pont St Louis as the grey water slid beneath us and Tom shivered and slipped a hand inside my coat, searched for my breast.

So this guy you ran into, what's he up to these days, what's he doing here?

I really don't know, I answered him truthfully.

You didn't ask?

Look, I said, and I realised the early morning now seemed pale enough to no longer feel true, it wasn't like that. It was only a few minutes. We barely spoke. It was – well, it was weird.

Tom put his hands back in his own pockets and looked at me carefully. I realised I had no idea what he was thinking.

In fact, you know, the more I think about it, the more I think I might have dreamed the whole thing, I told him.

Tom said nothing and he looked at his watch.

It's four-thirty in London. Do you want to try Fin now? He should be back at my mother's – just.

I knew he was trying to be kind. So I took his mobile and pressed it hard to one ear, dialled the number, cupped my hand against the other ear and turned against the wind. A boat went by under the bridge and a duck was pecking and pecking at something under the water. The first time I dialled, nothing happened, and I had to start again. Second time, Tom's mother's answerphone – wobble-voiced and halting – cut in.

He's not there, I said. He can't be back yet. It's OK. We'll try again at the hotel.

Tom put an arm around me and kissed my head and I hugged him back as if I meant it.

You don't think so really though, do you?

Think what?

That you imagined the whole thing.

I laughed and pressed my face into his shoulder, then stretched up to kiss his neck. It smelled good, the pepper and soap smell of home. Does it matter? I asked him and I heard my voice come out just about as laid-back as I'd hoped.

Tom held me away from him and looked in my face again. I didn't know what he was looking for. I tried to keep my gaze steady.

You tell me, he said after a second or two. And I thought what a tough customer he could be at times.

★ ★ ★

The hotel room was much too hot again. There were chocolates on our pillows, all the curtains were drawn and in the
bathroom my bottles and lotions had been arranged in an
oppressive semi-circle. Tom put both chocolates in his mouth
and fiddled with the air conditioning while I kicked off my
shoes and lay down on the hard and absurdly smoothly
made-up bed which was now bathed in apple-green light.
I dialled Tom's mother's number again and this time Fin
answered.

Before I could even get two words out, he asked me if
he could watch the match tonight.

What match?

It's against Azerbaijan. It ends at nine forty-five. I'd be
completely ready for bed.

What does Granny say?

Granny says – Granny says I should ask you.

You mean – has Granny said no?

I heard Fin suck in his breath.

She's being really mean.

I rolled over on my stomach and put my fingers in the
impossibly thick white carpet.

Darling, I said, Fin sweetheart, this isn't fair. You know
it isn't. You can't play one of us against the other. It's up
to Granny, it's her decision.

Tom looked over at me with an annoyed face and I
shook my head at him to show I wasn't necessarily going
to give in. Fin was sniffing.

But she said it was up to you! he said.

Is Granny there?

No.

Where is she?

73

Dunno.

But, sweetie, you must know. Did she go out? She would never go out without telling you. She must have told you where she went?

I can't remember.

Fin — now think. Where did she say she was going?

No idea. To the shops? Yeah, I think to the shops.

I sighed because I wished Fin would pay more attention to things.

Look, I said, I could talk to Granny later about this, of course I could, I could ring her up — I looked over at Tom who was shaking his head and gesturing no — but Daddy and I are supposed to be here on holiday, on a break. We're trying to get some rest.

I heard Fin sigh on the other end of the phone.

You know that really, I said, and there was a moment of silence from him. Don't you? I said.

Fine then, he said in a voice that usually signalled the beginning of a sulk.

Tom sat down on the bed next to me and slid his hands up my legs. When I said goodbye to Fin and put down the phone, he kissed me and his breath tasted of chocolate. I looked at him.

You didn't want to talk to him? I said, even though I already knew the answer. He gave a lazy smile and shrugged.

I'm on holiday, he said.

Your mother had gone out, I told him, and Fin had no idea where she was. He just doesn't listen. He's hopeless. It's like there's a part of him that's always off somewhere else.

Like someone else I know, Tom said.

What's that supposed to mean?

Come here, he said and this time I tasted more chocolate on his tongue.

We had the kind of quick, thoughtless sex we reserved for holidays or late nights when we'd come home from a party or restaurant or been drinking or something.

I began by feeling lazy and not wanting it very much but, by the time he'd moved himself all over me and touched me roughly and put himself into me and whispered some stuff in my ear, I was startled by how very much I needed to come. Something about the lunch and the wine, and maybe the hard hotel bed with its absurd lighting. It was a swift, neat orgasm and as soon as I'd finished with mine he had his – groaning, holding my hips in his hands, while twisting his head and somehow dislocating off into a place of his own. I felt sad as I watched him go.

A few seconds of breathing and sinking and then we moved apart – it was so hot in the room – and he took my hand absently in his, squeezed it, let it go again.

Lovely woman, he muttered, and I knew that in seconds he'd be asleep.

I went through a phase, after we'd had our children, when I didn't know what sex was for any more. It wasn't that I'd ever thought that the act existed purely for making babies – and anyway Tom and I had had our nicest sex before we even thought of making Jack.

But now it seemed that it had become strangely senseless, selfish almost – just a quest for individual pleasure, a pleasure that was somehow reduced by knowing for a fact that we could always give and get it easily, just like that. Tom and I had always been able to make each other come. So what? I thought. So bloody what?

I wish you'd talk to me, I used to say to him.

What? Before or after?

Both?

What's to talk about? he said, and he was half-joking and he certainly didn't mean it unkindly but it was as if he really couldn't see beyond the easy fact of our two bodies on the bed.

One time, straight afterwards, I just burst into tears.

Tom was shocked and so was I.

What is it? Nic, what's the matter?

What's this? I asked him through my tears. What are we doing? What is it exactly?

He laughed and lay back down and touched my thigh, just a brief touch that was intended to be reassuring.

It's great, that's what it is, he said. It's great.

I know what you should do, Tom said, when I came back from the loo. He was searching around for the zapper to turn on the TV.

What?

I was completely naked still and sticky between the legs, but I pulled the curtain to one side and looked out. It was just dusk outside, the sky was mauve but soon it would change colour and the world would look sharper and blacker. I saw that the light was on in the room opposite – the room where I'd seen the woman last night or early this morning.

You should take a bunch of notes out of my wallet and

wrap up warmly and go out to the nearest patisserie and buy about six creamy chocolatey cakes.

I turned to him and smiled. It was such a Tom suggestion.

And something for yourself too, he said, and I started to laugh.

Yeah, he said, locating the zapper under the bed, flowers, perfume, whatever. And a bottle of champagne if you can find it. I think I saw an off-licencey place, back on that street, the one you come up before you turn left to get here.

Les Vieilles something?

That's the one.

I let the curtain drop back and turned to him.

We can't drink champagne right now, I said.

Can't we? Why not?

We'll be too drunk. Or I will. We're going to go out to dinner later, aren't we?

Tom turned on the TV, found the blue menu of channels and squinted at it.

Speak for yourself. I'm on holiday. I have no problem whatsoever drinking champagne before dinner.

Oh, I said, and maybe my memory was jolted by the word holiday. We haven't phoned Jack.

I'll try him while you're out. He won't want to talk anyway.

OK, I said, because I knew what Tom said was true and also because it gave me some kind of mad pleasure when he chose to speak to the boys. I pulled on my knickers.

Aren't you going to wash? he said.

Later.

Dirty girl. Unwashed and on a cake hunt. Now hurry up will you, I can't wait for ever.

I took the lift which was already there waiting and I zoomed straight down to the foyer where the white pebble fire was flickering and people were gathered with cocktails on the white sofa. They looked like they'd come in from outside or else were on their way out, jackets and coats on their arms, a look of party on their faces. I could make out some kind of electronic jazz funk beat and the swish of liquid and ice being shaken at the bar and for a moment I stood there, fascinated. There was a part of me that could have just forgotten Tom and his cakes and, even though I was still sticky with sex, gone over there and slid up to the bar and sat on a high stool and tucked my feet under and ordered whatever drink I could understand on the cocktail menu.

But I didn't do that. Instead I turned and walked out of the hotel.

The girl on the desk – a different one from the morning, smiled at me and so did the young bilingual guy who was standing there in his clean white jacket and chatting to her. They had a languid and satisfied look on their faces, as if they didn't mind their work but also as if some kind of special and interesting pleasure waited for them at the end of their day.

Suitcases were piled up in the hall, as if someone was arriving or leaving. Arriving, I decided. As the glass doors parted, the cold banged into me with such force that it knocked the white cloud of my breath back in my throat.

* * *

You and I, we once went for a walk. It wasn't cold at all, not like this, in fact I know it was a stifling summer's night, the kind of airless night where it's still hot in the city at midnight. It's been like that practically all the summer term – day after day, night after night – the kind of endless hot weather that makes the air feel crumbly, that makes boys drink beer in the day and makes it impossible to sleep at night, so much so that in the end no one even bothers trying.

The house has a flattish roof with a little concrete parapet all around. It's pretty hard to climb onto but once you're up there it's worth it. All you can see is sky and TV aerials, all you can hear is the faraway noise of traffic, the occasional sad sound of a radio.

One very hot night, about nine or ten of us take beer and blankets up there. There's Simon and me and you, six boys from the house, and a couple of other people whose names I don't really know. A joint is passed around and there, up among the chimney stacks with a view that stretches right over the city to the Downs, we lie and laugh and talk and smoke and drink and some of you get wrecked.

You are near me, I know that, I always know that, but you say nothing to me. This is quite normal. It's some time since our night of the pearl necklace – six months at least – and nothing else has ever happened between us and I don't think it ever will. I tell myself I don't care and most of the time I can almost believe this is true and in fact that night now seems as unlikely as the snow that fell around it.

Now it's hot, another season altogether and I've just

turned twenty and I've kissed one or two other boys since, though no one half as special or as good and all the while it's as if I've somehow been trying to make myself immune to you – as if you are something a person can actually take precautions against. You'd laugh if you knew this.

But you're near me now, tonight, up on the roof. I can feel you looking, or at least I can feel where your gaze might fall. If only. Whenever you move, I feel it, the possibility of what you might do next. Though in the end, sick of the strung-up feeling it's giving me, I turn away. I move as far away from you as it's possible to move.

Even though it's night the sky is pale, lit up from somewhere or by something we can't see. The soft mysterious light of the city. Someone has brought a guitar up there and every time a plane flies over, both the music and the talking are drowned out. Actually the conversation is going nowhere and though at first I was liking it – just the pure romance of all of us up there on a hot night and the lazy thing of not having to try hard when you know people well – in the end I get restless and distracted. Despite or because of the fact that you are up there too, I decide I've had enough. I know that it won't be long before everyone is stoned and then the talking will peter out and there'll be no point to anything.

Hey, where are you going? somebody asks me as I get up unsteadily and pull my red patterned cheesecloth skirt down around my legs.

For a walk, I say without looking back. The air's so hot it makes me dizzy. I fumble with the hatch thing so I can climb back down into the house.

I'll come with you, says a voice I recognise and I look around and realise with a rush of surprise that it's you.

We walk and walk in that hot hard night. We say very little to each other. I don't care. I feel able to wait for you to speak, to make the moves, even though you have your hands in your pockets and your face is a pale mask, impossible to read. Maybe it's that life is an always increasing mystery to me back then, or maybe it's that we couldn't be further from the people we were on the night of the pearl necklace, but somehow it's extraordinary to me that you are here, walking with me.

We walk through the ugly Victorian streets and into the Georgian part of the city, past houses covered in wisteria so thick the scent seems to knock you off your feet as you pass. Even away from the house, down here in the streets, the night has a violet quality – as if a strange light's being poured on us from somewhere.

We walk right down the main street where the pubs are still spilling out and people are grabbing each other and shouting and a man is vomiting in the gutter by Lloyds Bank, and I realise I'm glad of your company as I might not actually have dared walk this far alone – I'd probably have turned back after a few blocks. Though I'd never say this to you, of course.

We walk along the edge of the square and finally, still wordlessly, onto the bridge itself and I think it's there that we stop and lean our bare arms on the railings and look down – anywhere rather than at each other – and you tell me about your little brothers and how you worried about them and your mom after your dad died. I don't know why you tell me these things, but you do. I look at your face and as usual I can read absolutely nothing in it, but still the words come out. I am dazzled, distressed, glad. Somehow I know you've told no one else these things.

And I think it might be then that I tell you about that afternoon in Italy and the moment when I knew about the abyss – because I remember that you look at me with surprise and recognition and say how incredible that is, because you've known it too. You know that feeling of despair, of the world turned dark and tilting. And I know from the way you say it – the abruptness and hesitation in your voice – that you aren't making it up just to keep me company or to make me like you or something. I believe you completely – I believe that you've known how it feels for the world to swerve and tilt enough to tip you right out of it. And even though you say nothing to reassure me, I feel comforted. You know it too.

We stand there in silence for a few more moments.

It's so very hot and people in cars are shouting and hooting as they speed over the bridge. Earlier in the month a student jumped off and died. A first-year. I don't know what the figures are, how many people jump off in a year, but it's a lot, more than you'd think. You have on just a T-shirt, thin and torn. I have an old cotton cardigan, bought at a charity shop, flung around my shoulders. My feet are dirty in flip-flops. I wait for you to kiss me or to say something else but you never do. Instead we stand in silence for a second or two more and then you just smile at me and without saying a thing, we turn and walk all the way back to the house.

★   ★   ★

The first patisserie I came to in rue Vieille du Temple had a large queue of people spilling right out of the door and it was far too cold to stand there and wait. The second one looked half-closed and there was quite a poor selection of cakes in its dusty window. I looked around for a shop that might sell champagne but could see none so decided instead to have a look around at some of the other shops – there were places which sold bags, antiques, candles and one shop, painted all white, which seemed to sell every possible flavour of tea.

I peered in the window and saw a lady with black hair talking and laughing on the telephone. She saw me looking and turned her back to me. Next door was a friendlier-looking shop with Miffy rabbit and Tintin figures and varnished wooden puppets in the window, but even Fin was too old for toys these days. I needed if possible to find a shop that sold something to do with football or basketball. A French football shirt would have been a great idea, but this didn't look like a road exactly stuffed with sports shops. As for Jack, he'd recently become quite impossible to buy things for. I decided his present might just have to be chocolate bought as we left Gare du Nord.

Some of the shops seemed to be closed, others were clearly reopening for the evening. It was completely dark now and snow was falling fast through the navy blue air but so very fine that it looked more like dust or powder in the creamy lamplight. I picked my way carefully over the pavement where most of this morning's snow has already compacted and gone icy and I try hard not to slip and at the same time I wonder why my heart is beating so very hard, really punching at my ribs. And then I know.

As I round the corner onto rue de la Perle, there you are. Just you, just standing there in the falling snow – gazing straight out in front of you, your eyes fixed on the cold air, as if waiting for me. Waiting for me and yet – you couldn't possibly know I was coming around that corner, could you?

This time I am so shocked my knees almost give beneath me. A hot pain shoots up from my belly to my chest. Nothing in the world could have prepared me for this, a second time in one day. You. I make a small sound but I don't know what it is.

Hi, baby, you say, and you're looking right into my face or at least I think you are.

You seem unsurprised to see me. This time you have on a long leather coat and your hands are thrust deep in the pockets. There's snow flecked all over your fair yet greying hair and a little on your glasses and the snow is melting where it touches the leather of your coat and you have no scarf on and you look a little cold despite the coat, though nothing like as cold as you used to look back in the days when you had no coat.

I stare at you and this time I do almost feel afraid. As if you know and understand this fact, you take a quick step forward, raise a hand to me.

Don't. Don't run away, you say softly.

I'd like to answer. I'd like to find my voice enough to remind you that I'm not the one who has a habit of running away, but the words simply won't come out. I feel myself put my hand up to my mouth. A woman in an orange coat passes me in a hurry and knocks me with her bag and tuts and I step back, off the pavement. As I

84

step back up, another person curses, a bicycle bell rings.

You take another step closer to me.

I'm sorry, you say, and your voice is soft and warm. Really, I didn't mean to scare you.

I say nothing, but I can't move away from you and still I can't speak. The snow is falling harder now, bigger flakes, blown back against the buildings, drifting. It's going in your face. If I turned away from you, it would fill my face so I couldn't see.

Come – you stretch out a hand and take mine and your touch and your pull are so light yet so impossible to resist – here, let's go inside where it's warmer.

You put one hand on my arm and in a moment or two I'm aware that you have somehow moved me into a bar, a small dark brown bar packed entirely with men, music playing, three or four moustaches behind the counter.

You cup your mouth to my ear. I can't hear what you say so you say it again and I still can't hear you but I am so shocked to hear the sound you make and to feel the hotness of your breath on my ear that I start shivering all over. You take my hand again and lead me upstairs, up a little staircase to a place where there are two seats and the music is quieter and you can look down on what's happening below.

Sit, you say, but as you turn to go back down, I can't stop myself. Please, I can't help calling out to you, please don't leave me!

You smile. And then as if it's an answer, you simply unbutton your coat and pull it off and lay it across my lap where it sits, heavy and warmly damp and real. Then you go down the stairs. I watch the back of your head disappear and then I touch the coat – feel its weight, the rub of the leather. I stroke the silky label. The name written there is strange and old-fashioned and maybe American.

Seconds pass, maybe a minute, but before I can start to worry, you're back and you put a clear, icy drink in front of me.

Vodka, you say, and I feel you smiling at me. Drink it.

I stare at the drink but do nothing so you take my hands and pull off my gloves and put them next to the glass on the table. Then you put both my hands around the glass.

I laugh in spite of everything, I can't help it. Though you are touching me, I feel nothing.

It's cold.

Sorry.

I like it, I say.

You do?

Yes I do, I like vodka, but – how did you know?

Again, you just smile.

What's happening? I ask you.

These are the first words I've managed to say to you, the first real words.

Why am I here?

It's me who says it but it could be either of us. It could be you. Because what are we both doing here in this bar after more than twenty years? You say nothing, you just keep your eyes on me and take a long sip of your drink then place it back on the table and keeping both hands on it, still your eyes are on me like they can't let go.

Have you been following me? I ask you then, though the possibility is only just occurring to me. You look at me and shake your head, exasperated.

Foolish girl, of course I haven't. How could you even think it?

But —

I had to see you. I'm sorry but there it is. I needed to see you.

Why?

Because — I don't know why. Or I do know, but —

But — this morning?

This morning?

You completely disappeared. You ran out on me.

You look surprised.

Did I? Well, OK, I'm sorry. I freaked, you say, and you smile a mad little smile at me, as if this explains it all.

I was so scared, I whisper to you across the table.

I glance at your face and it's very pale. You look like you've spent a million years in a cave. Which maybe you have. And just then you take off your glasses and rub your eyes and suddenly there you are, almost exactly the way you were. I think how your hair is too slick, too brushed back. I want to fluff it up and muss it — then add threadbare clothes and the picture would be complete. You would be you again.

Scared? you say as if this surprises you.

You've no idea how scared I was, I say again.

I do. I know it. Baby, I'm sorry, it's just — I didn't know what to do.

Baby. My heart jumps again.

I don't want to scare you, not at all, you tell me, and you look so old and weary suddenly. I mean it, Rosy. If I scare you, I'm screwed. Scaring you is the last thing I want to do.

87

What then? I say. What are you doing? How did you find me here? What's going on? Don't try and make out it's to do with me because it's not, none of it is, I didn't make it happen – and none of it is normal. I just don't –

But you don't answer my questions. You look down at the people in the bar below and then back at me.

It's not at all simple, you say at last.

You're telling me, I reply, and you laugh.

You haven't changed, Rosy, not one bit.

So, I say, ignoring this, do you live here?

You laugh.

Are you crazy? Of course not. I told you. I don't speak a word of fucking French. That's why they hate us over here.

Then –?

I told you. I came for you.

I put my drink down and sit back in my chair. Your eyes are on me. Your blue eyes.

You came – for me?

Two men in leather waistcoats and thick woollen scarves ask in English if they can sit at the table behind us and you say of course and straightaway reach behind and move our coats off the chair. The men both immediately light cigarettes and, on the stool between us, our two coats, yours and mine, wool and leather, slump together. They look like two people, deflated and purposeless, who have collapsed on each other. I wonder if later mine will smell of yours, or whether there will be no trace. No trace, I decide – and realise with a slap of surprise that I have no confidence in the reality of this meeting, less in fact than I had in our last. I've almost finished my drink.

You haven't told me anything, I say, and you look unsurprised and you tell me you know that.

I have to get back soon, to my hotel.

You do?

This time you do look a little surprised – as if you imagine I'm a thing that you've conjured, instead of the other way round.

Of course I do. My – someone's waiting for me.

Your husband?

Sort of.

You take a breath and look down at your fingers. You have sturdy hands, strong hands, not that large. I know without even thinking about it that they will be strangely rough to touch. I know already that if we walked out of here together and I let you, you'd interlace your fingers with mine, flesh tangled in flesh – and that this is how we'd walk, down the street, together.

I need another of these, you say, picking up the glass. So do you.

I say nothing but I don't resist. In any normal polite situation, I'd have offered to get the next drink but this is neither polite nor normal and anyway, there's no way I am going downstairs into that bar. I am about to glance at my watch but I don't because I glanced at it just a second or two ago and I know exactly what time it is. I think that Tom will be watching CNN. Or maybe asleep, mouth slightly open, arms flung wide. He won't worry yet. He knows I like to shop. I know he likes to sleep after sex.

And another reason I decide to stay – if you need other reasons – is because I know that soon you will leave me. There will be no walking out of this place together – that much is already clear to me. I can already feel the moment when I'll have to rise and take my bag and coat and negotiate my way out of this place, where they will all turn to stare at me with open French curiosity, a woman alone in a place of men. I know that whatever I do, whatever happens next between us or around us, soon you will be gone. And because I know this, I'm almost surprised when you come back with two more vodkas.

But then again, your coat's still here.

Thank you, I say, wondering how on earth I will explain it to Tom that I've been drinking.

You know, you can't smell vodka on the breath? you tell me as if reading my thoughts.

Really? Is that so? I always thought it was a myth.

When I've been drinking wine with Tom and I try to kiss Fin goodnight he always screws up his face and turns away. I don't know whether the same is true of vodka as I hardly ever drink vodka even though I like it. Tom doesn't touch spirits, only wine or beer or – to my frequent disgust – Fanta and Coke.

Vanilla vodka and Diet Coke, you say then. That's my drink.

Seriously? I say and I can't help thinking maybe this would explain your new heaviness.

Yup.

That's way too sweet for me. I hate sweet drinks. Even coffee, I can't have sugar –

I hesitate, remembering this morning all over again, the

90

ashtray with two stubs, then the empty one, the single coffee cup, the pure white snow outside.

Tom, my – husband – drinks Coke, I add quickly, but I don't know how he can. I hate it.

Your sort of husband, you say.

I smile. Yes, my sort of one.

You're not married?

Well – look, it's a long story.

I'd like to hear it, you say, and you smile and settle back in your chair.

Not now. Please.

OK. But some other time, yeah?

Will there be another time? Will I see you again?

I ask this question quite bluntly and I wait to hear what you'll say. You look at me steadily and there's a simple patch of silence and then, Rosy, you say. Oh, baby.

Why do you call me that? I ask.

You mean baby?

Yes. Why?

You lay your forearms on the table and lean over towards me and for a moment or two you are almost the same, almost you.

You don't remember?

I don't know.

I need to say something to you, you say, I need to ask you about something. I need to do it now or I never will.

I smile, because suddenly you look afraid and the idea of you being nervous is new to me. But that's how you seem now – nervous, anxious, afraid. I wait and you sip your drink.

It's a – well it's a crazy and somewhat sappy thing – but

it's something I keep on thinking of and, well if I don't say it to you now, then I know for a fact it will never leave me alone.

I shut my eyes because suddenly I know what you're going to say.

There was a night, long ago.

I wait.

Yes?

A night when a certain lady was kind enough to let me share her room because it was –

Extremely cold, I say, and you laugh.

Extremely fucking cold, yes, and –

Go on, I say, and I'm holding my breath.

Well, maybe she'd had a little too much to drink but, well – Rosy, you know what I'm going to say don't you?

I look at your face and I feel a stillness come over me, a strange stillness so pure and welcome that I think I haven't felt it either before or since – before all the terrible stuff in our lives. Yes, I want to whisper, yes, yes, yes. But instead, She hadn't, I say quickly.

What?

She hadn't had too much to drink.

No?

No, I tell you, she barely drank at all in those days.

You look at me thoughtfully.

Are you married? I ask you now, because I really need to know.

Again you look down at your hands on the table and shake your head.

Not any more.

Kids?

A boy. A big boy now. Almost eighteen. He lives with his mom.

Do you see him?

Not enough, no, never enough.

I sigh deeply and I realise I'm glad you don't ask me how many children I have, because I don't want to have to talk about Mary, not now, and I don't think I could find it in me to say: just the two – two lovely boys, one big, one small.

The pearls, I say then, to help you along, do you remember the pearls?

You look at me and laugh.

You think I could forget a detail like that? The pearls, the wonderful pearls. It was all the fault of the pearls.

Was it?

Rosy, tell me something, did you notice what this street is called?

I'm about to say no, I didn't, but then it just floats into my head and I hear myself saying it, rue de la Perle!

You smile, but before you can say anything I do a brave thing. I touch your finger with mine.

I'd like you to know something, I say, I'd like you to know that I was entirely sober that night, that nothing I did had anything to do with drink –

You put out your other hand to silence me and when you speak your voice is low and hoarse, Stop. Hush. I mean it, I don't need to hear this. Enough.

Please listen, it's important, I say. It's very important to me that you know. That night was –

I've never stopped thinking of you, Rosy.

I stare at you. You reach in your pocket for a pack of cigarettes, pull one out.

Really? I say, and I almost want to laugh with surprise, But it's been so long. You've really thought about me since then?

You hold the cigarette in one hand, your lighter in the other and you look straight in my eyes.

All the time. I've thought of you all the time.

Having Mary was a breeze. She was an easy breeze of a baby from her sweet uncomplicated beginning, from the first definite prickling hotness in my breast, to the metal morning mouth, through to the complete inability to tolerate coffee or alcohol or the smell of certain soaps, through to the first time I felt the thrill of her butterflying in my belly.

I'd loved having the boys, each time had been more relaxed and enjoyable than the last, but I could honestly say I'd never felt so completely at ease with my pregnant self as I was now. I'd never looked so sweet and bloomy and exactly as nature intended. People say girls make you sicker, but it certainly wasn't true for me. I ate sensibly and I swam lengths in the pool and I put on the exact right amount of weight, so much so that they praised me at the clinic. I was full of bounce and energy – I carried on writing poetry and began to plan a children's book. I even thought I might get it written before she came. In the end I got nowhere near, but I kept on thinking and feeling almost overly bright and alive right up to the very moment I went into labour. And then I had the kind of birth most mothers can only dream of – minimal pain relief, laughter all the way through, and only two hours later a rush of water that turned like magic into my baby.

My baby, my little girl.

Hello Mary, I said.

The almost seven pounds of her lay in my arms with her head turned slightly to one side and I admired the blonde downy fur on her head, the criss-cross of little veins that showed through the silk of her skin. Her eyes settled shut then and she took a small breath and sighed and her lips parted and there was a bubble there – a whitish see-through bubble made of my milk. She slept with her tiny fingers up in the air, as if pointing to something startling and beautiful that no one else could see.

She came in the winter but the days passed quickly and soon it was spring. The perfect time for new babies. The hours of light were getting longer and soon I could leave the top blanket off her pram. The room was drowned in sunshine but still she went down for her morning nap and she slept. On warmer days I put her pram out in the garden under the apple tree. I put my head as close to hers as I could and tried to imagine how it might feel to wake under that canopy of leaves and gaze at the jagged blueness of the sky through blossom.

She slept and she woke and she fed and she slept. And in between? Well, in between she just gazed at me. I had no idea what she could be thinking but I could see the shapes forming in her head, the questions, the ideas. Her eyes were an almost indescribable colour, blue but not blue, almost a violetish blue – the rainbows you get in the gutter when oil has been spilled on the road. Not a very romantic description perhaps, but the only way I could find to describe the unique colour of my baby's eyes.

She smiled early. Babies are meant to smile at about six weeks but, just like our Jack, Mary smiled at three. It wasn't wind, it wasn't a fluke, it was a smile – warm as sunshine and perfectly timed to catch me unawares. But unlike our changeable Jack, Mary just kept on smiling. Just about nothing except hunger made her cry – and even then she was easily soothed. Just one touch from me and she'd calm down immediately. People said she was the perfect baby and I suppose if perfection equals absolute contentment, then she was.

People claim there are no patterns in life, that it's all random and meaningless, but I know better. You should watch out when strange things seem to happen – things that make no sense to the naked eye. The biggest mistake is to try to make them ordinary and excusable, to try to justify them somehow.

Three weeks after Mary was born, a friend of ours died. I say a friend but she wasn't, not really. She wasn't someone we could have claimed to know well. In fact even now I'm not sure where she lived or even what she did for a job. Something in music or teaching is what I seem to remember. But I'd met her enough times to feel, when I heard she was dead, a real sense of shock. Last time I'd seen her – months before, admittedly – she'd been standing in someone's kitchen talking about some soap she liked on TV. Leaning against the cooker, arms folded, laughing, agreeing that after all the programme was crap. I'd never watched the programme so I only half-listened, smiling and not paying a lot of attention. She'd had on a blue wool pencil skirt that I'd admired and she carried a carrier bag full of gifts for her nieces whom she was going on to visit. I knew her name was Rachel – or was it Rebecca? Something beginning with R, anyway.

No one knew she had cancer, said our mutual friend,

she kept it very quiet. She didn't even tell her own family, her mum and dad, can you believe? They were in shock when it happened. She went to house-sit for someone and she suffered some kind of a heart attack and died alone and, you know, the day I heard she'd died I was supposed to phone her. I'd written it on a Post-it to remind myself – phone R. And I didn't, and then I heard. I feel terrible. I'll never forgive myself.

I was sitting in another kitchen when I heard this, neither the mutual friend's, nor my own. It was sunny, a bright warm day, blossomy trees bending in the breeze. Aretha was playing on the radio. I had a muslin flung over my shoulder, Mary in my arms, her mouth wetly loosening on my nipple as she fell from food to sleep, a cup of cooling Earl Grey tea at my side.

That's so terrible, I said, and I meant it. I couldn't imagine how lonely and appalling it might be to die alone, to face all of that alone. I drank a glass of water and ate a biscuit and when Mary woke I kissed her head and changed her over to the other breast and allowed myself to be comforted by the feeling of her taking hold.

It wasn't until I got home and was getting ready for bed and cleaning my teeth that I remembered the dream I'd had the morning we'd conceived Mary – the dream that led, in fact, to her conception. The friend, the apartment, the dying, the phone conversation. I froze at the basin, brush in hand. Then I gasped so hard that Tom came rushing in, thinking I must have hurt myself.

Even though I'd been in a smoky bar, my hair didn't seem to smell at all, which was lucky. Also by the time I reached the foyer of the hotel, the effect of the vodka seemed to have worn off and I felt quite sober.

It was just like Tom to forgive me for the lack of either cakes or champagne.

Just as well really, he said, I think my cake urge had already passed by the time you went out. And let's face it, Nic, you're never any fun when you get too pissed.

He did not wonder where I'd been for so long. He seemed perfectly happy to accept that I'd managed to shop for almost two hours and still come back with nothing.

We'll get you something nice tomorrow before we go, he said as I showered and then we both dressed to go out for dinner. Some earrings or something, would you like that? And something small for the boys.

I don't have to have anything, I told him, and he laughed and said he was yet to see me turn down an excuse to buy new clothes.

When he asked me what the weather was like out there, I told him that it was still freezing but that the light was very strange. He laughed again.

Yeah yeah, he said, but sweetie do I need the big coat, or will I be all right with just my jacket?

I think you need the coat, I said as I stepped out of the shower, and even though he pulled the towel off the heater and straightaway wrapped its warm softness around me, still I felt colder than I ever remembered feeling.

The bilingual boy was dragging someone's suitcase out of the lift as we stepped in. He smiled with his own strange mix of confidence and shyness and said *Bonsoir* but it was addressed mostly to Tom and not me. Then he moved off, pulling the case down the long corridor and vanished into the turquoise darkness. The lift smelled thick and hot, of someone else's perfume. As the doors closed, Tom pressed me against the wall which was not only carpeted but shag-pile carpeted.

Mmm, you're nice, he said.

So are you.

He kissed me on the lips and tried to get his tongue in and he pushed his hips hard against me and I tried to concentrate on what he was doing but I knew the doors were about to open and I pushed him off gently.

You should know by now, he said.

Know what?

That I'm not safe in lifts.

It was an old joke between us, the kind of lame and dull but sweet thing couples tend to say to each other and laugh about and on any other day maybe I'd have laughed more or at least pretended to.

Downstairs the white room and the white sofa and the white pebble fireplace were looking cool, like a spread straight out of a magazine. Mauve flames flickered and the lights were turned down low and the music was techno-something, a computerish beat and a growly French voice.

Tom saw me looking at it all.

We could have a drink down here before we go out, if you want, he said, and I said OK, though I knew he was just being generous and doing it for me, as deep in his heart he loathed this sort of bar, this sort of place.

Still, I brightened as we sat side by side on the high white upholstered stools at the long mirrored bar and he ordered us two Tom Collins. I realised I'd been longing to sit at this bar and feel how it felt.

You look like a little girl out on a treat, Tom said, and he smiled.

I've never had a Tom Collins before, I told him.

Oh you have, he said. You must have, surely?

I shook my head.

Seriously?

I thought how funny it was that Tom had seen me and my body from every possible angle, had been right in there and had seen his children come out of there, and yet there were still so many normal things he didn't know about me.

But will I like it? I said, and he laughed and picked up a toothpick and fiddled around with it, tapping it on the bar. First one end then the other so it slipped up and down through his fingers.

Well I didn't realise you'd never had one, but that's all the more reason to try it. You can't always have a Martini, Nic.

I put an olive in my mouth, chewed it, then spat out the stone. Tom pushed the ashtray towards me.

You spoke to Jack? I said.

He made a face.

If speaking's the word.

Everything's all right?

He sounds fine.

He did his homework?

You think I dared ask that?

I laughed and picked up another olive. Then – I don't know why I do this, I've no idea – but I turn my head and there you are. Behind us on the furthest sofa, the one beyond the white one. You're sitting there in the far corner of the large room, in your dark leather coat, the only man in the place still with his coat on, and you're looking kind of out of place even though you're holding a glass and you're looking straight at me.

I turn back quickly but even if I didn't feel it burning, I'd know just from Tom's face that my own is flushed bright red.

He stares at me.

What –? Nicole, darling, what happened?

I hold Tom's arm.

I feel – a little sick.

Darling, Nic, you turned around and your face just went – something happened. You have to tell me.

Tom has already slid one leg off the stool and is looking around to try and see what caused this. I don't blame him. It's exactly what I'd do in the same situation. He puts a hand on my arm and I glance in the mirror behind the bar to see if I can see you. I can't. It shows me the wrong bit of the room. The lilies obscure the area I need to see. My heart seems to swerve. I daren't look again.

I steady myself.

Really, I'm fine. I'm sorry. I mean it. I just turned and suddenly felt all sick and faint. Don't know why but it's gone now.

Do you need to go back upstairs? Tom asks me, his hand still on my arm.

I make a face which is supposed to be funny.

I'm not missing my Tom Collins after all that, I say. But Tom doesn't go for it, he doesn't smile.

You really scared me.

I scared myself.

Well, you scared me more.

I might just go to the loo, I tell him as the drinks arrive. I'm still shaking slightly as I pick up my handbag. It's a little red fake snakeskin one, with a silver clasp. It contains tampons and a lipstick and a tiny perfume spray.

Well don't be long or I'll worry. Are you sure you should go alone?

You really want to come with me to the Ladies?

Tom sighs and moves the stick in his drink. I can't read his expression at all.

Don't be long, Nic, he says. I'm serious.

I don't know what I'm expecting as I pick my way between the people and out past the sofas to the glossy dark marble staircase that winds in a shallow spiral down to the toilets. I knew for a fact that Tom would be watching my back and I suppose I imagined that you'd be sitting there still, in your coat, with your drink in your hand, watching the front of me.

But no. The sofa where I'd seen you was full up now but not with you. A crowd of very young people, teenagers almost, boys and girls, drinking together and laughing. The girls were skinny and blonde and mostly dressed in white and from the way they had their legs slung over the boys' laps, and the way the boys' hands drifted lazily over their slim shoulders and knees, it was clear to me that they'd all been there for some time.

Dinner was fun, nice. Tom and I held hands and looked at each other and talked slowly and carefully about anything but our children. I could tell he was pleased with me. It was almost like the old days. It was our last night, so I tried extra hard to make it happy. Actually if I am honest I didn't even have to try that hard. He was being so easy and kind and good – so much the Tom I find it easy to respond to – and I drank enough wine almost to forget how crazy and confusing the day had been, to forget about you. Maybe the earlier vodkas helped too. Or maybe not. Maybe I'd never had them. Maybe it didn't matter. After all, vodka leaves no trace on the breath.

We walked back under bright stars and through even thicker snow to the hotel and Tom stopped and kissed me in the street, full and wet and deep in the mouth as if he meant it. I kissed him back. It was the way we used to kiss often, before Mary. I knew that he was in the kind of mood where he'd want sex, but also that he would forgive me if I was too tired or drunk to do it. Actually I wasn't drunk, not at all, but I had this feeling that the room might tilt when I lay down. Luckily it didn't and this time it was I who, eyes closed, mind happily disengaged, ate both of the chocolates left on our pillows.

Home tomorrow, Tom said as he pulled off his good shirt and flung it in the open suitcase. He looked in the mirror, rubbing his chin and then scratching his chest with both hands. Don't really want to go. Could have done with longer really, couldn't we?

I don't know, I said, but in my head I'd already decided. I badly needed to see Fin and Jack. But I also wanted to get away from this place. I wanted to be home and I didn't want to have to think too hard about anything, least of all you. The last I see of you tonight is a million miles away, at the far end of the long white hotel corridor, as Tom slides his finger in to open the door. You have on the same long coat but your face is much too pale and as I stare at you, you seem to look right around me, over me, into me, through me.

I take a breath and turn away and the door clicks open.

There, says Tom.

I know I'm not drunk. The room looks entirely normal and nothing is tilting. I glance back behind me, expecting you to be gone. But no, you're still there, far away, your eyes fixed on the air around my head.

That's the last time I see you in Paris.

LONDON

The winter that Jack was born, Tom was still trying to raise enough money to go solo and I was working as a reader for a couple of publishing houses but it was poorly paid and the work was sporadic, so we were pretty short of money. Of course we hadn't counted on having a baby quite so quickly, but – being young and romantic – we were hardly going to delay our family just because of the state of our finances. We both agreed that real life was more important than the bank and that we'd struggle through somehow.

Anyway it was easy to make a few changes. We didn't go out for meals in those days and we'd never really been pub people. It didn't hurt much to give up the car and Tom started cycling everywhere. We managed to save a little on food. I'd never been much of a cook, but I cooked lots of nourishing meals which were basically brown rice or pasta with something on top. We laughed later at how boring it must have been, but our tastes were simpler back then. Just a glass of wine in the evening felt like a treat. It was a strangely innocent time.

For the first weeks of his life, Jack slept between us on a sheepskin in our bed and, after that, he graduated to a drawer – a deep old pine drawer pulled from the Victorian chest we kept our sweaters and underwear in. We put the pine drawer down by the side of the bed, where our bedside table usually was. We fixed it up with his sheepskin and some blankets, and then we put Jack in it. And then we laughed. He looked so funny, lying there and cooing at us from inside a bedroom drawer.

For about eight weeks, he fitted it perfectly. But as he grew, we found an old second-hand cot which Tom carefully sanded and repainted and for which we purchased – at ludicrous expense we thought – a brand new mattress. This was a necessity though, because all the magazines said old mattresses were unsafe. We bought a cotton mattress cover too, but we didn't buy cot bumpers as Tom said that was pointless and silly – just another marketing ploy to make new parents feel they had to buy things.

Of course, Fin and Mary never had to sleep in the drawer – they went straight from our bed to the cot. Fin had a de-luxe blanket with a kind of fleecy texture and a pattern of boats and stars on, which he loved so much we finally had to cut it up into small pieces so he could carry them around to suck. And by the time Mary came along, we even had a top-of-the-range wind-up cot mobile – a whole flock of pastel sheep which twirled above her to the tune of 'Für Elise'. But the fact is the drawer was perfectly good enough at the time – and later when Jack was a whole two inches taller than me, the whole idea that he'd ever fitted in that tiny space where I now kept my socks and tights was enough to bring me to tears.

But back then, in those days of not much money, baby equipment seemed shockingly expensive to us. I'd been changing nappies on a towel spread out on the bedroom floor and complaining more and more of backache, when Tom had this brilliant idea. He decided he would make me a changing table, using some old pieces of wood he knew he had stored down in the cellar.

I was sceptical at first. I'd seen the splintery and cobwebby old planks piled up next to the fusebox down in that grim cellar and I just couldn't believe Tom could make them into anything worth using. Not for our baby. Not only that but how could I be sure that anything he came up with would conform to safety regulations?

But he laughed and told me to shut up and trust him and he spent a busy weekend sawing and sticking and nailing. And then painting. The smell of eggshell filled the house. I wasn't allowed even to look at what he was doing. And then, when he'd finished, he invited me into Jack's room to see.

On the small white melamine chest of drawers where we kept the Babygros and muslin cloths was a sturdy white table which came just a little above waist height – definitely the most comfortable height for changing a baby. Beneath it – supported by sweet but sturdy wooden pillars made of dowling – was a deep and generous-sized shelf. On this shelf Tom had stacked piles and piles of our regular disposable nappies. It touched me to see how carefully he'd done it, putting the smooth white polythene ends all the same way round, how neat and satisfying he'd made them look. An extra ledge stuck out on the right side – just a convenient hand's reach away – and here he'd neatly arranged the wipes and creams and lotions we used when we changed Jack. The whole thing was painted a clean glossy white.

Non-toxic paint of course, Tom said in a solemn voice, as he folded his arms and stood back to watch me look.

With Jack wriggling hotly in my arms, I gazed at the table.

There's even a hook, look, to hang the dirty nappy bag, he said, showing me a large cup-hook sticking out of the edge. And then he stepped back again to let me examine it for myself.

I laughed. It's great, I said. Really. It's wonderful, perfect. Better than anything I've seen in the shops.

It was true. No one we knew had a changing table like it. The ones you got in the baby-furniture departments were flimsy plastic things with nasty patterns on them and much too low for comfort. They were badly made and expensive. But this – this was the king of all changing tables. It was the kind of changing table that made you stand outside of yourself for a brief moment and think that life actually could be different and better, if you only had the use of such a flawless and outstanding piece of equipment.

Tom stood back and smiled, then he reached out and yanked at the table. It slipped a couple of inches on the chest of drawers, then stopped.

See? Quite hefty too, he said, pushing it back. Very sturdy and stable. Should see us through a few more babies yet.

I laughed again. My pleasure was genuine. At that moment, on that day, his words filled me with nothing but warmth and gladness and expectation. More babies, more nappies. I could see them now, plump and sturdy little legs kicking like champions as I creamed their sweet, white bottoms.

We arrived back to find London cold and wet and rainy. They hadn't had the snow – just brown skies and browner streets. They were digging up our road again and the bin men didn't seem to have been and other people's rubbish – foil and crisp packets and the greasy white cardboard remains of a takeaway – littered our path. The house was freezing and smelled of cat, a faint odour of urine and stale dried food that only seemed to come when the humans were gone for a while.

We dumped the bags in the hall where, after the immaculate white of the hotel, the first thing you noticed was the wall, scraped and scuffed with the marks of many skateboards and muddy trainers. Tom turned on the heating while I gathered the letters and newspapers up off the mat.

At least the milk didn't come, said Tom, who never had faith in messages left stuffed in bottles.

I pushed open the pine door into the kitchen and saw black gritty paw prints all over the table, dull wefts of cat fur on the dark fabric of the chairs. A bowl of Weetos – the last hurried thing eaten by Fin the morning we left – still sat by the sink and because he hadn't finished the milk, its sour smell, combined with the mustier one of cat, punctured the room.

We'd been gone less than three days, but it felt as if the

house had already turned back in on itself and given up, forgotten us. I picked up Fin's bowl and put it in the sink, ran the tap, the base of which leaked as usual, a jet of cold water spurting out and hitting the windowsill.

Damn, said Tom, I forgot to phone the plumber.

I hate this place, I heard myself say as I watched a squirrel scuffle madly through the flowerbeds where, a century ago or in another world, I'd planted spring bulbs. I rapped on the window and the squirrel sat up, held its skinny foetal hands up in the air, jerked its head once in each direction, then carried on with what it was doing.

Don't be silly, he said, squeezing my ponytail as he walked past to put a load in the washing machine. You've just got back. You're tired. You need a bath and maybe a cup of tea.

I just need not to be here, I said as quietly as I could, and was slightly shocked to realise I meant it.

He looked at me.

It's a recognised syndrome, he said. There's even a name for it.

Oh yeah? I said.

Yeah. It's called wanting-to-live-for-ever-on-a-romantic-break-in-Paris.

Baby! Fin said it first and so we all copied, we all coined it. Every family has its family words and Baby was the family word for our girl. Not especially imaginative or original, as Tom was quick to point out, but still, who cared? It fitted her perfectly. It fitted the unique babyness of her – the softness and the sweetness and the blondeness. The pale, dimpled parts of her that made you want to kiss her, big long soft kisses so you could breathe her in. The chubby feet, the fat round ankles, the small pot belly. The sweet bendy fingers that always had fluff and crumbs trapped in them. The top of her white-blonde girl head which smelled of honey and was somehow robust and fragile both at the same time.

Tom said that as soon as she was crawling or walking we would really have to try and revert to her real name. He said that we couldn't go on calling her Baby for ever or she would end up aged fifty-five wearing marabou slippers and drinking gin at three in the afternoon.

Why would she have to drink gin? asked Jack, who seemed to find that idea even more alarming than breast milk.

So when you say baby, when you call me that, it stops me in my tracks. It's a name I haven't heard in a while, a name that almost literally seems to pull my breath out of me, out of my lungs, my chest. On that evening in Paris that no longer feels at all like yesterday, you lean your arms on the table and you look at my whole face and you call me that, you call me baby – and my heart contracts and the whole world shrinks away from us.

Baby? Baby?

Is that what you called me on that other night when the pearls spilled all over the carpet and you took one in your mouth and you told me to come and get it?

I walked right up two flights of stairs to the top of the house and pulled Fin's old brown bedroom curtains shut. Then I opened them again, just a crack and pressed my face to the blackness of the old Victorian window. It was dark outside and the window was spattered with rain, not snow, just rain. The rooftops melted into the sky, barely visible in the grey night light. I found I was touching my mouth with my fingers, feeling the softness of my bottom lip, a place where I could no longer imagine a pearl or a tongue for that matter slipping around.

Hush, you'd say. Stop thinking.

But what if I can't? What if I can't stop thinking?

Baby, come on, you can.

All right then, what if I won't?

Shhh.

Lex 2 – that was the name of the cat who came after the poor old first Lex died – entered the room with a small throaty noise and jumped straight on the desk by the window, sliding along for a second and displacing Fin's cut-out basketball and football pictures till a few of them floated to the floor, followed by the thud of his school organiser and a pencil sharpener.

Lex 2 mewed at me pointedly as if I was supposed to understand what she was saying and I saw that her muddy footprints were already all over the windowsill. I pushed her away and found that tears were falling down my cheeks and I blotted them with the sleeve of my jumper and then I shut my eyes for a second and when I opened them again nothing had changed at all and the black rooftops were still there, with their clutter of TV aerials.

I wondered if it was snowing in Paris. I wondered if rue de la Perle was still thick with snow. Then I picked up Fin's biro-scribbled school book and put it back on the desk, but I left most of the sports pictures on the floor.

★   ★   ★

It was better once the boys were home from school, making their noises, complaining about stuff and banging doors. The house started to shift itself around them – at first unwillingly, then more easily. Everything loosened. Slowly the smells disappeared and the heating ticked over and the water got hot and the radiators began to creak and bubble, the kettle chuntered up to the boil – family filled every crack of the space.

Tom made them come straight in the kitchen with their bags so we could empty the dirty washing out of them. The boys always carried their stuff around in carrier bags, which drove him mad.

I hugged Fin and felt him waver, unsure of how hard to hug me back.

You feel even bigger than when we left you, I told him, mainly to cover over his embarrassment.

Mum, he said, it's been two days.

Tom got his toolbox out and managed to screw the neck of the leaking tap down temporarily so the spurt of water was reduced to a dribble. He scrolled down his phone to see if he still had the number of the plumber.

Such a drag to have to pay a call-out, if all it needs is a new washer, he said, and I saw that he looked hot and frowny and there was a black smudge of something on the sleeve of his shirt.

Fin had requested boiled eggs and soldiers for tea. Two eggs done for exactly five minutes and fifteen seconds, eight or ten buttered soldiers – white toast not brown, he said. He always asked for this exact thing when we'd been away and I never minded, I knew it was his way of taking charge of me again, of marking out his territory and reassuring himself all over again that life could be solid and dependable and good.

You shouldn't always give him exactly what he wants, Tom muttered, looking up for a second from his phone.

We have eggs and we have bread, I said. What's the problem?

It's a hassle for you.

It's not, I told him, and he held both hands up in the air.

OK, he said. Just trying to save you work, that's all.

Fin sat in the chair and said nothing and tipped it as far back as he could without falling.

Don't. Don't tip your chair, I told him, and it came out snappier than I meant it to.

Tom said nothing.

Jack came in and before I could even ask him, he said he wasn't hungry. He stood stiffly while I hugged him then he dumped his coat and rucksack on the floor in the hall.

But when did you last eat? I asked him.

He shrugged.

It's OK. I've had stuff.

Stuff?

I noticed he had a huge spot on the side of his nose, bigger even than the one he had before we went away. I asked him if he minded if I hung up his coat for him.

No, he said.

She means would you mind hanging it up, Tom said, and Jack made some kind of a noise.

Do you need me now? he said, addressing Tom, not me.

Why? said Tom.

It's just – I have stuff to do.

Well, Tom began, but Jack was already halfway up the stairs and seconds later music thumped from his room.

While we waited for the eggs to cook, Fin tried on his new football shirt over his school jumper. I told him I was sorry I couldn't find a basketball one and he said it was OK.

I don't even know if they have basketball in Paris, he said. I mean are there even any black people?

Of course there are black people in Paris, said Tom, laughing, and I could tell he was getting ready to launch into one of his lectures about geography or ethnic minorities but Fin wasn't listening. He wanted to tell us about the horrible time he'd had with his grandmother.

I'm never staying with the Fusser again, he said – because this is what we call Tom's mum behind her back – I'm too old for it and she's too cramping of my style.

I reminded him that staying with friends wasn't any better, in fact if anything it was worse.

That was Josh, he said. I hate him and he has horrible parents. It would be fine if it was Fred or Louis or Gita.

Who's Gita?

He gave me a quiet look.

Gita's a girl, he said.

Later he watched me make the sandwiches for tomorrow's packed lunch. What's that you're putting in? he said.

Tuna.

Hmm.

OK?

Yeah.

I cut two more slices of bread for Jack's sandwich and got a tub of hummus from the fridge.

Who's that one for? Fin asked me.

Jack. I don't think he'll want tuna.

Well I'd much rather have that one.

I sighed.

I thought you didn't like hummus at the moment?

That kind I do. The non-organic. At the moment I prefer that kind to tuna.

I put down the knife and wiped my hands.

He's playing you, Tom warned as he opened the fridge and got himself a beer. I heard myself sigh again. All I ever seemed to do these days was sigh.

Are you playing me? I said to Fin. Because if you are, it's really not fair. Will you seriously not eat the tuna? I've already made it now.

He shrugged.

OK, I said, because Tom was still in the room. You're having the tuna and that's that.

I wrapped both sandwiches and put them in the fridge and Fin watched me, rocking dangerously backwards on his chair again. I said nothing.

You know, Mum, he said when Tom had gone, I think Lex 2 is, you know, pregnant.

Seriously? I said.

Yup!

I walked over to him and held his chair still so he couldn't rock and he laughed. I kissed the top of his head, something he still let me do if no one else was in the room. As soon as I let go of the chair, he started rocking again.

Fin, I said, but he ignored me.

She's definitely pregnant, he said.

I don't know if she's old enough, I told him.

But she hasn't been done? Fin said.

She hasn't, no, it's true.

He rolled his eyes and took a breath.

Well, I think she's going to have about eight. Eight kittens. Can they have eight?

I don't know. I'm not sure. Eight sounds like a lot.

Well I'm sure she is.

Has she got fatter?

Not just that but, you know how before Josh's cat gave birth her nipples got very big and the fur around them seemed to go? Well, I just turned Lex 2 over and her nipples are exactly the same – very big and not much fur.

I'd better have a look then, I said, thinking the last thing we needed in this house was more cats.

If she does, can we keep 'em? Fin asked. I'd do all the work and the looking after and all that. I mean it, I'm not just saying it.

We certainly couldn't keep them, I said. We'd have to find homes. But the kitten part would be quite fun. Maybe you could have them in your room? Still, don't get too excited. We don't even know if she is pregnant yet.

Well, said Fin, I've seen that tomcat shagging her about eight times in the garden.

Fin! That's not a nice way to say it.

He smiled at me.

OK. Humping then.

I went up to Tom and put my arms around him, pressed my nose against the warmth of his neck.

I love you, I told him, and he laughed.

Hey, funny woman, what's up now?

I drew back a little.

Nothing's up. I'm saying I love you.

Hmm, he said, and I was about to move away but he pulled me closer and tucked a long wisp of hair behind my ear. I knew he was doing it affectionately but I couldn't help it, I pulled it forward again. He didn't notice.

Come here, he said, and his voice changed and his hands slid under my breasts.

No, I told him, not now.

Why not?

Why?

I want to hold you a moment. I want you to stop wriggling.

He kissed my ear.

Tom, I said, I'm so tired. And I still have to do the boys' beds.

Do it later. I'll help you.

No, I said, not later. Fin's shattered and will crack soon. Really, I mean it, it has to be now.

Tom looked at me with eyes that said he gave up, that he didn't know what he was or wasn't doing, that he'd run out of ideas to please me. I knew those eyes so well – hurt but cold, baffled but somehow resolved.

What? I said.

No, he said, it's you, Nic – you tell me what.

What do you mean?

What? he said slowly. What have I done now?

Oh Tom, I said, don't take everything so personally.

I mean it, he said, I'm baffled. I literally don't know

what happened just then, during that little interaction of ours.

I laughed but my heart curled in on itself.

Interaction? I said, and I knew I sounded spiteful. He said nothing, just looked at me steadily.

Is that what it was? I asked him. An interaction?

He took his hands off me.

You can sneer at my language if you have to, Nicole.

I wasn't sneering, I told him, and he sighed.

Then – I just don't understand why you can't take love from me.

That was love?

He did his calm sane face, the one that made me feel I was a lunatic.

I was being loving, yes. I was trying to.

You have to try?

He said nothing and looked at me, even calmer this time and a small part of me felt even more furious with him.

Half an hour later, beds done, I was at my desk for the first time in several days. My study is the smallest room in the house – a kind of half-room on the first landing. I don't mind its smallness, not at all, in fact I like it. The little space always seems to concentrate my mind and it not only looks out over the garden but has a skylight in the ceiling as well. Some days I lie on the floor on the old threadbare carpet and watch the planes pass overhead. Just seeing them go over on their way to somewhere else seems to calm me.

On the wall – which is painted pure chalky white – is my favourite photo of the boys when very young, tucked into our bed and watching TV. Jack is about six, Fin about three. You can't see it's the TV, just that their attention is fixed on something else and that it is the same thing they are looking at, though each is looking in his quite different way. Jack is half-smiling, his body relaxed, in green and red Thomas the Tank pyjamas, his mouth hanging open and a dopey glaze over his face. Even now he watches TV in the same way – trusting, giving himself over completely to the experience.

Fin watches quite differently – a thumb stuck in his mouth, his lower lip wet and fat – but with one eye on the TV and the other, half-anxious, half-excited, on Jack. As if he can't quite relax into the experience – as if a part of him is there in the bed watching TV, whilst the other part is outside of himself, intent on taking the whole thing in and feeling the finality of it all.

Tom would have said it was ludicrous and that I was reading far too much into a three-year-old boy sucking his thumb, but I wasn't at all sure. Even at eighteen months or two years old you could see the exact same thing in Mary, that quality which I can only describe as a kind of heightened awareness, a sense of being a small part of something larger, a fragment of a whole.

I turned on my computer and started to clear my desk a little. There was dust on the phone, Lex's scuffy garden paw marks on the mouse mat and a pile of stuff I hadn't dealt with – mostly bills and things from before Paris – on the keyboard. There were also a few printed-out drafts of the poems I was pretending to write, but I knew without even looking at them that none would ever be finished. I turned them over and shoved them down the other end, under the pile of books which I kept on promising myself I'd read.

My computer whirred into life and I double-clicked to open my emails. I could hear Fin shouting something downstairs and beyond that the hum of the TV. Sixteen emails were coming into my inbox one after the other. Normally I'd go through them in order, quickly to start with, then again more slowly, relishing, reading each one properly. At this second stage, if I'd got time, I'd usually reply – I always preferred to deal with them on the spot before I forgot or lost interest or else they slipped right off the edge of my screen and therefore my memory and were forgotten. But now, tonight, I do none of these things. Tonight, before I can even begin, I stop.

Because I see your name.

Right there. Sixth email down. Your name on my screen, in bold. I can feel shock in my chest, my hands, behind my eyes. An email from you. Written yesterday. My heart bumps. It's you. You're back. Already. I can't believe it. You've gone and written to me.

Hey, Rosy!

(or Mrs Rosy as I guess you most probably are by now)

Remember me? Long time, yes? Well, how're you doing? Hope you won't mind that Simon Riley gave me your email – I think he said you and he had been in touch some time ago?

Why am I writing? Well, you may find this hard to believe but I'm a big fatcat businessman these days and I have to come over (on some business, would you believe) to see some other fatcats in about a month's time and I'll have some time to kill in London and I wondered if you wanted to meet up? A drink? Dinner even if you're not too busy.

Or, OK, let me say it. If you feel no particular urge to see some dumb-assed no-hoper from your student days again, then don't reply to this. I won't be hurt (well, OK, maybe just a little).

What is it, Mum?

Fin was suddenly standing in the doorway and he must have seen my face because he was gazing at me in a worried way and trying to see what was on the screen. He had on what he wore for bed these days – saggy flannel pyjama bottoms handed down from Jack and a stained old T-shirt in faded black and white with a photo of a dog on it.

I moved my head in his direction and I tried to smile.

What's what?

You look – really weird.

I put my hands up to my face and for a few seconds I wondered what Fin could see on me.

Are you crying? he asked me with real concern, and I smiled again and took a breath.

No, sweetie, of course not. I'm fine, I'm OK. Just a little bit frazzled and tired, that's all.

Oh.

He gazed at me uncertainly.

Where's Daddy? I asked him.

Dunno. Downstairs I think.

Tell him I'll be down in a minute. Tell him to pour me a nice glass of wine and I'll be down.

Fin turned to go.

I came to tell you something, he said, but I forgot what it was.

I smiled.

Oh well, I said, it'll come back to you.

Oh I know, he said. It's Lex. It's definite.

What's definite?

Lex 2. You know, kittens. You feel underneath her. I absolutely swear I'm not imagining it. It's true.

Well great, I said slowly. That's just great.

You don't mind? You'd let me have them in my room?

Maybe, we'll see.

You're not listening, are you?

Sweetheart, I said, just give me a moment to finish something off and then I'll be down, I promise.

He leaves and I stare at your email. I read it over and over and it's still there, still on my screen, though it makes no sense to me, still it's there, its bold backlit letters on my computer screen. I scroll up and down but it stays there still and it does not change.

Remember me? Long time, yes? Well, how're you doing? Mrs Rosy as I guess you most probably are by now.

For a moment the world is crashing down around me.

I press Reply and in the new box that is brought up, I write:

Is this really you?

Do you by any chance like vanilla vodka with Diet Coke?

Rx

And I send it before I can think any more. Then I went downstairs and joined my family and we watched a programme on TV about the Berlin Wall which Tom said was educational. I hardly heard a word of it. Twenty minutes later I went upstairs to get Fin to clean his teeth and to send him on up to bed and on the way back down I passed my study and I couldn't help it, I went in and I push the door shut and quickly press Send & Receive. Straightaway, as I know it will, as I know it must, your reply pops up.

Dear RX

How in fuck's name did you know that?

It was strange but I had no real memory of Mary's first birthday. Even though it hadn't been all that long ago, still it had gone for me, dissolved as if it had never happened.

We were staying with some friends somewhere near Sussex, I know that – in a massive but dark and cluttered house belonging to the stepmother or stepfather of one of them. We'd been given the whole house for a long weekend while they were abroad. Three or four couples and their various kids. It was practically a mansion – long dark corridors leading to more bedrooms than you could count, a vast kitchen with racks of herbs drying overhead, dodgy central heating. A huge long garden with a tangle of currant bushes and a pond at the bottom. The pond kept all the parents of the younger children on the edge of hysteria, but I know our boys had a wild time. Unlimited access to other kids, endless pizza, minimal parental supervision.

It's like *The Lion, the Witch and the Wardrobe,* Jack breathlessly observed as he flew past the kitchen carrying a plastic axe and stopped briefly to check we were still his parents.

Yes, I said, but don't go climbing into any wardrobes.

Why not?

Because it's someone else's house and we have to respect their things.

The strange thing is, I remember that conversation with Jack, but nothing of Mary's birthday.

I do know there was some kind of a celebration or a party, because there's a photo of me wearing a turquoise velour cardigan, my hair very long, longer than it is now, bending over this blonde baby and blowing out the single pink candle on her cake.

The baby sits upright and alert in the high chair and holds her head very still, an expression of intense concentration on her face. She frowns and gazes at the candle, not with excitement exactly, but as if it might tell her something precise or interesting or important. What I don't like about the photo is that my hair is in the way. The long curtain of my hair obliterates what you might otherwise have seen – the rest of the baby's face, her mouth. Her peachy mouth.

As it is, only her eyes are visible – wide and black, watching that flame. Waiting for the moment to happen. And the next, and the next.

It's odd because though I can't recall the moment of the photo, still I do have plenty of other memories of that time, of that house. The ploughed fields, iced every morning with frost. The cows in their sheds, which Fin insisted on visiting eight times a day. There's a photo of him in his red anorak, thrusting a handful of straw through the bars with his face averted.

I remember parents taking ages to get their kids settled for bed – lengthy baths and endless bedtime stories – and me being so glad as usual that I had Tom, no-nonsense Tom, who was able to get two boys washed, teeth cleaned and more or less quiet in their beds in the ten minutes it took me to feed Mary. After that, it was downstairs for a drink.

Grown-up time, Tom used to say, and everyone thought he was joking but he was actually quite serious about it. And we'd sit and hold hands on the big saggy sofa as the fire crackled and – entirely alone – we waited for any of the other parents to come down.

I do remember kneeling on the rush matting in that huge and draughty sitting room, with its big stone fireplace, and wrapping our daughter's birthday presents. I know the paper was blue with white daisies on. I even remember choosing the paper – I remember the moment of being in the shop and pulling the sheet off the stack. But I don't remember what the presents were, or in fact anything that we gave her ever. I know, for instance, that Jack got a pull-along train for his first birthday, and I'm pretty sure that Fin got a yellow inflatable car. And those birthdays were far longer ago, so why couldn't I have told you what we gave Mary?

I can only guess I was used to kids' birthdays by then and I was tired and busy and didn't take enough notice. With your third one, you get lax. You assume your baby's first birthday is just the first of many – that next year there will be two candles on the cake and so on. You assume a lifetime of cakes awaits her, a long line of lit-up candles stretching practically into infinity. You assume a lot of things.

I decide to say nothing to you about Paris. What could I possibly say that wouldn't sound completely insane? Hey, don't you remember that we actually saw each other a couple of days ago? Are you forgetting that you appeared and disappeared and scared and upset me and, well, see how there's really nothing I can say?

Either there are two of you, or you are messing with me, or I imagined the whole thing – I dipped into a place in Paris that wasn't really there. Narnia-land. It wouldn't be the first time. Either there are two of you or I'm going crazy, heading back into the land of the unbalanced. I know which Tom would vote for.

I don't feel mad though. I feel sane, entirely sane – more sane than I've felt in some time.

Just a hunch, I email back to you about the vanilla vodka and Diet Coke, a lucky guess.

Like hell, you write. I think you've been talking to Simon Riley, you add, referring to the mutual friend who apparently had put us in touch. He came over recently on a visit. Just for a day or so, passing through. But long enough to get to know all my shameful fat-ass habits.

I say Maybe, and leave it at that. I don't mention that I barely know Simon Riley, not really, and certainly haven't heard from him in at least three or four years.

I ask you whether you're married now, whether you have any kids.

Divorced, you write back. One son, pretty big now. His mom doesn't really tolerate me too well. It's kind of complicated.

You ask about me – about my kids, about my life. What have I been doing with myself all of these years? I pause for a moment then I write that I have three children.

You ask for their names and ages and I tell you that's kind of complicated too and will have to wait till I see you. You ask if I still write.

127

You remember that?

Sure I remember that. Your little typewriter tapping away when all the rest of us were wrecked or asleep.

I tell you that I do, but only poems.

Mrs Rosy! you email back the very next day. You're too modest. I looked you up on the internet, you're a published poet – you won a prize for chrissake.

I explain that it was a small prize and it is now some years ago.

Ha! You're not getting away with it like that, you write. I'm impressed. I'm fucking impressed.

But what about you? I say. You're a big businessman now.

It's all about money, you reply and I sense a weariness between your words, the business I mean. It's just bean-counting, nothing fancier, nothing more. I used to have to wear a suit and tie but hey, now I'm more important I get to dress down – jeans and sneakers – and I get to shout at people too. You'd laugh if you could see me. But some days if you want to know the truth, it really gets me down. I dream of jacking it all in and playing guitar.

Then why don't you?

Oh Rosy. I haven't the balls and I have to pay my ex so much fucking money. I guess I need to grow some balls if I'm ever to do it.

I remember that you used to play guitar before, and I ask you if you ever tried to make a living from it.

The short answer? you write. No. Though it's still my big passion. A secret middle-aged kind of passion now – in fact my son plays way better than I ever did. But enough about that. I'm not good enough anyway. I never was. Unlike you, with your poems, Mrs Rosy.

I'm not sure I can write any more of those, I tell you and for the first time I realise it's what I believe, that I'm telling myself what I know to be true.

Have you ever been to Paris? I write, finally.

I think I went to somewhere in France once, years ago when I was a kid, you write, with my mom, I mean. Why? Have you?

We went there for our anniversary, I write, last week in fact.

Nice, you write, and I notice that your tone cools a little. How many years have you been married?

Not exactly married, I write back. It's complicated.

Hmm. You'll explain when you see me?

That's right.

You tell me you should be over in two and a half weeks' time. You're just waiting for confirmation on flights, meetings and so on. Your schedule is entirely in someone else's hands, but you'll probably be over for four days. I put a mark by these days in my diary, but I don't write your name – just a mark. I keep all four of the days free.

You make me laugh. Even at this great distance of years and miles, you really make me laugh.

As the days pass, I'm surprised at how easy it is to write to you, to give you full and honest and unthinking answers, to share stuff with you that I'd have trouble sharing with anyone else, even Tom, well OK, especially Tom.

Tell me three things you love, you write one day. They can be anything, but the only rule is you must come straight out with them, you mustn't think too hard about it.

My children, I write immediately, and – feeling myself hesitate, I shut my eyes, and – the sky.

The sky?

Yes. The sky. Seriously. Any day, any colour. It lifts me. I think I would die if I couldn't see the sky.

Don't say die, Mrs Rosy, I mean it. Please don't talk that way about yourself.

What I mean, I write back, is I suppose I love weather. I notice it. Light and dark and cold and hot, it all affects me – really it affects me quite a lot, beyond the normal I mean.

That's nice, you write, I like that.

Don't laugh, I write.

I'm not laughing.

I can hear you laughing.

You can hear me?

It's in the words – between the words you write.

That's not laughing, Mrs Rosy, you reply. That's just me smiling. You make me smile.

Do I?

Yeah. You do. You make me happy. Writing to you makes me happy.

I don't write straight back to you when you say this. There's a twenty-four-hour gap. I find that I want to think about you a little, I want to think about what you've just said. This dialogue has begun to make me breathless.

You didn't tell me the third thing? you write when we start up again. You said your kids and you said the sky. You only gave me two.

I hesitate.

I can't think what the third thing would be, I write, and a hard cold feeling lodges itself in my belly.

You can't?

I'll think about it, I write.

That's no good, you reply. It doesn't work if you have to think about it.

I decide that I have to stop myself answering your emails so instantly. The key, I decide, would be to slow down a little. I soon work out that, since you seem to get up very early, your day must start around 3 p.m. my time. So if I log on at around 4, there'll almost certainly be one from you – either written first thing in your morning or maybe the night before, as I slept. And if I reply to it that afternoon, then you'll send me another before evening. That's the thing with us: each email just seems quite naturally to elicit a reply. And so it's hopeless, there's never a stop, the dialogue goes on and on. And they get longer, the emails. Now each one has at least two PS's. And then there's the meaning that lies between the words. If I wait for a note to settle, I can see more in it – it will seem to grow larger on the third or fourth reading. In fact I find I can read each one of yours at least ten times and still new meanings will filter through.

You write so well, I write to you. I mean it. I'm not just saying it. You're such a good writer.

Shame on you, Mrs Rosy, you reply. You're messing with me. You're the writer lady and I'm the dumb-ass Yank.

No, I say, you choose your words so well. Or at least, you don't appear to choose them at all. You express yourself so easily and I understand every single word.

It's the best thing in life, you write. It's what everyone wants — to be understood, to feel understood. But that comes from you, you know — it's the way you read, the way you pay so much attention. My writing is quite ordinary, I know that, and I'm sorry but you won't convince me otherwise.

It's the best sort of writing, I reply to you. Well, it's the kind of writing I like best anyway.

Then you should prepare to be disappointed when you meet me, you write. I swear I'm much dumber in the flesh.

I can't think what to say to this.

One day there isn't an email at 4, 4.30, or 5 and I'm shocked, despite all my good intentions, at how madly disappointed I feel. Every half-hour I check and, furious with myself, I am about to turn off and leave the room when you send me one at 6 instead, apologising and saying you had a difficult breakfast meeting and were too rushed to write before it.

I flush with embarrassment. Even though you are so many thousands of miles away, I find I am hot to the skull. Is it really possible that I've become so dependent and demanding?

It's OK, I write back a little too quickly. You don't have to apologise. Really — I don't expect you to write every day.

Well you should expect it, you reply, because I do. I expect it. I have to write now, every day. And I don't think I could bear it if you didn't reply.

Another day I realise we've exchanged six emails before 8 p.m. This really scares me. I decide that I must try not to write for at least twenty-four hours. It was going to be extremely hard, I thought, but I would be strict with myself. The only way was to go nowhere near my computer, not even turn it on. And so there it waited all day, blank-faced and accusing and sad. In the end I got sick of walking past it and I shut the door.

I tried to focus on my family. I helped Fin prepare an old grocery box for Lex to have her kittens in. With our somewhat blunt kitchen scissors, we cut out one of the sides of the box and bent the flaps down and then we lined it with an old towel. Fin wrote KITTENS BORN HERE in thick black marker pen across the top, and as usual I reminded him that it was going to be a few weeks yet before they came.

I know, he said. But then again Mum, you never know, she might have them early.

Very very unlikely, I told him, It's only human mums who sometimes do that – and for a second the old familiar ache that was Mary flashed across my heart and I realised with a small quick shock that I hadn't had a painful thought about her in some time.

Fin poured himself some lemon squash and topped it up with water from the tap, but he ran the tap too fast and it overflowed and went all over his sleeve. He mopped it with the kitchen towel which he threw down on the floor.

Pick that up, I said, and he did.

I just wish they would hurry up and come, he said with a sigh. I wish it didn't have to take so long. I wish it was days not weeks.

The time will go quickly, I told him, you'll see – and

I realised as I spoke that by the time Lex's kittens were born, I'd have seen you. And that I could not possibly imagine how that would be. I could not imagine doing it and I could not imagine not doing it either. I thought if I had to wait too long to see you again I might burst. But at the same time I was filled with dread. And without knowing I was even doing it I glanced at the kitchen clock and did what I'd done automatically for the last few days – subtracted eight hours to see what time it was for you.

Why are you looking at the clock? said Fin.

To see if it's teatime yet, I told him.

Tom came home. What's up, Nic? he asked me.

What d'you mean what's up?

You're all on edge.

Am I?

Yes, you are. You're jumpy as hell. Is something worrying you?

Not at all, I'm fine, I told him, and I kicked my study door firmly shut because Lex had gone and pushed it open again.

Later in bed I pulled him to me and I tried hard to make it up to him. I kissed his face, his dark, unruly brows, his closed eyes. Parts of him looked old these days but other parts still looked young. I held his hands in mine and I turned them over and over.

What're you doing?

Looking at your hands. I like them.

After his hands, I touched the heavy hotness of his balls and he smiled and then he laughed with pleasure and surprise and when he was hard, I climbed on top of him and fitted him into me and we made what felt like a kind of love and I knew that he was glad because I'd started it – he was always wishing I would start things – and when he came I tried with all my heart to adore him, I tried to make it all true.

But I found myself watching his face a little too closely – the way it twisted away as he experienced pleasure, the way his mouth moved and puckered, and I wished he didn't have to look like a stranger then, I wished he could carry on just looking like Tom.

Name three things you love, I whispered to him as tiredness made his mouth fall open and the wetness began to leak out of me.

Sleep, he said, and he stroked my head once and turned over and was gone.

When I turn on the next day there are four emails from you, each increasingly frantic and sad. You are afraid I might be sick, or that something has happened to one of the kids, or even that I just don't want to write to you any more. If it's that last one, you say, don't worry, I can deal with it, I'll try hard to understand. But please, Rosy, I just need to know that you and your family are OK.

I gaze at my screen and my hands tremble.

I write back and tell you I'm sorry, that I'm fine, the kids are fine, we're all fine. I tell you I was just busy for a day, that's all.

Have you really nothing better to do than write to me? I write then, attempting a lighter tone, teasing you.

Your reply when it comes is succinct enough to make my heart contract.

No. I've quite literally nothing more important to do with my time. I need this. Please, Rosy. Do what you have to do with your kids – feed them or help them with their homework or whatever, what I mean is, don't neglect them – then come back and write me one more tonight. One of your long and crazy ones, OK? Please, just do it for me, OK?

Alone in my study I begin to laugh.

Long and crazy? Is that what you want? Are you begging me? I write, and I press Send and then I wait, breath held, finger in my mouth.

Absolutely, comes the reply, I'm on my knees. You can't see me but I swear I'm on my knees and it's not a pretty sight, this fat-assed businessman on his knees.

You're not fat, I write.

Just wait till you see me before you decide that.

OK, I write, but it'll be at least an hour. You'll have to wait till I've cooked pasta for the boys.

I write it simply and jauntily, but my heart is banging in my chest.

I'll wait, you write. I've got to go into a meeting now, but what's going to get me through it is knowing you'll be writing me. Smiles, kiddo.

You're very busy up there, Tom said, and I could tell he assumed I was finally writing poetry and was genuinely pleased for me.

I kept my eyes on the boiling water, tipped in the pasta quills. I decided that tonight I might go up after supper and actually try to work on a poem. I didn't want to lie to Tom, that was the last thing I wanted to do. And anyway, for the first time in a very long time, I could almost imagine writing something.

Then one day it all shifts into a higher key. I don't know why. Or, that's not entirely true, maybe I actually do.

One day you write to me much earlier than usual. An email comes at midday, when I'm just not expecting it, not at all. And as your name pops up there, I register a little rush, a quick sugar hit. The feeling that the sight of your name always gives me. For a moment I have to stop and take some breaths. This is how it has become for me – the fix of you – it has to be coped with physically because it changes me, it changes everything.

You tell me that you woke at 3 a.m. and couldn't get back to sleep.

I was quite rested, you write, I just knew that I was absolutely awake, that there was no point whatsoever in trying to go back to sleep. It was very windy, stormy, cans rolling around in the neighbor's yard. I lay there listening to the cans and the wind in the trees and just enjoying the feeling of you right there where you seem to have placed yourself, in the calm center of me.

Is that really where I am? I write back in a whisper. In the calm centre of you?

Center, you write back, correcting my English spelling. But yes, yes Rosy, you know it, don't you? You know that's what you've done, you know that's where you've put yourself?

I wonder if I do know it. Sometimes these days I don't know what I know any more. I sit at my desk for a moment,

137

head bowed, pinching the tears from the corners of my eyes. Outside it's got very cold again, almost as cold as Paris. They say it might snow. The trees are black as rope against a white sky.

Calm center. I like that, I write.

Hmm. Yeah. I like it too.

I don't understand it though.

Neither do I. I don't know how you did it but you've become central to my life, Mrs Rosy. Just this — just writing to you, knowing you again, it's far bigger than I ever thought it would be. I feel I know you, almost as if these years between are gone, are nothing. I don't know — can such a thing be possible? After all these years?

It's strange, I write back, hesitating a little. I am about to write something else but I stop myself. Don't you think it's just so — strange?

Yes, you agree, it's strange. Very strange.

It scares me a little, I write.

Yes, you reply, it scares me too.

I ask you then about your wife, why you and she got divorced.

You really want to know? your reply comes shooting back. It's not a nice story. What I mean is, I don't come out of it at all well.

Don't tell me if you don't want to, I write, realising my breath is always held these days as I punch the keys, realising that I am now living each day for the moment I can sit in this white room and move my fingers and feel you there.

She cheated on me, you write. There was nothing subtle about it. I came back early from a meeting and found him

138

there, in our bed. Both naked — it pains me to tell you this — just like in some crap TV movie. The young guy who gave my son extra help with his math for chrissake. I'd quite liked him before that, would you believe — or let's just say I thought I did.

I heard them before I saw them. Made me sick to the stomach. I lost it completely, threw stuff around in front of my son, smashed my foot right through a cupboard door. I tell you, it was not a pretty sight. I left that night and moved into an apartment with an old friend, a guitar git friend of mine. I was heartbroken. I drank every night, easier to pass out than get to sleep. After that — this is the bit you might not want to hear, Rosy — I slept with as many women as I could.

You did what????!! I write.

I slept with as many women as I could. Just as I'd always wanted to. Why not? Face it, Rosy, it's what men do. And there was no reason, finally, for holding back. Don't worry, you add, I wasn't very good at it. Or at least, don't get me wrong, I'm OK in that department but I was a horrible man at the time so, in the end, well, not a lot of women would sleep with me and I don't mind telling you that because it's the truth.

At this point, on the evening you are telling me the story of your broken marriage, Tom came into my study to give me a piece of paper he'd found in Jack's blazer.

Parents' evening dates, he said, unfolding the blue scrunched-up sheet and placing it on my keyboard. I don't know how long he's had this. Better reply and put it in the —

139

And then he stopped. Something about my face must have caught at him.

What're you doing? Who're you writing to?

No one, I said, and a little too quickly I hit the button that would reduce the screen, just, you know, people, stuff.

I heard myself and I thought I sounded like Jack – Jack when he's hiding something. No, I thought, worse than Jack. Jack's sixteen.

Tom looked at me and said nothing and then he left the room.

Got to go, I type quickly. I'll write tomorrow.

I press Send and then I shut down my computer and turn you right off and put my head in my hands and then I feel the tears come.

Lex 2 was certainly pregnant, there wasn't any doubt about it. And if she hadn't been already then it would only have been a matter of time. Every single moment she spent in the garden, a tomcat skulked close by.

Fin didn't like it at all.

I wish he'd get away from her now, he said at lunch. I mean, shouldn't he leave her alone now she's pregnant? I don't want them all over her, shagging her and that.

Fin, I said, I don't like that word.

What word?

Shagging. It's horrible. I don't like it.

What should I say then?

I don't know. Mating.

Fin twirled spaghetti on his fork and laughed to himself as if I knew nothing.

I just want my cat to have some peace, that's all.

Tom explained then that the animal kingdom didn't really work that way, that Lex's instinct to mate was strong and that she didn't know she was pregnant, after all.

But she is, right? Fin said to him.

Tom poured the rest of a can of beer into his glass.

I'm sure she is, he said. You only have to look at the shape of her.

Especially if you look at her from above, Fin said.

She's got a lot more solid, I agreed, and Tom looked at me in cool surprise, as if he'd forgotten I was there. He'd been acting like this since the other night – remote, polite, attentive. As if I were someone he'd come upon in the house and was prepared to accommodate, but had no real connection with.

She used to be a skinny cat, Fin observed. But now she looks like she's swallowed a whole full-scale model of herself.

What a fucking moronic thing to say, Jack said.

Shut up, said Fin. Shut your stupid face.

That's enough, said Tom. You're right, Fin. That's a very apt description I would say of a cat in the first stages of pregnancy.

Jack snorted.

It's like she's the same but there are two layers of her, Fin said, trying again.

She won't like you once she's had kittens, Jack told him. Do you realise that? Her whole personality will change, you'll see.

Oh Jack, I said, that's completely untrue and a very mean thing to say and you know it.

I don't think he meant it like that, did you, Jack? Tom

said, and I took a small breath because Tom never normally took the children's side against me.

Jack shrugged.

I don't know how I meant it, he said, which amounted to him admitting that he'd intended to be mean. I stole a satisfied glance at Tom.

Jack hadn't finished his food but he pushed his plate away and tipped back on his chair, his arms folded.

Well we'll see, won't we? he said to Fin.

Shut up, Fin said again.

That line you wrote me – I slept with as many women as I could – I don't know why it moves me but it does.

Pretty shocking, huh? you write. Now at least you know what sort of a man I am.

No, I write back. It's heartbreaking. I can't explain but – that line is exactly a part of why I like you.

These things I've told you, you write, you know I've never told anyone else – no one, not even a man friend. I don't know why I'm telling you all this stuff, Rosy. Only I guess if you think you like me, well I'd rather you liked a real version of me. Not some crap made-up version of the man I'd like to be.

I like you, I write, I do. I like you so much. And I like it when you write: Smiles, kiddo.

You do? That's just a funny thing I used to say sometimes to my boy.

Well, I like it, I tell you. It makes me laugh.

You know something? you write later. I'm looking forward to meeting you again but I'm going to be fucking terrified as well.

Me too, I reply. So — practical details please. What time does your plane get in? Where are you staying? Will you need a day to get over jetlag and all that? How busy will you be? I mean, how many meetings exactly do you have?

In reply, you send me the address of the hotel where you're staying and the time you think you'll be there. You tell me that you may as well be honest — that you're going to need to see me straightaway.

How soon can you get there, Rosy?

As soon as the kids have left for school, I write, I'll set off. I can be there soon after you arrive.

This time, after I've replied, I sit in my study and I do something I've never done before, not ever. I delete our last few emails, sent and received.

Nicole, are you in touch with that man you saw in Paris?

Tom asked me this as we were getting ready for bed. I was standing there half-undressed and you were so near the surface, so close to the edge of my thoughts, that the question made me jump.

I tried to look normal as I laid my T-shirt over the back of the chair, but for a moment I'd forgotten how the action went and I realised I was doing it too carefully.

Him? Oh, no, no. Paris — running into him there was the strangest thing. I don't know what happened but no, I never saw him again after he disappeared.

This is all true, I told myself as I pulled at the clip of my bra. This is all totally true.

Tom flumped down on the edge of the bed in just his underpants. His shoulders were hunched. He pulled off his watch and held it for a moment in his hand, looked at it as if it should tell him more than just the time.

I'm sorry, Nicole, he said, but – can I ask you something?

I said nothing. I just shrugged.

Would you ever lie to me?

I put my bra on top of my T-shirt on the chair. It looked all wrong just as the T-shirt did.

I don't think so, I told him.

You don't think so? You mean you don't know?

I tied my hair back so I could clean my face. I noticed that when I lifted my arms my breasts looked a whole lot better, and also that in the mirror, despite everything, my eyes looked dark and excited, a kind of liquid happiness I'd never noticed before.

I pulled my knickers down and stepped out of them.

Oh look, I said. What I mean is, I never have, of course I haven't – but how can anyone ever know what they'll do in the future?

Well, great. That fills me with confidence.

Tom, I turned to him, and I reached for the cotton slip I wore in bed, I'm not lying to you now.

We looked at each other in silence for a moment.

Tell me who you've been writing to, then, he said, because I know for a fact you've been writing to someone.

My blood bumped as a terrible thought occurred to me.

You haven't been reading my emails?

Tom looked shocked.

Jesus, Nicole, of course I haven't, I never would. How could you even think it? What a bloody hurtful thing to say.

I looked at him and he sighed.

144

I'm sorry, Nicole, but I don't have to spy on you to see that you're always writing to someone, he said. Don't you realise it's completely fucking obvious? Since we came back from Paris, you're always locked in that room of yours, emailing away.

I took a breath.

OK, there is someone I'm in touch with, I told him. Just an old friend – I mean someone else, another one. It's not a secret or anything.

Tom looked surprised. Maybe he hadn't expected me to say this much. Or maybe he had.

A man? Another man?

The way he said it irritated me.

Yes, I said, OK, a man. But that's not significant. He's just a very old friend. And you know, it's kind of nice, getting back in touch with people from the past. It feels, well, it feels neat – in a full-circle kind of way.

Neat? said Tom, repeating my word with a blank look on his face.

Yes, I said, it feels good. Warm. Satisfying.

Neat isn't a word you ever use, Tom said. It sounds strange.

Does it?

You sound strange, Nicole.

I blushed now and wondered whether it was a word I'd picked up from you. I wondered then whether I should just tell the truth, say you were coming over on a visit – what after all was so wrong with that? But something stopped me. Your visit – how it would be and how I would see you, it was something I hadn't allowed myself to think about.

Tom was frowning.

145

But – I don't get it, he said.

What don't you get?

You mean, this is yet another man? Not the one you told me about in Paris?

I told you, I said. The Paris guy, he disappeared.

People don't disappear, Nic.

Maybe I imagined him then, OK? Maybe he was a ghost.

What a completely crazy and stupid thing to say.

Well, maybe that's what I am. Crazy and stupid. You'd like that, wouldn't you?

Tom looked at me with an amazed face.

What the fuck's that supposed to mean?

Oh, nothing. Just – what's happening to us, Tom?

Tom sighed and turned his watch over and over in his hands.

That's not a question I can answer, Nicole.

What?

All the answers lie with you. They always do.

I write and tell you that our cat Lex 2 is having kittens. I explain that the 2 part is because the first Lex died. I tell you that Fin will want to keep one but I'm not sure we want another cat in the house. I tell you I'm postponing this dialogue with him as long as I can.

You write back and ask me to describe Fin to you in every possible aspect. Is he like you? you say. I don't know but from what you've written so far, he sounds a lot like you – perceptive, sympathetic, protective.

Am I protective? I ask, surprised, because I've never thought of myself like that before.

Oh absolutely, you say. It's so obvious in your attitude

to everyone – your kids, your husband-who-isn't-a-husband, everyone.

I think about this and realise I really like this idea of myself, that it gives me a kind of strength, just thinking about it makes me feel better about things. I realise I wish Tom saw me that way – strong and dependable and noble almost, rather than this flaky and unreliable person whose language and ideas change at the drop of a hat, who always needs to be sorted out.

So I do exactly as you ask. I write you a lengthy description of Fin. It contains just about everything there is to say about him, from the moment he was born through to now. When I've finished, it runs to more than three pages and includes stuff I didn't really even know I thought and felt. Mother stuff. I smile and feel my life has turned mad. Can you really want to read all of this about one of my boys?

I realise with a small jolt of surprise how easy it is to adore someone who's interested in your kids.

Your last email that day says the thing I've been waiting for. Or at least, when it comes, I realise I'd never thought about it but now I do, it's obvious. It's the single element that's been missing up to now.

Something I have to ask you, you write. I hope you won't mind. It's a hard thing to talk about after the way we've been writing to each other like this, but it's been on my mind and if I don't say it, well, I don't know what I'll do.

I sit for a moment in silence. I look out at the garden, the white sky beyond my room. My heart thumps.

I know, I write back quickly. I know what you're going to say.

You do? It's just – there was a night, back then, a freezing night and –

You don't have to say it.

You remember it too?

In my study that night, I bit my fingers for a moment and then I took a breath and created a blank document on my screen. At first I called it POEM. And then I thought for a moment and deleted that and changed it to NOTPN, because that's what this was going to be about, there was no doubt in my mind about that. Night of the Pearl Necklace.

Once I'd started, the words came with no effort at all and the poem shaped itself loosely and easily, words slipping out, rhythmic, light, as if they knew what to do without me needing to move or guide them. It began to feel as if another heart was making them happen – not mine but another separate one I barely knew, a heart inside a heart perhaps, like Lex 2's body, a double thing, full of the life inside itself.

My hands worked fast, fingers crazy to keep up with the voice in my head and my blood rushed and my face grew hot with the simple electric happiness of writing. I hadn't felt it in a long time, that hand, mind, screen connection – except, perhaps, when I'd been writing to you.

I wrote for more than an hour, maybe two, and in all that time I gave not a single thought to Tom or the boys or even Mary. Not to myself either – especially not to myself – and that was a relief, to be released from myself and to go to quite another place, the place in my head where the words were, where you are. It's a good place –

calm, gentle, certain, cradling. I could so easily shut my eyes and give in to the cradled feeling and stay there. In fact in some ways I almost think I will because, by the time I've finished, I know that what I've written is only the beginning of a much longer poem – a poem that will last as long as I can possibly make it last.

I know nothing else about it, only that it's true, that I don't want it ever to stop, that it has saved my life, and that it begins with snow.

Just after her first birthday, Mary began to stand, pulling herself up on furniture, holding on with her two small hands and moving with small wobbly steps around the low grey-lacquered coffee table. I bought her some little striped sock things with a suede bottom, non-slip, warm and comfortable with plenty of room for her bones to grow. You should never put a baby in shoes till they have been walking for a while. It's amazing how many people don't seem to know this simple fact.

With the socks, her balance was better. But she was cautious. She moved around, step, step, step, beaming all the time. She never stopped beaming and moving and stepping, but neither did she ever let go.

I remember the look of her hands holding on.

It's a bright day and light spills into the room and her hands are holding hard onto the coffee table and she's smiling and smiling and I'm calling to her, trying to get her to let go and come to me – just two steps – but she won't even think about it. Her fingers grip the table as if they will never let go.

I know, Tom said. She'll wait till she's thirteen and

strong enough to lift the table, then she'll just walk around holding it.

We all laughed. It was funny to imagine Mary at thirteen, a long and lanky teenager, welded to a lacquered coffee table.

But it wasn't just the table. Anything of the right height would do. One day she was holding onto the wicker trunk we used as a toy box and she reached in to get something, a brick or a ragbook maybe, and she just toppled over and fell in head first. All you could see were her two small legs in their cord dungarees – old ones that had belonged to Jack and Fin – and striped socks, sticking up out of the box.

It took her about four dazed seconds to understand what she'd done and then she took a single long breath and screamed and screamed. Fin thought it was the funniest thing he had ever seen, but he rushed to rescue her, pulled her out and sat her on his lap and stroked her hands and her corduroy knees till she was calm.

He and his baby sister, they had a strange little thing going. Certainly he was Mary's protector. He'd never have admitted it in a million years but it was no coincidence that he lurked behind her all the time, ready to jump to her rescue. He was patient with her, far more than he was with anyone or anything else in his life with the exception perhaps of Lex 2.

Later, when Mary could just about walk unaided, her best thing by far was to pick up a picture book and back slowly towards Fin so he could pull her up on his lap and open the book for her. Then he'd talk her through all the pictures and though she was barely thirteen months, she'd listen intently, with just one long thread of dribble wobbling from her mouth.

I wrote all of this in the email to you. And then I realised how strange it was, improper almost, that I'd told you all of this, and yet you still didn't know about what happened to Mary.

Who knows, maybe after the long hot walk we took that summer night when we stood together on the bridge and shared so much of what we cared about, maybe it wouldn't have been long before you asked to sleep in my room again. And I'd have said yes, there's no doubt at all that this is what I'd have said. I think you knew that then. And maybe by the time the following winter came, we'd have spent many nights together and maybe we'd have done a lot more than just kiss and maybe we wouldn't need pearls any more, just our own two bodies, relieved of our previous shyness. I think I'd have loved you then.

But it doesn't happen that way.

Because some weeks or months after the long hot walk, you start going out with Linzi. No one can understand how you can possibly like Linzi. Or let's just say it's me who can't understand it. Linzi is a boy's girl – the kind of girl who'll come over in the evening and hang out and smoke and drink with all the boys and then make sure she's still there in the morning. Not always in the same bed either. It's a joke among many of the boys that Linzi is a shared thing, that you all share her. She is talked about with a mixture of derision and awe and, looking back, I can see how mean this is and how, as another girl, it might have been better if I could have acted as a fellow spirit and taken Linzi's part in this, protected her against such disrespect. But I don't. I only think of myself. I only wonder why she doesn't just pick up her annoyingly small gold rucksack and leave.

I don't think I'd mind if you just slept with Linzi. But it's worse than that. Once she's woken in your bed, then she's always there after that, padding half-naked from kitchen to bathroom and back to your bed. You and she are definitely going out and there's no room for anyone else and though I hate myself for hating her, and though I don't want you for myself, still it's so clear that she's no good for you.

You and I don't even get to talk any more.

Linzi wears see-through clothes that barely fit her. She's tall and slim with waist-length dark hair and she makes sure everything always hangs off her, buttons always coming undone, skirts hitched up. She has a shrill and irritating laugh and everything she says is somehow shambolic and false. She pretends to be all sorts of things – intense and sexy, breathlessly funny. But everything she claims to be is stolen from other people. Her spontaneity is entirely calculated. She pulls the sorts of careful tricks that only other girls can see right through.

But you were always so in love with Linzi, I protest to you quite early on when you write and say you wish we hadn't stopped being friends. That's why you and I were never close again after that winter, that summer.

You write straight back:

Mrs Rosy, I wish you could see me laughing, because I am, I'm laughing now. I did not love Linzi. To be honest I did not even like her all that much. But – and here's the thing, now you'll be the one to laugh at me – I lost my virginity to her. You didn't know that did you? Before Linzi I'd never slept with a girl, not properly. So what could I do?

I was too young and stupid and inexperienced – and certainly way too much in awe of what she offered – to turf that girl out of my bed.

Tom continued to be cold with me. In the morning he'd rise deftly from the bed before I could touch him and then he'd go downstairs and pick up the paper off the mat and make the boys' breakfast before I could help – as if the very act of getting there first and doing all the work should somehow show me.

I knew he was angry because of the deadly efficient way he ran things – rinsing out the breakfast bowls the second the boys had finished with them, counting out change in piles for bus fare and swimming money. If I tried to get involved, he'd tell me coolly that it was all organised and that there was no need to worry and that he'd sorted it all out in advance.

But now and then I'd catch him looking at me with such pain and confusion on his face that my insides would swoop and crash. What could he be thinking? What was going through his head? What did he think I was doing and was it better or worse than what I thought I was doing?

One time after supper, I couldn't bear it any longer and got up and went to sit on his knee. This was something I did a lot in the old days. Just like then, I put my arms around his neck and laid my head on his shoulder and he did not resist. The boys made noises of excitement and disapproval.

Phwoar! said Jack. Get a room, why don't you?

Oh yuk, yuk, said Fin. Oh gross.

Hey, what's the matter? Tom asked them as his hand

rested gently on my thigh and I put my lips against his neck. You worried we might have kittens or something?

Fin giggled with surprise as he tried to think this one through.

Tom was trying to be light, I could feel it. I could feel his jokes and also that he wanted to respond to me, he really did. But as he held me to him, I also felt him tremble and when I kissed his temple, I tasted sweat on his brow.

On the day I knew you were rising early to catch your plane, I woke in a kind of panic.

Are you OK? Tom called when I spent a little too long in the bathroom.

I feel a bit sick, I said, I'll be OK in a minute.

But it wasn't true, I didn't feel sick, not at all. Instead I felt almost drunk, dizzy. Outside the window a small brown bird was hopping on the sloped roof of the kitchen extension. Hop, hop, hop. Up and down. I leaned my arms on the ledge of the window and watched the strange mad movement of the little bird, and then I had to look away again because my heart was turning over and over so fast I could not catch my breath.

In the bathroom mirror my eyes were bright and I looked about ten years old. I didn't know whether that was a good or a bad thing. I put cream on my face, cleaned my teeth, brushed my hair and twisted it back on itself into a looped-up ponytail. I don't want to be a bad person, I told myself.

When I'd got the boys off to school and Tom had finally ridden off on his bike, I drove to the supermarket. I didn't know why I was rushing but I was – rushing madly up and down the aisles as I filled the trolley with the kind of things our family eats, filling it up as if it was the last time I'd ever get a chance to shop. It was as if time had divided and there was today when I didn't see you and then tomorrow when I would and all the food I was putting in my trolley would somehow have to be eaten between those two times, those two worlds.

The short drive back home was draggingly slow, impossible. And then, just as I was going into the house a man drew up in a van and walked slowly across the road to bring me a parcel addressed to Tom that had to be signed for. I could hardly hide my impatience and I scribbled something that only half looked like my name and then I snatched the parcel out of his hands without even thanking him.

Once inside, I ran up and turned on my computer then ran back downstairs and made coffee, barely stopping to put in the milk. I put a slice of bread in the toaster, realising I was maybe hungry and that might be why I felt light and disorientated and my heart felt like it was thumping madly out of control.

I held my hands out in front of me and I could see them shaking.

The phone rang and it was Tom, his voice small and tight and faraway.

Just checking you're OK, he said.

That I'm OK? I repeated as I held the phone which felt suddenly strange in my hand.

That you're feeling better?

Oh, I said, remembering. Oh yes. I think so.

Have you eaten breakfast? he asked me sternly.

Just making it.

OK, he said, good.

155

I laughed.

You looked so pale this morning, he said, and I was silent a moment.

Well, got to go, he said, and for a small moment I almost wished he wouldn't.

Hey – thanks, I told him then, and there was another tight little pause and I could see his face at the other end of the line, I could just see it thinking and frowning and wondering.

OK, he said, see you later then.

I threw the phone down on the table and popped the toaster up to see if the toast was done yet but it wasn't even beginning to brown. In the end I can't wait any longer and I just pull it from the toaster as it is, warm and bendy and white, and run up the stairs two at a time.

I sit down at my desk and stuff the half-toasted bread into my mouth as I type.

I'm sorry. I wasn't going to write this morning. But there's something I have to say to you. Before you leave. Please, if it's not something you want to hear, well then forget I said it. But I don't care, I'll take the risk, because I woke up this morning and I knew I had to say it, today, before you leave. I mean it. I think I'll explode if I don't say it. Because anything could happen between now and you getting here. What if something goes wrong with one or other of us? What if your plane crashes? What if you don't make it?

So I had to tell you that, though I don't understand it and I can't say whether it's real or not and I've no idea what this is that's happening to me, still the fact is that right here today on this slightly dull morning in February,

I love you, I just love you with all my heart, there it is, I have to say it, I just do.

And then, without waiting to correct the spelling or read back what I've just written, I press Send.

After that I put down the rest of the toast and lay my head on my arms and I take such deep breaths that I almost sleep.

Your reply comes back less than ten minutes later. I'm not expecting it. It's three in the morning for you and you have to be up at six to catch a plane. You weren't meant to get my email yet. You shouldn't even be awake.

Baby, oh baby, me too, I was going to say the exact same thing except I wanted to wait and say it to you in person. But me too, I find I love you. I don't know how it happened but I've fallen completely and unexpectedly in love with you. I wish you could see that I'm smiling right now as I write this. Nothing so good has ever happened to me, not ever in my whole life and it's like I don't know what to do with it, I don't at all.

Now hush. Stop thinking. I mean it. I'm getting on a plane and nothing's going to happen. Life has kept us both safe for more than twenty years, this meeting of ours was meant to be. After that, who knows? But for now just know it. I love you too. I love you – so there it is, just believe it, OK?

I'm turning off now. I need to sleep a little and then I need to leave. Keep safe for me. I'll wait for you at the hotel. Come when you can, but please come. Whatever time you come, I'll be waiting. Smiles, kiddo – OK?

LONDON AGAIN

It was a freezing cold Sunday morning, winter. She was twenty-three months – ten days short of her second birthday. She'd been walking for a while now and rarely allowed us to strap her into her pushchair. She was even beginning to use a potty, though she still wore a nappy at night. She still had all the round and blurry softness of a baby, but you could see in her face and the way she held herself the child she was going to be – alert and beady, quick, passionate, mostly happy if not ever exactly content in that lazy-cow way that some kids have.

She had none of Fin's strange and tragic side, and was an easier child in many ways than Jack. Easier to please, anyway. For whereas Jack had this mad, thunking need for people – any person, all the time, any time – Mary could be alone with herself quite happily for hours, playing, laughing, holding a toy in both her hands and gazing at it from all angles and chatting to it.

She slept pretty well and hardly ever woke us up in the night any more, but I know she did that night. A small cry, coming out of nowhere, followed by another. It hooked its way into my sleep and at first I ignored it and turned over, but when it came again I found myself pushing up out of bed still barely awake but knowing it was her.

No, Tom put out an arm to stop me. His voice was soft with sleep. Leave her.

I lay back down but stayed tense, my head stiff on the pillow, listening. Our house was draughty. The old Victorian windows didn't fit. Even in the bedroom the air was icy on my cheek, it felt almost like outdoors. Then it came again. Maa!

This time even before I moved, Tom tried to reach out of his sleep and pull me back in, but I was awake now. And – maybe because it was rare for her to cry in the night, or maybe because the air really was so dreadfully and unearthly cold – I knew I couldn't leave my baby girl to cry any more than I could tell myself not to breathe.

I heard Tom roll over and give up, falling back into sleep. I got up and pulled on a cardigan that was lying on the chair.

Out of bed, I felt the air of the house thumping with cold – there'd been a heavy frost the last few mornings. The half-landing outside Mary's room felt especially chilly and I wondered whether this was what had woken her, whether I should turn the heating back on. But then I saw from the landing clock that it was half-past three already and it would be coming on anyway in a couple of hours. Besides she had on a warm sleepsuit and two blankets and I knew that overheating was worse for babies than cold.

Maa!

Moonlight was thrown into her room through a gap in the curtains – a blueish beam of light from thousands of miles away. She was standing up in her cot and holding on with both hands, rocking gently up and down, knees flexing, eyes fixed on the door, waiting for me. A glittery look on her face.

Maa! Maa!

Shush, I murmured in my middle-of-the-night voice, shush, it's OK, there, Baby, there.

I touched her hair. It was so light and soft it seemed to dissolve into my fingertips so I could barely feel it. Her head was warm and her cheek was wet. She gave a little half-sob and tramped her legs and reached up to show she wanted to be picked up out of her cot.

This Tom would never have done. He had his rules about night and he was quite right. He knew his babies well enough to know that if you do something once, once you give in on one single occasion, then that's it, they expect it all the time. We found this out to our cost with Jack, who had a small flannel bear he grew to need in order to sleep well at night. He discovered this trick of easing the bear out through the bars of the cot and pushing him so he fell on the floor. He'd then cry and wait for us to come in and pick the bear up. Then when we had, he'd wait a few minutes and do the whole thing all over again.

Tom said the only way we'd cure him of it was not to go. Tough love, but he was right. It took a couple of nights of tears and screaming but by the third night, Jack had magically learned to keep flannel bear in the cot and that was the end of it.

But Mary had never been like that. Mary never did things for the hell of it. If Mary made a fuss there was usually a reason and now she was fixing me with that sharp Mary look – a funny look she often did that seemed to say that she expected at any moment to be cheated or tricked. When she looked like that you saw, for a few fleeting seconds, the future adult in her face. Sometimes she wasn't like a baby at all, but a person who knew things and had chosen to keep them to herself. There was a look in her eyes sometimes that left me breathless – its power seemed to go beyond the normal mother-and-baby thing. I couldn't have told Tom this – he would have laughed and dismissed it – but there was something in Mary's eyes and the tone of her cry that night that told me what to do. We understood each other perfectly and on that particular night at 3.30 a.m., I'd been summoned because she wanted to get out of her cot.

So I did as she wanted. I lifted her gently, she was light and warm. She relaxed into me with a little sigh as I carried her over to the window and together we looked out at the dark garden. Her breath smelled wet and clean and her face was hot with tears or maybe the salivating that comes with teething, I don't know which. She'd been cutting a few more teeth recently but, unlike the boys, she usually slept through even that.

I kissed her – once on her head and then again on her pink appley cheek. I snaffled her and she did a hiccupy laugh. She smelled perfect – of clean, cut fruit, of honey, of fur. Her smell went beyond smell and took on shape and colour and became sensation. I wanted to ingest every scrap of her, breathe her in – a mother high on her own baby.

Naughty girl, I whispered. Look at you, you've woken me now.

She clucked and chortled. Ca, Ca, Ca! she said.

Cat's asleep, I told her.

Ca – she said again, more urgently, and she turned her head and tried to wriggle round in my arms to show me what she wanted.

Then I saw it. Looped on a hook on the edge of the changing table – the one that Tom had made all those years ago for Jack and which we'd got back out of the loft for Mary – was a plastic cat with a smiley face. You pulled the string which hung from the cat's pointy chin and it played 'Three Blind Mice' for about eight seconds before it stopped. We often pulled it when we changed Mary – especially since recently she'd gone through a phase of fussing and crying when we took off her night nappy. Sometimes just the music was enough, but if it wasn't then you could pass her the cat toy to fiddle with and it would distract her just long enough to get the nappy on or off.

OK, OK, I whispered, and I walked over and picked up the cat and gave it to her. Tom would have said I absolutely shouldn't have done this. Not in the middle of the night, not on demand like that.

Then I returned to the window with her in my arms and we stood there a good few more minutes. I shivered and gazed out at the night while Mary turned the cat over and over in her hands. The garden was too black to see much. There was only a sliver of moon left in the sky and faraway you could hear a fox screaming – or at least if I hadn't known it was a fox I'd have sworn it was a child in some kind of terrible agony and fear, but I knew it wasn't. Round here we were used to the fox.

Ca, said Mary happily as she jiggled the string of the cat, Ca, Ca.

Mm, I said, and pressed my face on the top of her head so I could have one more honey-fix before I left her to sleep.

I heard Tom get up and go to the bathroom. I heard the seat go up and then down again. I knew in a moment he would see I was still gone and would come stumbling across the landing to get me back to bed. I knew for certain that this would happen. And I suppose I also knew somehow on that night that this was stolen time I was snatching with my daughter – that something about the whole situation was skewed and that I would pay for it later. Easy to say that now but I think my heart told me things I could not have known.

Nic, Tom's murmur from the landing. D'you know what time it is?

I'm coming.

She OK?

Yes. Fine. Sorry, I'm coming.

I don't know why I felt the need to apologise to him but I did. Mary stiffened a little and I stood there for a few seconds with her rigid and frozen in my arms as we both waited for his footsteps to go back across the landing. And then she turned and, with the cat in one hand, she took four wet fingers of the other hand from her mouth and gave me a look of perfect understanding. And then the spell broke.

Bed, I said firmly. C'mon, Baby. Sleepy time.

I prised the cat from her hot damp fingers and tried to lie her down in her cot but she wasn't having it. She arched her back and wriggled and fussed and every time I gently smoothed her head to her pillow, she scrambled onto her knees and began to cry, both hands gripping the bars and then standing and trying to lift her leg over to climb out. She couldn't have made it yet, not over the top of the bars, but she wasn't far off and she was a strong and determined child and Tom and I were thinking we might soon have to put her in a proper bed.

Baby, I whispered more firmly. Shush. You have to sleep.

But she wanted the cat again. I'd done it now. She kept on reaching out towards it.

Shhh, I settled her down again and stroked her head, but still she shuffled and grunted and took a quick breath which I knew so well was the prelude to a full-blown wail.

I had an idea.

I put the cat where he was supposed to be, on the hook. But I pulled the chest of drawers with the changing table on top slightly closer to the bed. Not a lot closer – there was still a good eighteen inches between the bed and the chest of drawers – but just enough so that she could look up and see him hanging there, so that she could think I'd done something for her.

I pulled the cat's cord. They all ran after the farmer's wife, it played. Cat smiled and smiled.

Mary smiled.

Night night, I said.

She reached right out with her arm, fingers extended, as if to try and touch the cat, but since she couldn't, she slowly let her hand relax, until it rested back on the flannel cot sheet. Her fingers curled into their normal shape and she sighed. Then she lay there and gazed straight at me with her mad black eyes. She blinked. Her hand looked relaxed but I couldn't tell if the rest of her was or not.

I love you, I whispered.

She blinked again and her mouth turned down at the corners for a second and I knew what she meant.

Who cut off their tails with a carving knife, played the song from the cat.

Night night, Baby, I said once more. See you in the morning.

Did ever you see such a thing in your life . . . ?

I left my baby girl thinking I was telling her the truth, that I would see her in the morning. But I never saw her alive again.

Your flight was landing at Heathrow at six in the morning, so I worked out that you should be at your hotel by nine at the very latest. I decided that if I left the house more or less straight after Tom, then I'd be able to get there in time for you to have checked in and showered and changed.

The last few days had been rainy and brown but, as if the weather had magically tuned in to the mysterious thrill of you, on that morning a cold snap set in. Really cold. Every car in the road was iced over and the radio warned of blizzard conditions in some parts of Scotland and the East Coast and said no one should make any journeys unless absolutely necessary. It was said that the snow was unlikely to hit London but, as I set out to walk to the Tube station, a few dry flakes were already visible against the blackened buildings. I smiled. It made no difference. Nothing would make a difference. For me this journey was absolutely necessary.

How will I know you? I wrote a few days ago. I mean, will I recognise you? What do you look like now?

Fat, middle-aged, gray-haired, you wrote back.

No – really, I protested.

I'm not joking. OK, graying hair, brushed back. Sports shoes, dark jeans, jacket I don't know what color yet, no tie. Glasses. You'll be glad to know I haven't lost my hair but I'm so fucking blind it's not true.

Yes, I thought. Yes, I know all this.

By the way, you added in a PS, I have a small goatee beard, a puny thing grown over the last few months. I'm not sure if it suits me or not. What do you think, should I shave it off?

What I thought was that you were joking, teasing me, and so I didn't reply to this part. Actually I was confused. Why a goatee? In Paris you had no goatee. And why should I be the one to decide if you should shave it off or not?

For some perplexing reason the mention of the goatee threw you out of Paris and back into the realm of the real for me. You were a middle-aged man I used to know. And you were really coming here. Inside I began to tremble.

And anyway, how am I going to know you? you asked me then and I couldn't tell if you were teasing or serious. Tell me what you'll be wearing and how you'll look.

I wrote back and told you the truth: I'll have on a pink coat and I'll look – petrified.

The streets of London were hard and white by the time I came out of the Tube station and moved myself closer and closer to your hotel. A thin layer of snow had got itself onto everything – strange violet shadows cut the sunlight between buildings and pavement – and for a moment I could have imagined I was back in Paris, about to discover you waiting for me on rue de la Perle. Grey rooftops, shutters, black iron railings. I felt helpless or afraid, I didn't know which – maybe both, maybe neither. Maybe I was just excited – numb to the present moment, safe as a sleepwalker to whom anything and nothing might happen.

All I knew was that nothing could have stopped this moment, that I had to go to you. I wished I didn't feel so nervous. I wished it was evening so I could at least have had a drink.

I knew the road of your hotel – or at least I thought I did, I'd been down it on and off at various points in my life. I knew it was one of those wide red-brick streets that lead off behind the High Street, an area masked by shops on the one side and the grander terraced houses of the area dipping off on the other. Round here most were split into flats – expensive flats for Arabs or businessmen or divorced people. I knew that your hotel would be one of those dauntingly faceless places with an underground car park and a foyer that felt like an airport. A place for business conferences, the kind of place that would make Tom shudder. I knew this, it was obvious to me just from the address of it. A tacked-on lump of an address. You told me that your company chose it, that you have no say in these things. That budget is what it all comes down to in the end.

You would not be surprised to know that it took me a long time to decide what clothes to put on today. That when I woke up this morning my body looked its shakiest and saddest, its most middle-aged. That whatever way I turned in the mirror, no matter how I pulled my stomach in or closed my mouth and widened my eyes, nothing looked quite right. It was as though I'd never noticed the shadows under my eyes before, the two deep frown lines between my brows. My eyes were as bright as a schoolchild's eyes but the area around them looked about a hundred years old.

For a moment I wished we didn't have to meet after all, that I could just go on writing to you, safe and connected and happy.

I tried on every bottom and every top in my wardrobe – my newest and my oldest. I realised it was a long time since I'd thought about clothes. I pulled on a dress I hadn't worn since before I had Mary – ruffled, clingy, nice fabric. It still fitted but I looked like I had stolen it from another person – younger, happier, more daring. I pulled it off quickly.

In the end I put back on the jeans I had on when I gave the boys breakfast. Clean jeans. And though I'd tried my hair in every possible style – long and loose and brushed out, even twisted up in a chignon (something I'd never tried before), in the end I got frustrated and just twisted it back into its usual looped ponytail. Rather like you telling me about your marriage breaking up, I wanted to show you me as I thought I really was. I knew I looked OK in jeans anyway. I am a good person, I told myself as I sneaked a sideways glance at my bottom in the mirror. I've done nothing wrong, I said as I unpinned the dry-cleaner's label from my pink wool coat, the one I keep for best.

By the time I turned into the street, snow was falling properly – people hurrying, hailing cabs and the whole morning had gone strange and dark.

On the steps up to your hotel, I paused a moment. It wasn't that I would have dreamt of turning back, but suddenly I had no energy or courage left to move my legs forward. And it was going to take both energy and courage to walk through those sliding doors into the vast marble foyer with the sound of suitcases being wheeled along and the large speckled plants and No Smoking signs.

Finally I did it and the world blurs and I can see nothing but grey suits, grey men, a knot of greyness. But then one of them seems a little less grey than the rest and takes a step towards me and I know before I dare to properly look at his pale man's face and businessman's body, that this person is you.

Rosy?

My hands fly up to my mouth, I bite my lip, I know I'm blushing. You touch my arm in the pink coat – pink wool with a light covering of snow fast melting to wet now in the foyer's heat. You touch me so gently I can barely feel it. I can't look at you. Instead I twist my face off somewhere else and glance at the desk.

This is so embarrassing, I begin to say, but you tell me to stand still.

Hush. Stop. Let me look at you a moment.

You've already seen me.

No, no – I haven't, not like this, not in twenty years.

We walk across several mottled marble hallways to the hotel bar. The whole time we walk, you're smiling and looking at me. The bar is a dark place with no windows and some businessmen are drinking what look like brandies even though it's the middle of the morning. The girl behind the bar is standing and leaning over the counter reading the paper. The seats are brown fake velvet. Ashtrays everywhere. A cigarette machine beyond. We go in the furthest corner and I try to sit down next to you but you stop me.

No, you say, no. Here, opposite, I need to look at you, Rosy. It's been so long. Just do that for me, please?

OK, I say as my heart recognises something and turns over. If you want.

You go over to the bar and get two filter coffees. I hear you say something to the girl and I hear her almost laugh. I watch you carefully. From behind you could be any solid, middle-aged businessman. From the front you could only be you.

You walk back over with the coffees.

Remember how you used to like me to say coffee like an American? you say, smiling, as you sit back down and pass me mine. Remember how you used to make me say it over and over again – cwaffee? D'you remember that, Rosy?

You say this and then you stop and you just look at me. And I try to laugh but really I am just looking too, looking back at you. We've done so many words, written words, and now the fact of you here – the real solid fact – is too unbelievable. I'm so nervous I can hardly speak.

First I think this, then I hear myself say it.

I'm so nervous I can hardly speak, I say, and you look at my eyes and you smile.

I look down at my hands and ask if you want to see some photos of my kids. I know it's too soon to ask you this but it's all I can think of to say.

You tell me yes, that you want to see them.

But first, you say, looking around you and reaching for one of the ashtrays, I'm going to have to smoke. Do you mind, Rosy? I wouldn't normally, what I mean is, I'd try not to, but I'm so fucking nervous. I swear it's the only thing that's going to calm me down.

You light a cigarette and look at me.

You forgive me? you say. I nod.

I watch you inhale with your head slightly on one side as you shake out the match and in that second I remember you doing that, all those years ago, in exactly that way. I also remember it in Paris. That action of yours sucks me straight back to two pasts and suddenly I don't know where I am and I can't help it, I shiver.

Shouldn't be smoking, you say even though I've still made no comment about it. I actually threw away my lighter so I wouldn't be tempted. Only had one the whole of yesterday. Trying to stop. You don't believe me, do you?

I say nothing, just smile at you, I can't help smiling. You indicate the photos in my hand.

C'mon, show me.

I pass each photo to you and explain it. I show you Jack as a three-week-old baby in a pale blue velvet suit, fast asleep with a fur of black hair and sagging puppy eyes. There's Fin aged about three, lying on a beach looking at a *Beano* magazine. Jack and Fin together with their arms around each other, taken in Greece, long curly hair and brown faces, a million miles from winter and school. One of my favourite pictures – Fin scowling in swimming trunks and a Batman cape. You laugh at this one.

The Caped Crusader, you say.

He wore it all the time, I tell you, even at night. It got so dirty – covered in food. We used to have to sneak it off him while he slept and wash it and hang it to dry so there wouldn't be a scene in the morning.

There's another of Tom and Jack playing cards, a couple of months ago this one – both with serious concentrating faces, matching cans of Coca-Cola beside them. I nearly didn't bring this one but then I thought it wouldn't be honest not to show you Tom.

That's your husband? OK, I know, I know – sort of husband? That's him?

I nod and you blink at the picture.

Tom, I say, yes.

He looks nice.

You don't have to say that.

He does.

I show you Mary then, sitting plonked right in the middle of Tom's big upholstered desk chair, in a navy Babygro with the poppers done up to her chin, small legs sticking out in front of her, hands grasping the arms of the chair, mouth wide open laughing, two new top teeth showing. Her mad laugh. Shock of blonde hair.

You study this picture with special interest.

She looks a lot like you, you say. Same eyes exactly.

This surprises me.

Really? I say. No one's said that before. I thought she looked like neither of us, not really.

No? Well, I can't tell about your husband. But so very like you, most definitely. Same hair.

Mine's not real, I say quickly, wondering if you realise it's a lot blonder than it used to be.

You glance at my hair.

OK, same crazy eyes, then.

She's a crazy girl, I tell you, realising with a thud of worry that I'm enjoying the feel of talking about Mary in the present tense. She can be so funny, I add as my voice tapers off.

You stub out your cigarette even though you've only had about three puffs of it and you open your wallet and, without saying anything, pull out a cracked and ageing photo. A young and skinny boy perched on the top of a bench in bright sunshine, hair as white as light.

Zach, you say. That was years ago. I have lots more but it's the one I carry – I've always carried. It was a good day that day. He's eighteen now. Taller than me. Great bass player. Plays in a band. Lives with his mom. She took him to New York to live.

I look at Zach. He's about Fin's age in the picture, gap-toothed, laughing.

So when do you see him? I ask and, just as I expected, you look a little demolished. You take off your glasses and rub the space between your eyes.

Not half enough. I miss him like – well, Rosy, you don't know how I miss him. Some days it's like I've lost him,

173

like I've disappeared from his life and I never had him at all.

You put your glasses back on and you give me a stern look, peering over the top of them. You pat the banquette.

OK, you say, now you can come and sit beside me.

You've seen enough?

You laugh.

I've seen enough.

But sitting beside you seems too close. I wonder what we must look like to other people. Husband and wife? Lovers? Brother and sister? I think you're probably wondering the same thing and so we sit a little apart and in silence for a moment or two.

What are you thinking? you ask me.

I'm thinking – I'm trying – to decide something.

What?

I'm trying to decide if this is all real.

You screw up your eyes and take another long look at me over your glasses.

If what's real?

This, I say. Us, you. Everything we've said to each other so far.

Suddenly you look sad. Your mouth goes tight and it reminds me for a second of Tom's mouth – set against whatever's to come next.

Am I a disappointment? you ask me, Tell me the truth. I mean in the flesh, the way I look, all that?

Of course you aren't, I say. Not at all – though the real truth is I haven't yet decided.

You feel in your pocket for another cigarette.

Foolish girl, you say. Do you want me to be real?

I take a breath and knit my fingers together in my lap. I don't look at you. I daren't.

Of course. Of course I do.

You punch your own arm in its dark jacket. Feel me, then. Flesh and blood. Plenty of it, way too much I'm afraid. Silly girl, of course I'm real.

I put out a hand and touch your arm and it does feel real so I keep my hand there and then, without really understanding why I do it, I lay my head on your shoulder. Your jacket smells of fresh air.

Oh, you say, and your voice drops a little lower. Keep on doing that please.

I feel myself trembling again but it's mostly down in my legs so that's OK. This is the first time I've touched a man other than Tom in all these years and – I can't believe I've just done it so easily.

This doesn't feel real, I tell you quietly. Not really, not to me.

It doesn't? you say, and you sigh.

What?

Just – it feels so nice, you say, that's what.

We don't really know each other, I say.

We don't?

Well – we do and we don't.

Hmm, you say, and I feel your heart beating hard, or maybe it's your blood pulsing around your body.

I'm scared, I tell you then, still keeping my head there on your shoulder. You touch my hand on your sleeve.

I know. I know you are. Me too. Everything you're

175

feeling, I'm feeling it too. You don't have to do anything, you know. I mean, neither of us, we don't have to.

I know.

I just had to see you.

I know, I say again, and then, writing to you was – is – so good.

You put your hand on my head then, stroke my hair. And a feeling of unbelievable warmth passes into me, like something being poured straight in. I wonder if this is how it feels to my kids when I touch them.

I know, you say, as you stroke me. Hush. I know.

But –

But? Now you echo me and make a face and twist your head down to look at me.

I smile.

But – I was going to say, but it's so strange, seeing you.

You don't like me after all?

You're smiling but I know it's a serious question and I have to give you an honest answer.

I don't know, I reply, realising at the same time that something about the calm you've given me has let me say it.

We'll take it slowly, you tell me in a slightly sadder voice. We'll take it all slowly. I need to get to know you again, Rosy.

I know, I say, and a confused vision of Tom swoops suddenly into my head – Tom on his bike, urgent, sad, moving fast between the London trees.

Will you let me do that this time, you ask me, without running away?

I lift my head.

I never ran away.

Oh but you did.

What – you mean after the –

That was the night I was thinking of, you say with a smile, and you push my coffee cup towards me. I drink some coffee. It's not nice. I push it away again.

The one with the pearls? I say, and you smile.

That was the only night we had, Rosy.

I look at you.

I did not run away.

You say nothing, you just smile at me over your glasses – your little rimless glasses.

Can I tell you something funny? you say. Your walk. It's exactly the same.

I blush and something inside me clicks.

No, I say.

Yes. Oh sure, oh yes.

How do I walk?

With a bit of a bounce, that's all.

I do not! I tell you, even though I know it's true, I do.

Hey, it's nice, you say. I mean it. It's attractive.

I shake my head.

You have glasses, I say because I have to now, because I'm locked somewhere between the past and the future and all I want is to stay in this present with you.

Oh Rosy, I'm so fucking blind these days. You wouldn't believe it. I'm not good. I'm fat, I'm old. I drink and smoke too much, I know I do.

I've had three kids, I tell you, and my eyes are almost filling up with tears. Look at me. We're both quite middle-aged.

Never, you say. Not you, not middle-aged. You look perfect.

And then, just as I know you will, you reach out and – very gently – touch the crinkles next to my eyes.

You're older, you say after a moment, but you look – fucking adorable.

Neither of us heard anything that morning. Not a crash or a thump or even the smallest cry. Maybe the silence itself should have been our clue.

We woke later than usual to a room filled with the perfect bright clarity that comes with snow – and the whizzing and popping and chasing music of early-morning cartoons on the TV downstairs. Clearly Fin was already down. He'd have kept the sitting-room curtains drawn and wouldn't yet have looked outside, otherwise he'd have raced in to tell us and beg to go out in it.

I lifted my head and frowned at my watch. It was almost eight. Normally Mary would have woken and called for us by now, she'd be rattling the bars of the cot, anxious to be lifted out. But because she'd been so awake in the night, I imagined she'd slept in. It wasn't like her but neither was it completely unknown. I decided to give her ten more minutes and then go in to her.

I turned over and snuggled closer to Tom. He sighed and licked his lips and thrust an arm out behind him and stroked the inside of my thigh with his warm fingers but only for a second or two because before he could help it, he fell back to sleep.

We take the lift up to your room. The lift is carpeted up the sides, just like the Paris one, only this time the carpet is beige, mottled, coming unstuck at the edges. There's ash on the floor.

In the lift we stand apart.

You tell me your first meeting is at five. You ask me how long I can stay. I say until the boys come home. Till three, I say, the boys leave school at three-fifteen. I need to get back by four.

Who looks after the baby? you ask me.

I take a breath and for a second I shut my eyes.

It's a long story, I say.

And tomorrow? you ask me.

What about tomorrow?

Can I see you tomorrow?

You don't have work to do?

It's a long story, you say, and you wink at me and then, Hey, Mrs Rosy, you say, your coat is very pink.

You don't like it?

Did I say I didn't like it? It's good. I like it a lot. But you have to agree it's extremely pink.

The lift stops on the seventh floor but no one is there so the doors close again. I shut my eyes.

I can't believe I'm doing this, I whisper to you.

Doing what? What are you doing?

I don't know. Whatever this is.

You step closer and touch my hair. You hold my looped-up ponytail in your hand, then you release it and I feel the hairs on my neck shiver as you let go.

You don't have to do anything, you tell me. We'll do nothing. I want to talk. But I think I may just need to hold you – in the room, I mean. Is that OK?

The lift stops and the doors open and a man gets in.

It's OK, I say. That's fine. That will be OK.

We stand apart again and you smile at me and I smile back. The man stares at the doors not at us.

So much snow out there, you say in a normal voice.

Yes, I say more softly, and I'm about to say, just like in Paris but I stop myself. We had snow in Paris, I tell you, when we were there.

You did?

So much snow. Thick snow. Like today only more. It was unreal – it was wonderful.

You go a little quiet then and I can tell it's because I'm talking about an experience that didn't include you or at least that's what I think you think and what can I say?

We reach the nineteenth floor.

Here we are, you say.

Your room is a small beige cube with a smaller dark bathroom attached, but it at least has a huge wide window with a big view. The city is white and the snow has settled and it's no longer dark, the sky has lightened a little and the morning sun is just beginning to shine through. I go to the window and look out.

Whoa, I say, look at that.

You come up behind me and you look too. I see the close-up unlikely texture of your jacket sleeve, and I smell soap on your skin. You seem subdued and suddenly younger and shyer – shyer than you were downstairs.

I don't know what all these buildings are, you tell me. Do you know? What's that one over there for instance?

The one with the light flashing on top? That's Canary

Wharf. And that one's the Gherkin building – see, because it looks like a gherkin? Do you have gherkins?

The vegetable, you say, smiling. Yeah, we have those.

I don't know what's beyond that though, I tell you, and I can hear my voice is talking too hard and brightly. Don't know what the big white one is – that's the City I suppose. I don't know every building.

You're taking off your jacket and throwing it on the chair, undoing your tie. It's strange to see a man undoing a tie. Tom never wears one, or almost never.

I have to go to the bathroom a moment, you tell me. Don't move. Wait right there.

I take off my coat and lay it on the chair and then I stand and look at your things. A fat thriller on the bedside table, by someone I've never heard of, pages curling. A pair of brown socks on the chair. Your suitcase, half-unpacked, white T-shirts spilling out. A pair of black shoes, well-polished. White trainers, a little too clean. I think of you packing while I wrote to say I loved you. I think of how Tom would never read a fat thriller or have overly clean white trainers.

When I first lived with Tom, I tried to iron one of his shirts – as a favour and because I loved him and because I thought that in their hearts all men wanted to wear crease-free shirts. He laughed and crumpled it and threw it back at me.

Don't you think if I wanted it ironed I'd do it myself? he said. I don't think he intended this to be mean, it was just a fact. He was quite capable of using an iron. It was just his way of telling me I'd wasted my time.

When you come out, you smell of mouthwash. You've cleaned your teeth.

That's better, you say. Come here, Mrs Rosy.

I need to pee, I tell you, and I go in the bathroom where there is your washbag full of products with strange American names. Mouthwash. Eyewash. Everything is very ordered and neat. It strikes me that you are a very clean and neat person now and that's very funny when I think back to the night of the pearl necklace and the boy you were back then, with everything torn or frayed, your hair snaggling around your collar.

I go back into the room and fumble around trying to find the switch to turn off the bathroom light, as it makes such a noise.

You're lying on the bed fully dressed, hands behind your head. You look all wrong, too neat, too buttoned – still too much like a businessman. I feel strange. I sit on the edge of the bed.

You look funny, I say.

Funny how?

Grown-up. So like a man.

You seem about to laugh but then you don't. Instead you look straight at me and your eyes are very blue.

This is who I am, you say.

We look at each other for a moment.

I can't do this, I tell you, because it's suddenly clear to me that I can't.

Foolish girl, you say, and you put out a hand and touch my knee in my dark denim jeans. Look at you, that face of yours, so much going on in there, funny old Mrs Poet Lady. You're gorgeous but you're thinking too much and it's fatal, you know that?

I can't help thinking, I begin to say, and then I stop

because I feel it again – such warmth in my leg from your hand. Like something hot being poured in.

What's that? I say.

What's what?

What you're doing with your hand – it feels – incredible, like – I can't describe it – like –

You smile and you keep your hand there, move it a little, gently stroking. More hotness floods in. I feel my limbs start to let go a little.

I'm not doing anything, silly girl, it's you – it's what you're feeling. Don't you see? It's what you've decided to let yourself feel.

We lie together on the bed, the hard beige bed with its hard smooth white sheet and its ugly brown bedcover. We keep all our clothes on, just like twenty years before. You tell me all you want to do is talk and I agree and relax a little and then before I can think about it, I find I'm putting my arms around you. My wrists at the softest part of your neck, my thighs trembling a little against yours. My body feels thick and light and hard and hot all at the same time and you pull me to you and hold me tight and I begin to feel I need you closer. I almost tell you this but I don't.

Closer in what way? you'd ask me and I know your eyes would be quietly laughing.

I ask you to tell me more about your life story and so you settle me against you and you carry on from where you left off before – the bad ending of your marriage, the sleeping with as many women as you could.

I like that bit, I say, and you kiss my head, a quick noisy kiss and say, I know you do.

But first you tell me how, as a child, a boy of maybe ten or eleven, you had a friend called Mike and you both used to run along the rooftops, jumping from building to building.

Like Spiderman? I whisper, my face close to yours.

Right.

And your mum let you?

She didn't know. She had no idea. She'd have been crazy with worry. We were quite bad kids, Mikey and me.

I'm sure you weren't bad, I say, thinking of Jack and Fin and how many things I know for a fact they attempt behind my back, because they have to, because they're boys and they need to learn about the world in crazy unbalanced ways.

You move your head a little away from mine for a moment so you can look at me. You take your glasses off and fold them and lay them on the bedside table just behind you. I'm glad to see your eyes properly.

I look right into them and then I touch your chin with my finger.

I just realised – your little beard.

My goatee?

Did you really have one?

Yup. I shaved it off.

When?

Yesterday. Before I left.

Why?

I don't know. I thought it wouldn't do. You wouldn't have liked it.

How do you know I wouldn't have?

I just do, I just know.

You tell me then that you felt ashamed at writing to me all that stuff about your wife and her affair and what you did afterwards.

Ashamed? I say, gazing at the total blueness around the pupils of your eyes. But why?

You take a breath and seem to think about this.

I guess – I found myself telling you the truth but, well, it was the first time I'd faced those things myself. First time in a long time. And like I said, none of it was pretty. You're easy to tell the truth to, though, Rosy, you know that?

It broke my heart, I tell you, realising as I say it that it's true, it did.

Why? What broke your heart?

It broke my heart when you told me about sleeping with as many women as you could. Actually I think that's when I started to love you. It was at that moment I think.

You laugh softly and screw your eyes up at me.

Wait – let me get this straight. You loved me because I said I'd slept with as many women as I could?

It's a little more complicated than that, I say.

Then explain it, please.

You sounded so desperate. It was a desperate thing to do. It made me see how soft you are.

Soft?

Yes. You pretend to be hard but really you're soft.

Aha, you say, you fell for it. My soft-inside act.

I wanted to help you and rescue you, I say, and you think about this for a moment and you say nothing. You stroke my hair out of my face and shift yourself on the bed to get more comfortable.

185

When you were ten, you say, tell me, what did you most love doing?

I roll a little so I'm slightly on my back.

Most in the world?

Most in the whole world.

Fishing, I say straightaway, realising the answer is obvious even though I haven't thought about it in a very long time. I used to fish in the brook by our house. We lived in the country then. When my parents were still together. And I so desperately wanted a fishing rod for my birthday, only I wasn't allowed to have one.

But why the hell not?

Because I wasn't a boy.

You pull me a little closer to you.

Poor Rosy, you say. Poor little kid. I'd have given you one.

You're forgetting, you were also ten or OK maybe eleven at the time and jumping around on rooftops in another country.

Would have, I said. But hey, did you catch anything?

Mostly sticklebacks, but –

Mostly what?

Sticklebacks.

What in fuck's name is that? Stickle what? It sounds like some kind of a medieval thing.

I laugh and I feel you move your head just a touch closer to mine.

It's just a small common sort of fish with these little spiny things on top. But listen, what I was going to say is, one day I caught a trout – by mistake, in my net. Can you imagine? A big trout!

You laugh.

Wow. I know what a trout is.

Exactly.

I can just see you, little ten-year-old Rosy – wearing overalls, right? Overalls rolled up to the knees and standing in that fucking cold stream with your puny little net and this fucking great fish comes along and –

Wham. I got it. I surprised even myself.

I bet you did.

I did, I say, and I'm laughing a lot now, but you have to realise, there was quite a lot of skill involved.

I'll bet, you say. And you lace your hands behind my back and pull me right up against you there on the bed. I fall into you and I smell the scent of you and I realise with relief that you don't smell all that strange, not any more.

Rosy, you say. Oh Rosy –

What?

I love you. I – just – love – you.

I go very still and I look at your warm kind face.

OK? you say. Is it OK for me to say that?

I look at your fingers twined in mine, holding mine, and I hesitate, I feel so much like hesitating.

You can't love me, I say. Not yet. Not already.

Can't I? you say, and you're still smiling.

I don't know. It's not possible, not so soon.

You said it first, you remind me. You told me first.

I know, I say. And I meant it. I felt it. At that moment, I felt it.

I thought you were very brave, you say. To put your whole self on the line and tell me – something like that.

Did you? I say, thinking about this.

Yeah. Yeah, I did.

Well, just as I said, I felt it. I had to say it because I knew I felt it and it, well, it felt like the truth.

And now?

What?

Does it still feel like the truth?

I don't know, I say. It's – hard. I just don't know what's true and what isn't right now.

Moments pass and we listen to the silence in the room, the faraway hum of the world and its machinery outside. It's strange that it's morning. It doesn't feel like morning or afternoon or night. All we can see from here is the white blankness of the sky and it doesn't feel like any time of day at all.

What are you thinking now? you ask me.

I'm thinking of all the writing we've done, all the emails, I tell you. So many thousands of words. Do you think this could have happened without computers, I mean before the computer age?

Twenty years ago – that night – it had nothing to do with computers, you say.

I know, but this – now – the total understanding we seem to have reached?

I don't know, you say, but yeah, I guess I can see us both with our quills, scratching away –

Catching the noon post or whatever.

You look at me and go quiet for a moment.

I'm glad, you say. I'm so glad you wrote back to me.

I had to, I say. You've no idea how much I had to.

Why?

Because – I suppose I remembered you. That night. The pearls and the kissing, it was so unexpected. I never forgot it. I didn't think about it much over the years but it was always there somehow, underneath everything. It was always enticing to me, that memory.

You smile.

I like that, you say.

I thought you would.

So my genius plan paid off then?

Your plan?

To kiss you so goddam thoroughly that you'd come back to me eventually.

I smile and so do you.

It paid off, I say quietly. But the thing is –

What?

I don't know. It all seems such a waste. It feels so sad. All those years we lost, the way we just let them go.

Don't say that, you tell me, and then you go very still against me and I can feel you holding me.

There was a connection between us, wasn't there? you say then. I didn't recognise it, not properly, I didn't see it for what it was. But it was there – back then, I mean?

There was, I say. But that's just it, don't you see? That's what's so sad and stupid. You think – I thought – it's just the beginning. You imagine, when you're nineteen or twenty, that there will be so many more. And so you don't pay enough attention. You let precious things go. You know, I always thought it was just a splash, a drop – that there were so many boys waiting for me out there –

You laugh and stroke my head.

Hundreds more nights with pearls and kissing?

Yes. Exactly.

Whereas in fact –

In fact I was wrong, I say. There weren't.

No?

No. I didn't know it then, but this was unique and special, this connection of ours, and – and it would not come again.

Oh Rosy.

Well, for me it didn't come again, I tell you, and for a second I feel the tears come into my eyes. It was a one-off. Definitely. I never felt that again with anyone.

You look hard at me and your face is serious.

I feel exactly the same, you tell me. For me too. It didn't come again, the feeling, the connection. And I guess boys are even worse than girls.

Worse?

Well, at thinking there's so much out there for them, so many opportunities to, well, let's be honest, to get laid?

I smile.

So many women to sleep with?

Exactly. Precisely.

I sigh a long sigh.

At least we found each other again, I say then.

At least tonight, you say, wriggling your fingers behind me, our hands can take a break?

I laugh but your face goes serious.

Rosy, tell me something, you have to tell me the truth.

What?

You don't have to tell me about you and Tom, not if you don't want, but please just tell me you married for love. OK, not married, I know you didn't marry. But tell me you chose a man you loved. For the right reasons. And tell me he loved you – I need to know this.

The right reasons? I say slowly. What are the right reasons?

Because you felt it in your heart. Right here. Because you could not live without him.

Did you marry your wife for the right reasons?

No. I know this now. I married her because she wanted it so badly. Because I wanted to please her. And because I was afraid.

Afraid of what?

Afraid – of myself, I guess.

What do you mean, yourself?

Of what I might do otherwise. How I might be – without her. I'm not a good man, Rosy.

I think about this and that's when I tell you about Tom. How I loved him – how I do love him – how lonely he's made me recently. How he loves me too, I know he does, but he can't ever say it. How this is the reason he could not marry me either. How angry I now see that I am about this. Angry and sad. How I find myself living with a man who doesn't have any emotional dialogue whatsoever – no dialogue beyond the ordinary and practical and everyday – and how I've learned I need that dialogue, but that sometimes I feel ashamed and afraid of this fact. How sometimes I wonder whether simple love is enough – how I think I need to hold it in my hands, examine it, inspect it, see it, feel it. How I know this is wrong, that what I have – happiness, family, love – should be enough.

And then I tell you how deeply he seems to care for me, how committed he is and always has been, how well he knows me, what a caring father he is, how much I believe he loves me.

When I've finished, you look sad.

He sounds like a good man, you say. He does. He sounds entirely genuine and good.

He is, I say. I know he is.

He loves you a lot. Poor man, poor Tom.

Poor Tom, I say.

You hold my face in your two hands. You hold it like it's something intensely precious that you've never seen before and that someone just passed you to hold. As if you're trying to find the safest and most careful way to handle it. And again I feel warmth flood into my face – brightness and heat. I've never felt anything like it.

I'm afraid I love you, I whisper, I'm afraid – I've never felt this before, not ever.

I'm afraid I need to kiss you, Rosy, you say.

Without pearls? I whisper, and you smile, and the way you answer me is by what you do next.

I used to think kissing was just kissing – the smaller, slower activity that came perhaps before or as a prelude to sex, an expression of affection and trust and, yes, desire. But it was still just kissing – the safest and cleanest part of physical love, the part you could still stop at, could still retreat from if you needed to. Well now I know better.

When you begin kissing me in that beige London hotel room on a snowy February morning a whole twenty years after the night of the pearl necklace, something new happens. Something starts to unravel in me – I begin to come apart from a place so deep inside me I had no idea it was there. Strands of me, looping out in all directions. I turn into an inside-out version of myself, stretched and limp and helpless.

Or, maybe it's not new or surprising at all. Maybe it's just the obvious next part of the process you started on that cold night so long ago. Hey, give it back, I said, laughing. Come and get it, you replied, your bad blue eyes on mine as you stole my pearl and slipped it in your mouth.

My heart turned over.

Maybe we leave our imprints on each other, all of us, more than we can know – odd, indelible patterns of desire and longing, waiting just beneath the surface, always ready to reignite and remind us. Maybe once all the sensual pathways are in place, then it only takes one warm tongue, one light, unlooked-for touch, to trigger the zigzag of memory. Just one moment of two people seeking each other out all over again and colliding for a second and – whoosh – it happens. It's happened.

I don't know and I hardly care. All I know is, more than twenty years on you drop back into my life and all my certainties explode.

Is this nice? you whisper to me at one point when we've been kissing and kissing for several minutes. You have to lift your lips off mine to speak. I close my eyes and wait for them to come back.

Mmm.

Do I taste of cigarettes at all?

No.

I love you, Rosy.

Me too.

You love you too?

No, I just love you. I do. I love you.

Just saying the words makes me loosen up inside. A softening, a wetting. I smile at you and you smile back at me. We don't take our eyes away from each other. You brush my bottom lip with your tongue then and I open my mouth for you and it begins again.

Now without your glasses and close up and with me ruffling your hair, you're starting to look like the old you, the boy of nineteen or twenty from so long ago. This could almost for a moment be the you in the cold room in the ragged cords and frayed sweater, snaggled blond hair on his collar. I shut my eyes for two seconds then open them again and yes, there you are, up close to me still – smiling eyes. I remember those eyes – not just their colour but the shape of them and how they sit with the rest of your face. How deep they seem to look into me – that, especially.

Do you remember that time when we walked? I whisper to you, touching your soft, old hair, blond with a little grey in it, just as you said.

That night in summer? The long fucking endless walk you made me do?

I nod.

I was stoned, you say, as if you've only just realised this. I was totally out of my head that night, you know.

Yes, I whisper.

Yes, you say – and you run your hands over my breasts and it's like it's the first time I've ever felt them, the first ever sensation of what it is to have breasts. You pull up my T-shirt and you pull down my bra and you kiss me on the exact two places where I fed my babies. You kiss me there till I shiver. The feeling's so intense I have to look down to see what you're doing.

You told me about the abyss, you say then, and I freeze a moment and stop you kissing me so I can pull up your head and look in your eyes.

You remember that?

I was out of my head but I couldn't forget that. How could I forget a thing like that, Rosy?

I shake my head.

I can't believe you remember me telling you that.

I wanted to kiss you so badly that night, you say, and you touch my lips with your fingers.

You did? I say with surprise.

Oh god, so badly. But I was too wrecked and I didn't think you'd want it. And anyway I had no idea what you were thinking and then we walked back and you were crying –

I was not.

Oh Rosy, but you so were. Don't you remember? I walked behind you and I could tell. Your walk changes when you're crying. Even then I could tell – I knew what your sweet walk looked like when you were crying.

I stare at you as the memory comes back.

Please stop, I tell you, or I'll cry now.

You look at me with one hand still warmly on my breast, and with the other you lean back on the bed and prop your head.

It broke my heart, you say, that I'd made you cry.

Please, I say.

Silly girl. Don't you know? I've gone on thinking about

you, these past years I mean, it's like whatever else I've been doing or feeling or thinking, there's been this layer of Rosyness somewhere just behind everything, at the back of my mind.

This makes me laugh again. But inside I am amazed.

You? You really thought about me? Before now I mean?

All the time, you say with a sigh.

And then you take my face in your hands again, you hold me so gently, one hand on each cheek – Shhh, you say – and you wet my mouth a little with your tongue and then press gently on my lips till they part. You ball up my hair in one hand and touch me all over with the other. Your mouth slides so deep against mine that I forget which lips are yours and which are mine. And part of me wants to dissolve to nothing, the other part wants to stay whole for a little while longer just so I can climb up and up and perhaps when I reach the top, just somehow shatter against you.

We lie there and move against each other for what feels like hours, sliding in and out of each other's heads and hearts.

It must have been close to one o'clock when it happened. I remember thinking that my boys would have eaten the lunches I'd packed for them a hundred years ago that morning and would now be in the playground, running and shouting and throwing lumps of snow, getting damper and colder. Fin's cheeks would be red. Jack wouldn't have bothered to put a coat on. I know I saw the clock and thought of all of this from the safe warmth of your arms and then I begin to feel you do it.

You unbutton my jeans and start to pull them down a little and I say no, I whisper it, No, sweetheart, no.

Hush, I love you, you say, and you just push my hands away gently and carry on doing it.

But you don't take the jeans far down my legs, no, only a little, just so you can get your hand right in, put your fingers on me in there. I start to let you and then I stop and I tense up.

Hey, don't worry, you say. Rosy, I love you. Let me make you feel good, I want –

No, no.

I want to make you feel wonderful.

I don't need to, I say, panicking as I think of how anxious Tom always gets that I should have an orgasm before he can enjoy his. I mean – I do feel good, I say. Already I do.

Shh, baby, I mean it, hush.

And you slide your hand against me a little and then move your finger on me in what feels like almost the right place but you do it in the strangest, most different way. At first it doesn't feel that good – too hard and too un-comfortable and I move my hips a little and try to take hold of your hand and gently show you that it doesn't feel right, it's not what I'm used to, it hurts almost, a too-sensitive burning feeling and I know for a fact that it won't work. But you – you keep on looking at me with your tender, smiling face and you keep on whispering that you love me and I gaze at you and then it's like there's a click inside me and something slowly starts to twist and shake and build.

Very unexpected.

I gasp and I feel my face go hot.

And I don't know how long it goes on or how many minutes it takes, a few seconds or for ever maybe, but my whole body starts to loop and shake in a way I've never known – something almost unreachably beyond any coming I've ever done, almost unbearable in fact, but just about bearable because instead of going there on my own like I normally do, somehow I go there with you. Because all the time you're doing it, you never take your hands off me, you hold me in your arms and in your hands and you keep on looking at me the whole time.

That's it, you say. Let go, I love you.

I hear myself begin to cry.

Let go, baby, you say again. Let go. I love you.

I gasp. My eyes are open wide and so am I.

It's OK, you whisper in my ear, and I feel your kisses on my face. Don't cry, baby, I'm here, I love you, can you feel me, how I'm holding you?

Don't – please – don't let go, I cry as I find I'm going somewhere so hard and fast I can't imagine the future any more.

I won't. I'm not letting go, I'm here, I have you, I'm holding you, feel it, look, baby, I'm here.

I look in your face and your eyes are steady and warm on mine and still you're smiling so gently, even as my body climbs its big hot slope and I let go and I crash – I cling hard onto you as I crash – and you hold me too and all the time you're telling me you love me and it's wild, and I'm crying and laughing at the same time because it almost hurts but it's the best hurt I've ever felt in the whole wide life of me and yes I think, it is, it's wild.

★   ★   ★

It's quiet now. I'm here. You're here. I don't think I've ever been so here, so much in a single small place. For ten or fifteen minutes I sleep against you. Or, not quite sleep but breathe you in quietly, never moving a muscle. My legs are trembling. Then after a while you shift yourself under me and sigh a little and gently move my hair out of my eyes.

Your fingers move some strands of my hair. You look at my face. You've stayed looking at my face all this time. You look very serious.

Rosy?

Mmm.

Your legs are still shaking.

Mmm.

Are you saying you've never done that before?

I shake my head and because you sound so amazed, I curl harder against you and feel my heart wobble and the tears start to come as I tell you the truth.

I've done it, I say. Of course I have, I can always come. But not like that, never so hard. And never with someone holding me like that. I've never had someone hold me and look at me and say they love me all the time I'm coming.

More minutes pass. You hold me and you look at me and then you smile.

Your face, you say.

What?

Back when I was at school, if a girl looked like that, there was a thing we used to say — that she looked a bit jbl.

Jbl? What's that?

Just been laid.

Mmm, I say, getting it, I look like that?

Yes, baby, you say quite gravely, I'm afraid you do.

I think about this for a moment and then we both start to laugh.

But — what about you? I say.

What about me?

You haven't been jbl'd. What'll we do?

You smile and then you yawn.

Well actually, it's kind of funny, you say, normally I'd mind that. I'm real selfish and greedy when it comes to sex, I've warned you about that. But you know, something's different here — I can't believe I've managed to keep my dick in my pants but I have. Look at me. A changed man — because of love, because of you, Rosy. It feels pretty unreal but I guess it's real love that made me able to be good like that.

I laugh and then something happens that I don't want to feel — a shadow falls over us. Grief resurfacing.

Is it love? I whisper. I so badly want it to be love.

Silly girl, you say, kissing my head. Of course it's love. What else could it be? What else would make me keep my dick in my pants?

Somewhere outside faraway in a different world a clock strikes two. I feel your mouth on the edge of my ear, then on my hair. Two kisses.

I take a breath. I'm holding your hand, fingers laced. I only just realised that.

I have to tell you something, I say at last. I have to. Something terrible.

You don't speak but you twist to look at me in the bed. You've undone everything, pulled back the sheet and arranged the covers around us. We're still clothed though my jeans are around my knees and you've pulled the covers up to keep us warm. I think I've been asleep again for a few moments.

My little girl, I say, and I move back a little way out of your arms so I can see your face.

Mary?

Yes. Mary.

With the crazy eyes like you?

I put my hand on your mouth to stop you. I keep my hand there and I look in your blue eyes and my heart bangs so hard it hurts in my chest.

No, I say, and I hear my voice come out too loud. Don't talk about her. Don't.

You stare at me and I can see you begin to look almost afraid. And then I do it, I tell you the truth.

She was a strong girl. Strong and determined, right from the very start, always, even as a baby – you could tell from the kick of her leg, the breath in her, the open and shut of her small sticky fingers.

And somehow in the night, she must have got sick of just looking at the cat hanging there and maybe she wanted to make it play the music, but she must have got up in her cot and reached up over the bars and tried stretching up as high as she could to reach it. And though she couldn't actually get her fingers onto the cat, still she'd managed somehow to grab hold of the very edge of the changing table and ease it towards her, slowly, slowly, dragging it towards the cot.

She must have gripped the edge so hard with her small fingers. Very determined. Letting go and then grabbing hold again, not giving up. It must have moved quite slowly along the smooth melamine of the chest, which was just high enough above the cot to allow the table to tip suddenly before it fell. I wonder how many minutes it took her, before it tipped.

I can see her face – rapt, concentrating, a slight frown in her eyes and spit shining on her lower lip.

And at some point, when it got a little too far over, the table must have tipped right off the edge of the chest of drawers and landed in the cot, on its side, right on top of her. Three seconds it must have taken, a tip, a shock, just like that.

There was no crash or falling sound, nothing for us to hear, because it landed on the mattress and the blankets with Mary underneath. She would have fallen straightaway, knocked down by its substantial weight. I liked to think she didn't cry out because she didn't feel it happening, not for more than a second or two anyway.

I used to think, when I was an anxious new mother, that babies' heads were brittle as eggshells, easily cracked. But I learned later that this was a fallacy because, just like babies' heads, eggshells are actually engineered to be strong. I once saw a man on TV drop a hen's egg from a height and it bounced, it did not break.

Her lungs collapsed first and then because of that she suffered cardiac arrest. It turned out that her skull was also fractured, so even if we'd found her earlier she'd still have died. They were trying to comfort us when they told us this. They said it would have happened very quickly. They didn't want us to think it was just a matter of time, that we could have done anything, that we could have saved her if we'd come in earlier. They didn't want us to have to think about the if's.

The changing table was a hefty thing, made of good hard wood, well made and solid. It had seen us through three babies after all. The blow it dealt would have cracked a million eggs. Almost the worst thing of all was, Mary was nearly out of nappies – we usually just pulled her night-time one off her and these days it was sometimes easier to change her wherever she was, on the floor. I couldn't help thinking that we'd probably have stopped using the table for good in just a week or so's time.

I don't think I am crying. Not this time. This time I'm way past crying and I think instead that the person doing the crying is you. I think you hold me and I feel you shiver a little, your breath on my neck, and I put my hands on your face and I discover that the tears are yours.

It was my fault, I tell you.

Don't say that. Don't ever say that.

But it was.

You push the tears from your eyes again and take a breath.

Sometimes we do things, you say. We all do things.

I go over and over that moment, I tell you, I relive the moment in the night when I made that decision –

Hush, you say, and then you sound as if you're going to say something else but you don't, you just say Hush again.

Tom was going downstairs to get the papers and make us coffee, so first he went in to wake her. He was going to take off her nappy and bring her to me so she could come in the bathroom and be made to sit on the potty for a moment or two.

She liked to sit on the potty whilst I sat on the loo. Tom said I was in danger of making her into a child who could only poo if she had company.

She'd have sat on the blue plastic elephant potty in just her vest, the pale skin of her bottom slightly reddened from the damp nappy, and with her elbows resting on her fat knees, serious-faced, she'd have talked to me.

Lelly?

Yes. Elephant.

Lelly?

Yes, that's right.

It wasn't really a conversation that was going to go anywhere, but we had it every morning, the elephant conversation, just the same.

She might have done something in the potty right away and I'd have praised her. Or else she might have got bored and tried to get up and wander off, impatient with the whole process. Then I'd have had to judge whether to encourage her to sit down again or whether it was better not to push it but to give up and hope she'd remember the routine when the moment came.

And after that?

I suppose she'd have climbed into the bed with me and had a cuddle for a moment or two, me enjoying the feel of the curve of her back and the bounce of her thighs, smelling her warm sleepy hair. Then, getting bored with that, she might have slipped down off the bed and gone onto the landing to look in the basket of toys. Poking around in there. And more than likely after a couple of minutes she'd have brought something back to show me – usually something that used to belong to the boys. She had plenty of her own things but naturally she preferred boys' toys – especially cars, Transformers, Action Men, anything with bits. Whatever it was, it would be something that required some fiddling from me. She liked to get me to do things – undo things, pull things off, clip things on.

Her favourite thing was pulling off both of Action Man's green rubber boots then making me put them on him again while she watched.

Man! Man! She'd give the command with an imperious face, holding the doll upside down and jerking his feet in the air to show me what was required.

Or else, even better, she liked to fetch me Action Man's wetsuit – a frustrating garment which took a great deal of weaving and pulling from a grown-up to get on over his stiff plastic arms and legs, especially if that grown-up was lying in bed and still half-asleep.

Man! she'd say approvingly once it was on. Then she'd plop down on the floor and start to peel it off him again.

But none of this happened on that Sunday.

Instead I heard Tom cry out – a terrible cry without beginning or end, a cry I'd never heard before. I don't remember getting out of the bed but I have a memory of suddenly being on the landing, standing there and him trying hard to stop me getting in the room.

No! I heard him shout. Dial 999. Now! Don't come in – just do it.

I suppose he wanted to do the kind thing. He wanted to protect and save me from the terrible thing that was in the room. Maybe it was immediately obvious to him that she'd been dead a while, that it was hopeless. Or maybe not. Maybe in the deep shock of the moment he actually thought there was something someone medical could or should do.

But he knew, of course he knew, that nothing would keep me out of that room. He'd pulled the table up off the bed and let down the bars of the cot and he was kneeling there and trying to hold his daughter's head and feel her pulse without moving her body. For a moment I thought it was her breath I could hear but then I saw that it was his own that was coming in such quick harsh gasps.

No, I shouted, no!

Get the phone, he said, and I tried to but I couldn't move away so he leapt up and ran to get it and I heard him dialling and crying and dialling again. I heard some words, I knew he was talking to them and so I leaned over her and I put my hands on her cold cold head. I saw that her face was all wrong, her eyes half-open and all in the wrong place and that her skin was purplish on one side and lighter on the other.

Baby, I whispered to her now, Baby, it's OK – and I stayed very close to her and I just carried on saying her name to her and telling her that it was all OK, and stroking and stroking her cold cold head.

The room has got very cold now. The sky is greyer, not yet dusk but lights coming on over the city which is still frozen hard. You put on your glasses and you go over and pull down the blinds and try to find how to turn up the heater.

I sit up on the bed and look at my watch. Two forty-five. The boys will be leaving school in half an hour.

In silence, you help me pull up my jeans and put my boots back on. You pick up my pink wool coat off the chair and put it round my shoulders, adjusting it for me carefully and soberly as if I'm your child. You put both hands on my shoulders and you look at me over the top of your glasses and you smile at me and I smile back but it's not the same smile, not like before.

OK? you say.

OK, I lie, and then I shiver and you rub my arms for me and then hold me for a moment.

I've ruined it, haven't I? I say.

Ruined what?

All of it. This.

Oh my love, you say, but you don't disagree with me.

This morning when I put this coat on – in another place, in a house that smelled of laundry and cats and old windows, a house where I dared to tell you I loved you – well, that seems so very long ago. A place of hopefulness.

It's like we've been in here for ever, I say.

Yes, you say. Yes.

I can see from the pale skin under your eyes that you are tired.

You're tired, I say.

Yes, you agree, I am. I need to sleep.

Somehow just you admitting that makes me feel sad and excluded and exhausted.

You pull on a sweater and come down in the lift with me. I tell you that you really don't need to but you say you must, you want to. There's no one else in the lift. The doors close. The air smells stale. Your hair is still ruffed up, like a boy's hair. I think, you're not going to touch me now, and you don't.

Will we see each other again? I say, and you look down at the floor and you say, Of course.

When?

Just let me get this meeting done first. I'll call you. Later, OK? I'll call.

You can't call me. I mean, you'd better not.

Will you call me then? I don't have a cellphone here but call my room –

What? Here at the hotel? I'm about to say yes and then I think of something. Can I write to you? If I send an email will you get it? Today, I mean?

The lift arrives at the ground floor as you touch my face and say, Of course. Of course you can. I forgot. Write me something. Yes, do that. I'd like that.

It won't be long and crazy, I say.

I know that, sweetheart, I know it won't.

We stand outside in the freezing air, snow still on the ground under our feet.

Go in, I say, please. You'll get cold.

I need to sleep for an hour, you say.

More than an hour, I tell you.

An hour will do it, you say. And then I guess I ought to wash.

You make a face. You're trying to be light, but it doesn't come out right.

Go in, I say again.

And you look at me for a moment and then tiredness seems to take you over and you say OK, and you plant a kiss on your fingers and just briefly touch my nose and then you turn and I watch you go back into the hotel.

I don't like to watch you go. You walk wearily, your head down. From behind you could be any middle-aged businessman – slightly overweight, hair that used to be fair now streaked with grey, an unremarkable man, probably kind, but unremarkable. I try to take some comfort from this.

After Mary's death, Tom and I did the best we could. We found ourselves living a different kind of life for a while. We, who'd been such a careful family, a family who liked to do things properly, for a while we let ourselves go and we didn't do things properly at all. Without ever consciously telling ourselves what we were doing, we relaxed a lot of the rules of the house. We rented DVDs, got takeaways. We spent time together as a family and tried not to care whether the washing-up got done or not. For a while it was almost as if there was a holiday atmosphere – everything suspended and euphoric. It was like the glue of the family had come undone and we'd fallen apart and we'd almost been pleased with the pieces that we'd found. Certainly if you'd been a stranger looking in, you would not ever have guessed we'd just lost a child.

Some days I felt that it had all been a dream, a silly idea, a moment of terrible fantasy and that Mary might be back at any moment. I'd say her name secretly under my breath as I went up the stairs or put a bag of rubbish out on the path and I'd feel a kind of sneaking victory at being able to imagine she was still somehow there in our lives. I might even hear her naughty laugh, drowned beneath the drone of the vacuum cleaner and certainly most days the sweet animal warmth of her hair seemed still to be on my pillow and now and then I even thought I caught the warm ammonia whiff of her wet nappy – a smell Tom always teased me for enjoying.

But as time went on and life got back to normal, that's when I found it hardest. It was as if my grief had only pretended to give in and creep away but was actually waiting just around the corner, ready to pounce and hurt me when I was least prepared. So I'd take Jack and Fin to their music lessons, shop for food, tidy the house, cook supper. But it would only take one tiny thing – a look or a word, the shape of something that maybe didn't even have anything to do with her – and that would be it, I'd be paralysed, unhinged.

Fin or Jack might come upon me by the washing machine, unable to move, holding the basket full of wet washing, tears falling down my cheeks. One time I stood in a kitchen I barely recognised and poured apple juice on Fin's Weetabix and he screamed at me. Another time I drove through a red light and was almost hit by a lorry. My heart swerved. What if the boys had been in the car.

At night, Tom and I clung to each other. I don't think we'd ever touched each other so much. He had terrible night sweats. I'd brush up against his leg or his arm in the night and it would be soaked and burning up. Sex became a ferocious thing – a way of getting ourselves both out of our heads and off to sleep, and I think that's when we started being these two separate people in bed, two individuals who didn't have to speak, who could just go through the motions and then spring back apart again. We had this way of fusing together quickly and effectively, but it didn't have a lot to do with love.

Tom's way of coping was to mention her as little as possible, to turn to the present, to the children we still had. One day I found him in the hall, folding up her pushchair. He was on his knees doing it properly, undoing the little clips on the side and screwing them up again. It still had a couple of nappies and a knitted cardigan she'd worn the last time we used it, shoved in the plastic pocket at the back. Also a half-used pack of Bickipegs, for teething. He took these things out without looking at them, laid them on the stairs.

I should have done this weeks ago, he said. There was sweat on the side of his head. I saw that his hair didn't look too clean – flakes from his scalp had fallen on his shoulders, a man coming apart.

I said nothing, I just watched. He put the pushchair in the car and drove it round to the charity shop.

When he'd gone, I stood for a moment, looking at those things of hers on the stairs – the cardigan, the Bickipegs, the nappies – and I knew I should have moved them but I found I couldn't. I literally could not lift my hand or move from the place where I was. So I stood there frozen to the spot, like a woman in a fairy story, under a spell, rooted and turned to stone.

I took a cab home to make sure to get there in time for the boys. It hissed through streets which were brown and slippy with slush. I could still feel the heat and throb of where you'd touched me – it felt like it was somehow still going on, the feeling of coming. I sat in the cab in a daze, thankful that the driver wasn't trying to talk to me, amazed and almost embarrassed that my mind refused to focus on anything but my body, my blood, the mad rhythm of my heart.

When the cab stopped I somehow managed to take the right money out of my purse. But once inside our front door, I had to force myself to stand and take several deep breaths, to somehow place myself back inside this different day, this different place, this home I lived in.

Fin had been throwing snowballs on the way home. His gloves were sopping and so was his scarf and blazer and so were his grey school trousers.

I made him strip down to his underwear, so I could put some stuff in the washing machine, the rest on the radiator. After I'd done this, I stood and drank a glass of water straight from the tap. I remembered that I'd had no lunch. Suddenly I was starving. I took a banana from the bowl and offered one to Fin who refused and had a biscuit instead.

You're a thirsty woman, he remarked. Thirsty and hungry – and I laughed and agreed that yes, I was and then I tried to remember where I was and ask him about the snow.

It was great, he said, sitting at the kitchen table in his vest and boxers. I got Fred down the back of the neck. Ha! Up there by the, no the edge of the – you know – it was so deep it was crazy. Kids were just grabbing it and packing it down each other's shirts.

I tried to listen and to look enthusiastic.

Weren't you freezing cold? I asked him, and he nodded and took another sip of milk, wiped his mouth with the back of his hand.

Yeah, well, you see I like to be cold, cold and wet, man, it's great, it's wicked, man, it's wild.

Oh Fin, I said, and I finished the banana and touched my cheeks which were still burning.

When will Dad be home? he said then. Because I need to get him to fix my laptop. I need to get on the internet. It's kind of urgent.

Soon, later, I said, and then we heard the front door slam as Jack came in. When I asked him what sort of a day he'd had, he said OK, as he always did.

You look tired, I told him, and I noticed that his trousers were looking too short.

Well what d'you expect? he said, and went to the sink to get a glass of water, and then said Shit as the tap spurted and water hit the window.

Jack, I said. Language.

When's that tap going to be fixed? he said, scowling. You know it leaks.

I know, but when will it be fixed? Why does nothing work around here? And why are you all dressed up?

I'm not dressed up, I said, glancing down at my jeans.

You are. Your hair is all shiny and you've got a necklace and earrings on. And high heels.

You do look kind of different, Fin agreed. Not dirty or messy we mean.

Hey, well, thanks a lot, guys, I said, and I went over and squeezed Fin's shoulders and kissed the side of his face, something he hated.

Mum, please, he said.

I have to go and do some work at my desk, I told them, and Jack looked interested.

What work?

Just some work.

Even as I climbed the stairs I could feel myself fizzing inside and it was like my blood was still rocking, rocking and jumping.

Tom would not let me take a shred of blame. I tried to tell him straightaway, on that first morning, what I had done but he would not listen.

That doesn't make you any more to blame than me, he said quietly. I made the fucking table, don't you see? I made the frigging thing.

No one could blame you for making it, I told him as he put his arms around me.

A good kind friend from down the road came and collected the boys and took them back to hers and kept them happy and unsuspecting for the rest of the day. Well, not quite unsuspecting – Jack was constantly demanding to know why he couldn't be allowed back home. After the police had been – because they had to come – Mary was taken to the hospital morgue in an ambulance. We went with her. They used the siren even though she was dead.

The woman who came round with the police couldn't have been nicer. She had long black hair and a ring on every finger, even the thumbs. She stood in our kitchen and made us tea in a pot which we never normally used and which we left to go cold.

She spoke softly and she told us what we already knew, that we were in shock. She told us that the single thing parents say most often is If Only. That it is absolutely normal, the impulse to go round and round the edges of a tragedy, trying to roll back time and see how it could have been prevented. And nine times out of ten, it couldn't have. There's the moment before it happened and there's the moment after and there's no way of getting in between those two moments.

At five o'clock the boys came back and it was dark and cold outside. Sunday night. Jack looked angry, Fin looked scared. We sat at the kitchen table with them and I waited for Tom to speak and when he didn't, I did. We hadn't rehearsed what to say, for it seemed to us that there was no good way of saying it. All the same, sitting there then at that moment, certain things came to me. I said there had been a terrible and stupid accident and that Baby had died.

I described what had happened in the night with the table and I managed to tell it honestly without sounding like it was a huge thing or that anyone was especially to blame. I knew this was how Tom would want me to tell it. I tried to say that sometimes bad things happen to people we love, accidental things we can do little or nothing to prevent and that part of the preciousness of life is living with the risk of this. I tried also to say that Baby knew how very much we had all loved her and how good and loving and special her small short life had been.

Fin cried and cried but Jack didn't look at me at all, he kept his eyes down and his fingers played with a rubber band he had found on the table. After a moment I saw Tom put a hand on his and keep it there, to still his fidgeting but also to comfort him.

★   ★   ★

Your email must have been written very soon after I left you. You can't have slept for very long, in fact, now I think about it, you can't have slept at all.

Baby? Are you there? I'm missing you so much already – I love you, I need you, is there any way you can get back here tonight? Write when you get this. Please. Write to me now if you can. I'm sorry. But – please?

I stare at this on the screen and the whole moment – the room, the light, the darkness outside – it all changes, everything moves up a notch of happiness. And I feel my smile begin again, feel everything that's good start to happen – huge rolling welts of possibility lighting up all over.

I punch the keys quickly, madly.

I'm here, I'm – so in love with you. I'm – tell me, is your meeting over?

It's over, you write back. All done. Everything's good. I'm in love with you too, madly and hopelessly. I don't know what to do, Mrs Rosy. I need to see you. I want you so much. I'm sorry about earlier. When you'd gone this wave of sadness just came crashing right over me. I'm – just tell me what to do. I'm washed, I'm rested, I'm here, I'm waiting for you. When can you get here? Will you come? Please say you'll come?

I'll come, I write. It won't be till after seven, maybe closer to eight, it depends on the family and how soon I can get away, but yes, I'll come.

Far away, in another world, I heard Fin shouting at Tom. I heard Tom shouting back. I paused a moment and chewed my fingers as I tried to think.

I'm sorry, I write, slowly now, for what I had to tell

you, I mean. My timing was bad and, well, I didn't know how to but – if I'm to see what this is, this thing of ours, this thing between us, I have to tell you everything, the good and the bad. You do see that don't you? And it's been such a big part of what I've become – it's made me so confused about things –

Hush, comes the reply as I knew by now it would. Dear, sweet, crazy girl. Stop it right now. Too much thinking. Stop thinking. It's all OK, it's all going to be OK, I swear it is. I love you. I want to take care of you. I need you here so badly. Just come as soon as you can, OK? Go now and deal with your kids, then come to me. Take a cab and come here. I'll wait.

I love you, I write, and I send it straightaway.

Me too, comes the reply, I love you too.

I waited there at my machine for what felt like thirty seconds with the boys still shouting faraway upstairs. And then I couldn't help it, I pressed Send & Receive one more time.

A row of X's fills the box.

I'm going out, I told Tom from the drowned-out safety of the shower. Do you mind?

He stood in the bathroom doorway. I could see his blurred and hesitating shape through the glass of the shower doors.

Of course I don't mind, I heard him say, but I could feel him trying to decide what he should ask me next. He'd taken to treading warily around me, as though my actions were gigantic and unpredictable things, monsters of impulse which he must always be ready to grapple and manage as best he could.

I decided to be as frank as I dared.

I'm having dinner, I told him as I pulled my towel from the rail, with a friend – the old friend I told you about, remember?

Not the Paris one?

I took a breath.

No, I told him – not that one. The other one.

Name?

I told him your name.

And what's he like? Tom asked me. He put some clean washing away, snapped the drawer shut a little harder than necessary and then pulled down the blind. It drove him crazy that I never remembered to draw the bathroom blinds before I washed.

Um – well, he's greyish-haired, our age. A little over-weight, I told him truthfully, and he laughed.

Well, that's OK then.

I stood with the towel around me and dried my breasts, my legs and arms. Tom watched.

You look nice, he said.

Thank you.

I mean it.

I know.

What are you going to wear?

I don't know, I said. Does it matter? Something nice but not too nice.

As long as you don't go like that, Tom said, and normally I might have found this funny but this time I knew it was all my fault that I didn't.

You are waiting in the far corner of the hotel bar – the

218

very same bar as this morning, only now it's a quite different place, crammed with people laughing and smoking and talking, mostly men. Somewhere beyond their noise, a piano is playing, just a bland cocktail of hotel notes, shaken together and left to spill.

You have a paper folded open in front of you but you're not even pretending to read it. Two cigarettes have been stubbed out, barely smoked, in the ashtray. You move this quickly away to the other side of the table as I come in.

Sorry, I say. Have you been waiting ages?

I slide into the seat next to you. It's not so much that I need to know, more that I'm shy and self-conscious now and I have to say something – anything – fast. I can hear my breath banging around in my chest. I try to gulp some air to still it. It doesn't work.

Not long, you say, and when I take my eyes away from you, I can feel you looking at me, at my hair, my face, my black dress with the mauve and green stitching around the neckline. Just long enough for two large vodkas on the rocks.

You're not serious?

I am actually. I told you, Rosy, I wasn't lying when I said I do everything to excess. And here's yours, you say, as the barman comes over with two more.

But – you'll be plastered.

Plastered? You know, Mrs Rosy, that's a very weird word.

It means drunk.

Pissed?

Yes.

And that means angry where I come from. Hey, baby, look at you – you dressed up. Hey, you look beautiful.

You too, I say, and you laugh.

I showered and put on a clean shirt is all.

You go on looking at me. You make me turn my head so you can touch the back where I've twisted my hair into something like a chignon. I feel your fingers on the nape of my neck and something melts there. You glance under the table at my feet in their high heels. My stompy shoes, Fin called them. I feel your hand briefly on my knee.

Look at your grown-up hairstyle and your neat shoes and your earrings. Hey, but I mean it, you look so fucking great, Rosy.

I try to think of something good and funny to say but my neck and my knee are still recovering from your touch.

Why is it, I ask, that every time you put your hands on me something weird happens?

You smile.

I mean it, I say.

What kind of weird?

I struggle to describe what I feel.

It's – I feel a kind of hot and melting feeling, like something's pulling me straight to you.

This time you laugh.

That's called sex, sweetheart.

No, I say, no, I'm serious. I know what sex feels like and it's more than sex, it's beyond sex. It's like – it's almost medical, or scientific. It's like –

I hesitate a moment and I feel myself flush.

You bend your head to mine and place your hand on my knee again. My blood pulses.

What? What's it like, baby?

Nothing, I say, and I feel my hand go stupidly to my face. I'm embarrassed.

With your other hand, you reach up and gently pull my hand away.

No, you say, I mean it. I like the way you think kind of at the exact same time as you speak, so I can't really see the joins. Please try and tell me what it's like.

Well, I say slowly, what I was going to say is – and the reason I don't think it's sex – is the only other time I've really felt it is with my children, each of them, all of them, when they were babies, as if they were made to be touched by me. And for me too, the feel of them could still me and comfort me like – I can't describe it all that well. It was like the connection that our touching made went beyond anything normal or human. It felt – spiritual's the wrong word, I hate that word, but – unearthly. Hey – but then I suppose it's not so odd when you consider that they came out of me –

Is it the same now? With the kids I mean?

I think about this.

Yes and no. I do feel it now, the same thing about touching them, I mean – only not quite so strongly, or I don't notice it so much. Maybe because they're out there in the world and I know they're on their way to moving off and away from me. I feel it more with Fin right now but then Jack has become so – unconnected to me. I imagine if Mary were still here, well –

You'd feel it with her?

Yes. With her because she'd be little, yes.

You touch my hand with yours and I go silent then,

and I find I can't quite meet your eyes. It was a long speech, full of things I didn't quite know I thought until I'd expressed them. I worry you'll think it silly.

It's not to do with love, I add quickly. My love for Jack is as strong and fierce as it ever was. But it's like the line that ties us has gone very loose.

You're staring at me hard and there's a look I haven't seen in your eyes before.

I understand that, you say.

You do?

You just described it perfectly. I love the way you choose your words, Mrs Rosy, such a poet you are – I like how I can almost see the thoughts starting up in your head, in your eyes.

I'm laughing, I can't help it.

You can?

Yeah, and I feel it too but I couldn't have expressed it like that. But it's how I feel exactly – how I always felt – about my boy, right from the start, even in the hospital, even though his birth was far from perfect because already his mom and I were at each other's throats. But – well, holding him that first time, I can't express it as well as I want to, not really – but it felt like some kind of a circle had been joined up in me. A circuit connected, yeah? Like you said, it felt scientific, chemical almost.

I smile.

Actually I don't feel it much at all now, you say then, but that's because Zach's gotten so big and we're both of us male – we're kind of the same now you see so we cancel the feeling out. But I guess that's a man thing.

You smile at me and you take a long sip of your drink. I smile back and pick up mine.

You think that's a sappy thing for a man to say? you ask me then. You think I'm drunk – sorry – plastered?

Not at all, I say, I was actually thinking the opposite. I was thinking how good it makes me feel, talking to a man who dares to talk about feelings.

There's no daring involved, you say.

Well maybe that's what I like so much.

You don't answer this. Instead you gaze at me as if you've only just seen me now for the first time.

Sorry, you say, I need to touch you. Right now I mean.

You slide your hand over my knee and I jump a little inside.

I felt it with you too, you say then.

With me?

Yes. The first time I saw you again, here in the hotel after all this time, even though I was so fucking nervous, chain-smoking like you wouldn't believe it, still, it was like – seeing you was like a recognition of something I'd forgotten. It was like the wiring was already there and in place and some-thing just connected – zing. And I knew I could relax because it felt absolutely right.

Me too, I say, exactly that. I felt that too.

I know, Rosy. I know you did.

You ask me if I want to go out to eat.

What do you like? Do you like Indian? Chinese? Thai? What? Tell me what you like. What's your favourite food, Rosy? Tell me and I'll buy it for you. I want to feed you and then I want us to talk some more and then I want to kiss you again.

I sigh.

What? you say. What is it?

What's what?

That big shadow that came over your face – what is it, what's the matter? Look, it's cool, I'm rich now. I have all this British money – pounds, pence, everything –

I shake my head and you put your hand on mine.

Oh jeez, but I can't bear it when your face goes like that.

Like what?

Sad. Disappointed. Like a little kid who didn't get a fishing rod.

This makes me laugh.

I'm not disappointed. I'm perfectly happy – more than happy. I'm – it's just, oh well, there's just so little time.

What time do you have to be back home?

I look at my watch.

Not too late.

What's too late?

Well – midnight at the very latest? I said I was having dinner.

With me?

With a friend. Yes, with you.

You told your husband about me?

Yes. In a way. I mean I told him very little, obviously, but – he knows you exist. I thought it best.

I hesitate. I'm about to tell you that I hate lying, to anyone but especially to Tom, but in the light of the past twenty-four hours it has begun to seem like a ridiculous thing to say.

You look at me hard.

Well? So what's the problem then? Like I said, it's cool.

I hear myself sigh again and I look at my watch.

You want to go away from me? You're not hungry?

I don't want to go away from you, oh no. It's just – oh no, I can't say it.

My hands are on my face again and once again you remove them.

Foolish girl, what can't you say? You can tell me anything – I mean it. You can tell me to fuck right off here and now if you have to, you know you can.

I take a breath.

I love you, I say.

You put your arms around me.

Oh baby, me too. I love you so much. I can't tell you – this afternoon when you'd gone, do you know how long it took for me to miss you?

Tell me.

Only about four fucking minutes. I tried to shower but I had to be so quick. I had this stupid feeling that you might come straight back and knock on my door, or phone from downstairs in the lobby and I might not hear it. Even though I knew it was impossible, I knew you couldn't because you had to be back for your kids. After that I logged on and kept on checking my messages like a lunatic. Then I couldn't wait any longer and I wrote you that email.

This time it's you who sighs and your face suddenly looks tired.

I'm in love with you, Rosy. I never meant this to happen and it's breaking me up if you want to know.

Baby, I say.

I take both your hands in mine and this time I smile.

Hush, I tell you, using your own words back at you which makes you laugh inside yourself. Hush, foolish boy, it'll be OK, it will. OK, you want the truth? Well you're right, I'm not hungry. It's because – what I really want is to lie down with you.

You start to laugh.

Oh Mrs Rosy –

Naked and – lying down. I want to be in a bed with you. Right now.

Really? That's really what you want?

It's what I want. Am I blushing?

Yes. A lot.

Oh god –

You move closer and you put your arm around me, pull me close, kiss me on the side of my head, and I smell your skin and hair and the scary sweetness of you.

You want to do what we did earlier?

No, I say, more than that. I want us to do it properly.

Properly? You mean –

Yes.

You're still laughing. Now you put down your drink and you pick up my coat and put it around my shoulders. You do up the top button even though it doesn't really do up like that. Then you kiss me on the nose.

OK, OK, it's cool, it's all cool, it can be fixed, but – just tell me one thing – sorry to have to ask – do we need, do I need, to –

Yes, I say, you do. We do.

★   ★   ★

226

You say it's OK, that you'll go to the men's room, that they're sure to sell them there. But almost straightaway you return and tell me the machine's broken.

Stupid fucking hotel, why'd they put me here?

Oh dear, I say, it's so long since I've –

Hush. I'm thinking. OK, I have a plan.

You finish your drink and take me by the hand.

OK, we're going for a walk and we're going to find two things, a bottle of wine and some – protection. After that, after we've scored, we go back as fast as we can to my room and – well, I'm gonna rock your world, OK?

OK, I say, laughing, and then I glance again at my watch.

Don't worry, you whisper, you'll be home in time.

There's a lot of snow outside, I whisper. Do you realise? Have you even been out since you arrived today?

No.

I thought not.

Why are we whispering? you ask me, and I tell you I don't know.

I was right. Outside, the street is deep in settled snow, a silence on the world, a hush, a whisper. It feels so strange that for a moment I don't know where I am, where I'm coming from or where I've been. Suddenly out in the cold your presence beside me seems a little less solid.

Are you even real? I ask you suddenly, remembering Paris, and you grasp my cold hand with your warm one and your voice seems to come from somewhere else.

How would I know? you say, and I can't tell from your eyes if you're joking or not. All I know is right now I very much want to be.

None of this is real, I say, but mostly I say it to myself and I'm surprised at how little it bothers me.

We make our way down the big wide road where buses are travelling very slowly through the icy night, but all the chemists are shut. I suggest we try and find a supermarket. I'm pretty sure there's one further down the road.

You put your arm around me and I nustle against you. It's easy to walk along with you like this, we fit perfectly.

Hey, we fit perfectly, you say.

I know.

Mrs Rosy?

Yes.

You know something really funny?

What?

I bet you either of our kids – I mean Zach or Jack – would be able to supply us if they were here. Ironic, huh?

I steal a quick look at you and for some reason I don't like this thought.

Goodness, I really hope Jack wouldn't.

But he's sixteen, right?

He's never had sex.

No? How can you be so sure of that?

I think of Jack's room with its painted war figures, its Nirvana posters, half-drunk mugs of chocolate milk on his desk, graphic novels on the floor, bedsheets scrunched around a scuffed old Gameboy he still plays with late at night. The thought of his room sends an ache of worry through me.

He's never even had a girlfriend, I say.

Well – as far as you know.

OK, all right, I can't be sure. But I have a strong feeling.

You think he'd tell you?

Don't really know. I think he might. I don't think he'd go out of his way to hide it from me.

You're very close to your kids, aren't you?

So are you to your Zach too.

No, I mean, your thing is kind of different. It's partly because you're a mom of course, but it's also a Rosy thing, an animal thing.

I laugh.

I'm like an animal?

You're very instinctive, very visceral, yes.

I think about this and wonder if it's true.

I can tell from the way you talk, you say. Smell and touch, it's big for you.

Well, when they were much younger, I say, I could tell each of them apart, one from the other, simply by their smell. The tops of their heads – each had an entirely different scent. I could never have described why but I knew those different smells. Tom never believed me, didn't think it was possible, and we always had this big jokey plan that one day he'd blindfold me and test me. But of course we never found time to do it and then –

Then what?

Well, then – Mary died, I say.

You stop right there in the snowy street and you hold me tight in your arms.

Sweetheart, you say, sweetheart.

It's OK, I say.

I wish I could make things better for you.

You do. You have.

And I breathe you in and feel the closeness of your arms around me. We stand there together for a few more minutes and I listen to the sound of our feet which barely seem to make an imprint on the newly fallen snow.

No wonder you are so in need of love, Mrs Rosy, you say after a moment or two. I'm startled by this.

Am I?

You hold my face in your hands and look at me. Your own face is dazed and pale in the white light and for a moment or two you look like a ghost.

You really have to ask that?

I say nothing, I just stare at you.

Isn't that why I'm here? you say.

Is it?

You pull off your shoes and carefully remove your glasses and place them on the bedside table, and then you sit on the hotel bed and open the blue, red and white carrier bag which contains condoms, a bottle of wine and two packs of dried butter beans. I throw my coat on the chair and unclip my hair and shake it out and plomp down next to you on the bed.

What the fuck are these? you say, holding up the beans.

Oh, sorry, I say, and I squeeze myself a little closer to you on the bed. It was me, I put them in. To make it look a bit more normal –

Beans? To make it normal?

Well, more household, I say, laughing as I hear how crazy this sounds. I was just so embarrassed – at how obvious it looked.

Obvious?

Well, like the shopping of two people who were about to – you know.

About to what?

You chuck the beans on the floor and push the bag aside and pull me down next to you on the bed. I hear myself start to giggle.

I need to go to the bathroom, I say, and I try to say it like an American.

No, you say, you're going nowhere until you tell me – about to what?

I laugh again and you press yourself on me and kiss me on the lips. Such a soft kiss, and yet the hot sensation of it reaches right down as far as the backs of my knees.

I like that, you say, as you ball up my hair in your hand.

What?

The way your lips just part so easily when I kiss you.

Mmm.

It's like – it's a given, that you open yourself to me, there's no fuss at all. I like that. But you haven't answered my question. About to what?

I open my mouth for another kiss but you just press your tongue gently on my bottom lip and then take it away, teasing me.

Do you mean about to fuck? you say, low and quiet, as you work your way further on top of me. Is that what you mean?

Yes, I whisper back, though my breath will hardly come out to form the word.

Well, say it then.

I can't.

Say it.

I'm a mum. I can't say it.

I could make you say it.

Oh yeah?

Yeah. I could, Mrs Rosy, believe me, I could.

You are lying right on top of me now. I shift myself slightly beneath you and I look into the sly, lit-up blue of your eyes and realise you look different to me, not like you any more but like something out of my head from long ago – more like the boy from the night of the pearl necklace perhaps.

Can you feel that? you ask me.

Mmm.

Can you? What can you feel?

I can feel – you.

My what?

I giggle again and try to catch my breath.

I can't say it, I whisper.

Why not?

I don't know. I just – I don't know what it is.

You don't know what it is?

I don't know what you call it.

My cock. I call it my cock.

Oh. OK.

So can you feel it? Can you feel my cock?

I smile and I try to kiss your ears and your hair but you keep on stopping me even though I'm trying to pull you closer to every part of me.

Yes, I say and I'm laughing again, OK, I can feel it, OK? Your cock. I can feel your cock.

It wants you.

I know.

But not yet.

Oh – please.

Please what?

Please do it.

You laugh.

Do what?

Anything. Please – just go on kissing me.

But you come off me a little then, and you lean up on your elbows and you look at me.

Rosy?

Yes.

Do you like it when I talk a little dirty to you?

I shiver because suddenly there's too much space between us.

Mmm, yes, no, I don't know.

This time you let me undress you. You let me pull your black wool sweater over your head and you hold your two arms up like a child to allow me, and after it's off you try quickly to smooth down your hair but I won't let you, I muss it for you all over again – because I'm in charge and because like that everything's as it should be and you look like you.

Then I start to pull off your white T-shirt, but just before I do that, you ask me to turn out the light.

Why?

Oh Rosy, because I'm gross. Because I'm several pounds overweight and I don't want you to see.

Shh, I say as I struggle with the stupid stiff buckle of your belt and slide your jeans and pants down your thighs. Ridiculous man, foolish boy, have you no idea how much I love you?

233

You groan but I tell you to shut up or else I'll put on more lights.

I'll have you floodlit, I whisper, as I kneel and take hold of your springing-up cock in one hand and your balls in the other, and with my lips plant kisses all the way down your chest and belly. I mean it. If you don't do as I say, I'll have you lit from above and below — and then — then I'll have you magnified eight zillion times for the whole world to see.

In the end we make love twice, but the first time is hectic and difficult. We just can't seem to get it right. Every time we try to put the condom on you, it just slips off and in the end you have to hold it on with one hand as you go inside me. This makes me laugh and it makes you swear.

Take it off, I tell you in the end, and you look at me and your poor face is hot and red. Just do it, just take the stupid thing off.

But — I can't do that, you say, and I can hear the mix of anxiety and arousal in your voice.

It's OK, I say, and I kiss the fronts of your shoulders and move my hands over your back, down to the soft crease where your buttocks begin. Just come on me instead. Here —

You don't have to, you say.

I do have to.

I pull you to me and I use my hands to make you come. It doesn't take much, it takes no more than a few seconds, and when it's over we lie there together, warm and wet and laughing a little. Between my breasts is all slippy with it and our bodies slide a little but every time I slip too much away from you, you laugh and pull me close again.

You make me so happy, Mrs Rosy, you say after a minute or two. Really happy like I've never felt, not ever. Do you know that?

I slide myself slightly out from under you and there's a squelchy sound and I feel the breath leave my body in a sigh.

I know it, I say, I love you, I know it.

I don't understand this, you tell me then.

Me too, I agree, I don't either.

What's happening to us?

I've no idea.

I mean, I don't know what to do about it, is what I mean.

I'm silent for a moment when you say this, then, Do nothing, I tell you, for now.

Outside the window the city is cold and peppered with flashes of neon, and snow is falling again.

I think we sleep for a few minutes then. When I wake it's with a shock because my baby girl is in my arms – not only the warm elastic shape of her, but also the perfect protective contentment I used to feel when I held her. So often, even though Tom was against it, I used to take her into our bed if she was cranky or fretful in the night and within what felt like seconds, her limbs would settle and fall against me and I'd feel the soft shape of her breath on my cheek. My girl.

Instead I wake and feel the hard warmth of your chest and your arms around me and I have a second of confusion and panic.

Baby?

When I push myself up in the bed and take a breath, I wake you too.

235

What? you say and you start a little. What is it?

Nothing, it's nothing. Oh, I thought – I felt something strange, that's all.

You did?

It was nothing. It was a dream or something – it was in my head.

You yawn and rub your face and hold your glasses to your eyes so you can look at the time on your watch by the bed and then you reach for a bottle of water and drink from it. You offer it to me and I gulp it thirstily. I hadn't realised how thirsty I was.

We haven't drunk the wine, I say then.

Turns out we didn't need it, you say. We didn't need the pearls either, you add then in a soft voice.

I smile but Mary is still all over me, against me, inside me.

What time is it?

Don't worry about the time, I'm in charge of the time and there's plenty of it.

But –

Come here, you say, and you kiss my face on the pillow and put your tongue in my mouth and then you put your hands all over me, on every bit of me and then, finally, inside me.

This time is exactly the opposite of the first time. This time I don't even remember you taking out a condom or putting it on or anything. There's no fuss and no difficulty at all and it's like we've done this in our heads so many times before it's as slow and easy as a dream.

All I know is I trust you and I'm feeling so sweetened and relaxed that when you look straight in my eyes and enter me it's a quick dark shock, but nothing compared to the next few moments when you turn me inside out and shake me up and then take me somewhere I never even knew I wanted to go.

The snow is falling harder and the city is turning white. Right now the flakes are so thick you can barely see out of the window. I roll over on my stomach and look at your watch. Then look at it again. No time has passed at all. How is it possible?

Oh god, your watch has stopped, I say.

I don't think so.

Then – how can it still only be nine?

You seem unworried. You reach for the zapper and put on the TV, find the clock display.

It's nine, you say. Look, sweetheart, there it is. Nine. I told you, plenty of time.

You zap off the TV and the air in the room crackles for a second. I stare at you.

I don't get it, I say. After all we've done.

Don't be scared, you tell me.

I'm not scared. I'm just –

You get up and go in the bathroom and close the door. I hear you use the toilet and then I hear the water running. Then I hear you brush your teeth.

When you come back in the room you smell of mouthwash. You pull on your pants and jeans and stand at the window for a moment. As soon as you're any distance away from me you look so strange. I realise that it's only when you're close up to me that I feel OK about you.

Come back, I say, please. Come closer. I can't believe in you when you're right over there.

And you do. You turn and you smile at me and you come right back and the moment you hold me again it's all right.

It's like I'm in this play and I've forgotten who I'm meant to be, I whisper to you.

Me too, you whisper back, and you grin and pull the covers up around me and put your hands on either side of my face and you kiss me and look at me with such curiosity and love on your face that I start to curl back up again inside.

Did you mean it? I say. About the genius plan?

Course I did, you say. I thought, if I can just get her to kiss me once, for a whole night, while I'm skinny and wrecked and broke, then I'm set up. I let twenty years pass, I get rich and fat and middle-aged – and I come back to claim her, simple as pie.

I look in your eyes and I laugh.

Simple as pie, I say.

Simple as pie, you say, except –

Except what?

Well, I'm thinking now that maybe it wasn't such a genius plan after all.

Oh? Why not?

Well, because like you said before, the twenty years were something of a waste – the divorces, the grief and the loneliness –

The women you had to sleep with, I say quickly, and you laugh and then for a moment you look sad.

What kind of a boy were you? I ask you then. I mean as a little boy?

I was real skinny, you say.

No, I'm serious. What were you like?

You think about this.

I think I took responsibility. I had the world on my shoulders. I had to take care of my mom and my brothers. I looked after everyone I guess, but I think deep inside I resented it somewhat.

You did?

I was a kid, Rosy. It was too much. I'm not blaming anyone but – that's why I was such a dumb fuck when you knew me, such a stupid mess I mean. Something had to give. I had to break out somehow.

I turn to look at you and you smile at me. A sudden picture comes in my head – of a small skinny blond boy jumping from roof to roof. The rooftops are wet, the sky is black, the boy's bones are brittle and snappable. I shudder.

What?

Nothing.

No, it was something, I know it. Some strange thought just went through your head – a Rosy thought.

I laugh.

I can't bear to think of anything happening to you, that's all.

Nothing's going to happen to me.

You could have fallen so easily. Back then. It was a dangerous thing to do.

I didn't fall, you say. And look at me now, no longer a superhero. I guess it's unlikely I'll get up and go do the same thing now.

Would you lie to me? I ask you then. I mean ever, would you?

As I say these words, the day when, quite recently, Tom

asked me the very same thing comes rolling back to me and I flinch a little inside.

I would not lie to you, Rosy. I've told you everything I know about everything.

You have?

I have, you say sadly. Really. I mean it, Rosy, there isn't any more.

And you stare at me and your blue eyes have turned so black, almost liquid in the half-darkness. I'm suddenly afraid because it's as if you're not properly there any more.

Stop, I say, don't go!

You laugh.

I'm not going anywhere. Where would I go? Anyway, you know what? You keep on all the time about what's real and not real but I'll tell you something, I don't think you're real, not really. You want to know why? Because you never eat anything. You live on air, Rosy, thin air. Aren't you even hungry now? After all that fucking?

Are you hungry?

Hey, don't answer my question with a question.

I sigh.

I don't know, I say.

Minutes pass and you take off your jeans and lie down beside me and I feel you stroking my thighs with your hands.

That feels so nice, I say. Please don't stop. Do it higher and on the inside, please – and I move your hands a little further up till they're almost in between my legs – do it up here.

Sweet girl, you say, sweet foolish crazy girl. Why has no one ever loved you enough?

And you go on doing it and I shut my eyes and then you stop and take your hand away.

Hey, maybe I should make an honest woman of you, you say suddenly.

What?

Well, you're single, right? You're not married? And neither am I, not any more. So I could marry you, make an honest woman of you, how would that be?

I feel my face go hot and my stomach go over.

Goodness, I say, you'd really marry me?

You don't like the idea?

I can think of nothing more wonderful, but –

But what?

I can't do it. I have a family.

Sweetheart, baby, I know that. It's the only hurdle. Let me think about it. We need part B of the genius plan.

Moments pass. I tell you I think I maybe am a little hungry after all.

Great, you say, so am I. I'm always hungry. Let's get room service.

No one has ever wanted to marry me, I say quietly.

Well, they're all fools. The world is full of sick and crazy fools.

You're a fool, I say. You're a crazy fool.

Maybe, you agree. But I'm not sick, and just think, Rosy, if you were a nice cosy married lady and you ate food like other people, well, I guess you'd almost pass for normal.

The best that room service can offer is ham sandwiches. Thick slabs of ham in white bread, curling at the edges. They come on a large silver tray with a paper doily and some cress and yellowing halves of tomatoes. I pull out the meat and give it to you while I just eat the bread and mustard. You find a corkscrew in the minibar and we open the red wine.

If you want to know my serious feeling, you say. About the thing of what's real and what's not, what this thing of ours might be, then I guess it has to do with when I was a kid as well, losing my dad, all of that, and your little girl too, Rosy, in fact it has to do with everything –

I look at you and put down my glass and I wait.

Yes?

Back then when I knew you, I was a mixed-up mess. You know that now even if you never knew it then. I'd been through so much grief and done so many drugs and when I ran into you, at nineteen or twenty or whatever age it was –

Twenty, I say. You were twenty and I was nineteen.

OK, twenty. When I ran into you, I was way too fucking dumb and closed off to see what a precious thing you were, how you might be worth having.

You could have had me anyway, I begin, because I'm anxious for you to know what the night of the pearl necklace meant to me. But you stop me.

Hush. Sweetheart. That's not what I mean. I'm trying to tell you how dumb I was. But also how strange things happen in the world, Rosy, they really do. I've come to see life differently now and I know for a fact that sometimes a thing you think could only possibly ever go one way, can actually go either or even both – that there can be second chances. And I think that grief – this grief and loss I'm talking about – it can be a force for good as well as sadness. Stuff can be conjured out of grief, quite literally, out of the salt and sweat of the actual tears you cry.

I stiffen and sit up and you rub your eyes and smile at me. You laugh for a second.

I know, don't tell me, it sounds crazy, doesn't it?

No, I say, it doesn't. But – tell me – how exactly do you mean?

I mean, I guess, that maybe we made this happen, you and me, this – all of this between us.

Why? I say, and I don't know why my heart is sinking fast as you speak.

Why? Well, I don't know why. Because we both needed it? You needed me to come and find you now – right now at this point in your life – and I needed you.

I stare at you.

That might be enough, you say.

Might it?

Loss, you say. It does strange things to a person. You don't need me to tell you that, Rosy.

I push away the plate because suddenly I'm no longer hungry. I hunch myself up against the end of the bed, pull my knees to my chest and I think hard about this. The air in the room has turned very cold and as if you sense it, you put your black sweater around my shoulders. I'm shivering, we're both shivering but this time you don't come and hold me, you just watch me and look at me. You look so far away suddenly, moving further every minute.

Larger truths come sliding into my mind and I hear myself start to speak.

When it first happened, I say as quietly and slowly as I can, when she — well, it was such a shock. Not the losing her but — the speed of it, the — no warning. I'd think over and over of all the things I'd done with her, just small things, without knowing it was the last time — even that night in her room, holding her and talking to her —

And I used to trick myself, all the time. It was the only way. So I'd see and feel — even smell her, almost every second of the day. I'd tell myself she wasn't really gone, that she'd be back. I knew it wasn't real, not really. I knew it was just a trick, just my way probably of coping with what had happened. But it wasn't much help to Tom or the boys. I lived in another world for a while. I mean, it made me go very far away from them.

I take a quick sharp breath and wipe a tear off the end of my nose with my sleeve.

I think I left Tom very much alone, I tell you. And I feel very bad about that now, very guilty.

And then, well, time passed — so much time, too much time — and I was expected to start to mend my life — it was like the whole world was saying, Rosy, OK, enough! And expecting me to start to do this, speak of her in the past tense, all that.

And you didn't want to?

In some ways I did, of course I did, I could see it was necessary, for me, the right thing for all of us, especially the boys, but —

You sit up on the bed and you're still looking at me but suddenly you're close up as well which maybe must mean you're holding me, and perhaps I am crying more than I knew though I can't feel it, I can hardly feel myself in the room any more.

I'm better now, I hear myself say. I don't do it any more, I swear I don't, but –

Baby, I hear you say, baby, Rosy, sweetheart, it's OK, hush, it's OK, I'm here.

Don't go. Please don't go.

I'm not going.

Minutes pass and I can see the snow flying past the window and I see that you and me are holed up in this tiny space in the middle of a world that's turned entirely white.

I wonder if we're safe, I hear myself saying.

We're safe, you reply, though your voice is still coming from another place, from a dream.

I keep thinking we're in Paris, I say, and you laugh softly as if you know what I'm talking about.

But – but sometimes, I say at last, I feel myself falling apart all over again. And then it's like I go a little crazy, not very responsible or even very kind perhaps, certainly not very motherly and then, well it frightens me, this love I still have for her.

And then I think I would give anything – literally anything – I would give my whole life and everything in it that I love and value most just to feel her and see her again, not for ever, just for a bit, just to pick her up and feel her alive and in my arms, against me. It's a kind of greed, but – well, just to have another chance – it's like – one hour with her. I would do any deal, however bad, however crazy. I would sign my whole life away if necessary, just for an hour or ten minutes, to hold her again. Or ten seconds, even. Anything, in fact. No price would be too high, not if it was really her, my baby, not if it was her and it could feel real.

You say nothing. The air between us sharpens and falls away.

That's how much I miss her, I say, and then I think about this for a moment and then I add, That's nuts, isn't it? I mean, that's not normal. It's nuts and it's crazy.

You take hold of me then and you keep on holding me so very tight I think I will have to stop breathing until, at last, something inside me gently explodes and my whole body relaxes.

Maybe nuts, you say, maybe also just love.

I got home well before midnight, even though it felt like I'd been gone from the house for several days or even weeks. Time kept on stopping and starting and waiting for me to catch up and then stretching and stretching itself to accommodate whatever it was I needed to feel. I just didn't know what to think about it any more.

This time when the taxi dropped me off I had to keep my eyes wide and staring open and concentrate hard as I counted out the fare. I shut the door and said goodnight to the driver, who hadn't said a thing about the fact that I was crying – and then I walked up the path in my pink coat. One foot in front of the other. It's easy, I told myself, just a few more steps and then I'll be at the door.

It was strange – the path was a little icy but there was hardly any snow around our house, just a light crystalline fluff on the bins and some of the cars. Nothing like the dense softness and whiteness which had settled around your hotel.

I wiped my eyes and glanced up and saw that our bedroom window was dark. Tom had probably given up and gone to bed. I wouldn't have blamed him. But then a twitch at the curtains on the top floor told me Fin was awake and checking for my return. He should have been asleep three hours ago. Straightaway I felt worried and guilty.

The house smelled of cooking, a risotto Tom had done for the boys. Lex 2, who seemed to have grown much fatter just in the course of a single evening, brushed hard against my legs as I locked the front door and turned off the porch light. Then she followed me through to the kitchen, tripping along just far enough in front of my feet to make me have to nudge and kick her. After I'd shaken down some food for her, she left me alone.

In the kitchen, dry-eyed at last and suddenly more hungry than I could ever remember being, I stood by the cooker and spooned the remains of the risotto straight into my mouth from the serving spoon. Flakes of rice fell down the front of my coat and I had to go over to the sink to brush them off.

Then, unable to bring myself to go upstairs to bed quite yet, I poured a glass of cold milk and sat and drank it slowly at the table, staring out at the dark icy garden and pressing my lips and nose to the cuff of my coat in the hope that there might be some trace of you still lingering on me.

There was a small noise upstairs and I tensed and listened, imagining Tom might have heard me and be on his way down. I finished the milk and put the glass in the dishwasher and quickly checked my face in the big wall mirror, glad to see no sign of tears. I was just about to turn off the light when Fin appeared in the doorway, shivery and barefoot and bare-chested, wearing just his blue flannel pyjama bottoms.

Oh darling, I said, you made me jump.

Hi, he said, and he gazed at me with a blank and worried look.

What're you doing? I asked him. You should've been asleep ages ago.

He stared straight at me for a second and then he looked around the kitchen with a wild, unhappy face which made my heart contract.

I saw you, he said.

You saw me?

Yes. Just now. I saw you come home.

Well you shouldn't have been awake, I began to say, but I stopped again as I saw how afraid and upset he looked.

Where's Baby? he said, and I tensed up again inside and took a quick breath.

What?

I saw you, he said again.

But darling – saw me what?

With her. I saw you with her.

Who?

Baby! he almost shouted at me, I saw Baby –

You – what?

Just now, with you. Coming home. I saw you carrying her.

I stared at my son and I just didn't know what to say. I could not find any words at all for this.

I thought you had brought her home, he said, and then, without coming any closer to me, he sobbed.

★　★　★

Next morning, the snow had almost gone but the sky was dark and loaded with cold. I cooked an egg for Fin, found some clean underpants and a tie for Jack and had a quick row with him about whether he should take a piece of fruit to school. Fin and I didn't mention the night before, in fact he seemed to have forgotten all about it. Instead he was fussing about a plastic bag to put his dirty old football in.

I'd rather you didn't take a ball to school, I told him as he scrabbled around under the sink for a suitable bag.

Why not?

Because I'm worried you won't concentrate on your work if you're always thinking about football.

Oh, Mum. People are allowed to take in balls, what's wrong with you? Do you want me to have no friends?

As the door slammed hard behind Jack – who always left the house a good ten minutes after Fin – I climbed the stairs intending to go straight in the shower but fell back into bed instead and pulled the duvet up around me. Tom's newspaper slid to the floor.

Tom was already showered and dressed. He walked around the room with his toothbrush in his mouth, now and then glancing at his watch. I told him about what Fin had said the previous night.

Clearly a dream, he said. Don't talk to him about it. Sorry – what I mean is, don't make a big thing of it, Nic, best just to let it go.

OK, I said, and I put my hand down in the place between my legs where yours had been the night before.

But what?

I didn't say but.

Nicole. I heard it in your voice.

249

OK, but – but nothing. Really, I mean it – I don't know what.

I moved my hand a little and shut my eyes and waited to see if anything happened.

You all right? Tom said.

Mmm.

You're not getting up?

Soon, I said, and I yawned and turned over onto my side so my hand could stay without him noticing. I tried to shut my eyes and think of you.

OK, Tom said, and he picked up his paper and bent to kiss me, I have to go. Talk later, yes?

For a second I tasted the zing of his toothpaste. Then he left the room and all my energy left me too. And even though I moved my hand in the place where you'd moved yours, even though I tried so hard to bring back the magical humming and hotness, nothing happened and after three or four minutes of touching myself, I gave up and cried into the pillow instead.

There's an email waiting for me.

Where are you, baby?

I'm here, I write. I'm here. I miss you.

Can you come here this morning? you write back straightaway.

I can but – don't you have meetings?

I'm free at eleven, then I have another scheduled for twelve or twelve-thirty, I won't know exactly for a while. I have to give a kind of presentation to this guy but it won't last long. I badly need to see you, Mrs Rosy.

OK, I'll come.

Hey, baby, hey, Rosy?

Yes?

I love you. I am so in love with you. You know that?

Me too, I feel so much for you. I've never felt like this before, it's mad. Can I tell you something embarrassing? Just now, earlier, I got so lonely for you, I tried to do what you do – I tried to touch myself there, you know, the way you do. I tried it with my hand for a while but in the end I gave up, it didn't work.

Hey, but I tried it too, you write back. And you know what, I thought of you, and it worked.

We sit on a bench in the park opposite your hotel. You have on a clean grey suit under your coat, a thin dark tie, shiny black shoes. You've shaved and you smell of a scent I don't recognise. I have on jeans and a red woollen cardigan and my hair looks bad as I didn't have time to wash it before I left. I have a thick blue rubber band around my right wrist which Jack gave to me the other day because he has a lot of them. It says Strong, but I don't feel strong, not at all.

The sun bumps in and out of the clouds but the light is weak and cold. Few people are in the park and there's still snow on the ground under the bare black trees, but the wider paths have been gritted and a man with a barrow is sweeping. A small dog totters past wearing a coat on its brown hairy back. We both watch it in silence. Your hand is warm around mine.

I ask you what time you have to go.

Not for a while, you say. Slow down, baby.

I need to know.

Why? So you can hurt yourself by starting to say goodbye already?

I almost laugh because this is so very true.

So I can prepare myself, I say. For the moment when I have to watch you walk away.

You put both your arms around me and draw me closer to you on the bench.

Oh baby, you say, and I feel your mouth on my neck. I'm not walking away. I'm not ever walking away.

Tears spring to my eyes.

Don't say that, because you will, you know you will. You have to go back home. You have to go tomorrow, don't you?

Hush. Don't think of it now. Can you see me tonight?

I don't know, I say, I suppose so – and I wonder what on earth I'll say to Tom and then I decide it no longer matters, that I can't avoid it for long, that I'll have to tell him sooner or later.

You take both my hands in yours and you look at them.

Tell me honestly, Rosy, does it make a problem for you, to see me tonight?

No, I lie.

You pause a moment as if you don't believe me.

What are we going to do? you ask me then.

Tonight?

No – what are we going to do with this?

I have to leave Tom, I hear myself say, even though it's the first time I've really had the thought and it makes me turn quite cold inside.

You'd really leave him?

I have to. What else can I do?

He's a good man, Rosy, and you have kids together.

I pick this thought up, turn it over, lay it face down so I can't see it.

You left your wife, I say.

That was different. We weren't happy. I mean, we'd never been happy, not really. We were at each other's throats right from the start.

Tom and I, I – well, I don't think we make each other happy any more.

But I think you love him. I do. It hurts me to say it but I think you do.

I can't do this, I say quietly, and as I speak the words I can begin to feel they're true. I can't be with him and love you like this. I can't – have an affair. I never expected this to happen and – but, well, it's not fair on him, or me, or the kids – or anyone, I add, and I think that my words sound stupid, like someone in a bad movie.

You're silent for a few moments. We both watch the man sweeping the leaves.

I can't be without you, I say. It's as simple as that. I just can't.

I watch your face and I can see you're thinking hard.

What would have happened, you ask me, if this had never been, if I hadn't come along?

If you'd never written to me?

Yes.

Why?

Do you think you and Tom would have carried along quite happily?

I think about this. I think of Baby and then I think of Paris and a black confusion comes down over me.

I don't know, I say. How can I ever know that?

Guess, you say.

I can't, I tell you. It's impossible. It's like you said, you make things come to you when you need them. And I needed you and you came. And yes, after all these years we made something strange happen and I don't understand it at all but I think we needed it. We found what we both needed.

Did I say that? you say.

Yes, I say, you did. You know you did.

I could buy you a house somewhere, you tell me a moment or two later.

Don't be silly.

I mean it. For you and your boys.

You couldn't.

I'm rich, Rosy. I could buy you ten houses and not even notice it.

Crazy fool. I don't want your money.

I know you don't. But – I could jack in my job and come here. I could. I could just give it all up tomorrow.

You'd do that for me?

You don't believe me?

I do, but – I don't want you to do that. Your job is everything to you.

You're so wrong. It's nothing.

I know, but –

But what, Rosy?

Back then you had so little money there used to be a hand-scribbled list on the peeling plaster of the kitchen wall of what you owed everyone else in the house. This for a beer, this for the milk bill you could never pay, this amount promised towards the household kitty for cleaning stuff, and so on. We almost didn't notice that, though you worked harder than any of us – took jobs in the holidays, pub work every weekend and right through Christmas, including Christmas Day – still always in your life you were in perpetual arrears.

You know why I never asked you out properly? you told me later, I mean it, do you want to know the real reason, Rosy?

You didn't like me.

Foolish girl. Silly girl. Excuse me, but I thought you were just gorgeous. No, the reason was I couldn't afford it.

But – I wouldn't have wanted you to spend any money.

Don't you see? I was so fucking proud. But I couldn't even afford to buy a round of drinks in the frigging pub. Do I have to tell you how hard that was?

When, you left the house and moved in with Linzi – leaving us in the lurch and having to find another person to rent your room quickly – we all thought it was because you were crazy about her and also perhaps a little selfish.

I couldn't pay the rent, you tell me. I literally couldn't, I was down to nothing. The landlord – do you remember him? – was coming round and I didn't have it. I had to run and Linzi was there when I needed her. And I hated it. Hated accepting charity, hated taking stuff from people I disliked. I hated having to fake that I liked her more than I did – it wasn't fair on her and I hated myself for it. In the end we came to despise each other and that was all my fault.

I used to see you around the place, walking down the street with that funny, bouncy walk of yours. You never seemed to notice me. I was always on the other side of the street from you and I guess you thought I was stoned or crazy or still with Linzi or something.

I didn't know where you were living, I say then. I never saw you in the street. I didn't even know you were still around.

One time there was a party – in one of those crumbling old terraces that sloped down away below the bridge – and that girl with the bell on her bicycle and the enormous breasts, always wore purple –

Emma! I say. Emma in the year above, I remember her.

Well, she was there and some others and we were all up in her room getting stoned, lots of us, girls too, and I remember the door was flung wide open suddenly and it was you – you'd come in looking for someone and I was lying there smoking and drinking and I felt a little compromised I guess, but I almost called your name –

Why didn't you? I think I remember that party. People all clustered on the stairs? Lots of bicycles in the hall?

You laugh and squeeze my knee.

Rosy. That would describe just about any party at any of those houses.

But why didn't you at least say hi? You should have. Why didn't you say something? Oh, I say, suddenly remembering the bleakness of those days, I'd have been so glad to see you.

You think about this.

You looked so fucking pretty. You had on a dress. Kind of flowery. I noticed because it was so rare – you were actually dressed like a girl for once –

It was old, I say wistfully, that dress. It was from the

256

antiques market. I saved up for it. It was so old it finally fell apart.

It was me who was falling apart. I was wrecked that night. I'd had enough of the whole place. I was ready to move on. And you didn't look –

Didn't look what?

Like someone I knew any more.

I'd have loved to talk to you, I say again, and you're silent for a moment, you run your fingers over my knee and up onto my thigh and I feel my bones tighten.

Well. I didn't know that then, did I?

Foolish, foolish boy.

Foolish girl.

And I swore right then and there that I'd make money, that I'd put getting rich before everything else, everything. That was how I chose my career, Rosy. My uncle, who I didn't get on with all that well but who felt sorry for me I guess because of my dad, he had a slight connection to someone in banking and they said they might have a position for me. My first job was adding up these columns of figures in a firm in Chicago – just columns and columns of them. I had no idea what the figures were or what they meant, all I knew was I had to sit there and add them up.

So I did it, I applied myself to it and I added them up. I added and I checked and I added then checked again. Some days I worked so hard adding up the figures that I was still there in the building after everyone had gone home. It was a strange time. I got to know each one of the cleaners by name.

And I did it so well, all this adding up, that I got promoted. And that was it – the figures had to do with money, with finance – I wasn't entirely stupid, that much I'd worked out. And they liked me and next thing I know, I'm a banker. I get headhunted, but this firm pays to keep me, and so it goes. Suddenly I'm earning enough to buy my own apartment, suddenly women are interested – they'll even sleep with me. And that's it, Rosy, I don't ever really look back. So tell me, why on earth can't I buy you a house?

Baby's gone, I told Fin. She's gone and she can't come back. You know that really, don't you?

He said nothing. He just looked at me in a sullen way with his big greenish wide-apart eyes which made him seem a lot younger sometimes than his eleven and a bit years. Then without even blinking or drawing breath, he started to bite his fingers, tearing hard at the cuticles with his teeth, till a bright spot of blood appeared.

I took his small and dirty hands gently in mine. Even from here I could smell the school smell of his hair – corridors and bus tickets and boiled food.

Don't, sweetheart, I said. Please don't do that.

He looked down at his fingers where the blood oozed and wiped it on his trousers. Then he bit his lip and took a big breath in and I saw his chest move.

Mum, he said finally. You have to listen to me.

OK. I'm listening.

At first, he said slowly and carefully as if making sure I could follow him, I didn't believe it either. At first, when I saw you with her, I thought I was dreaming, I really did. But then – then I pressed my forehead on the window and it was so cold and I felt it, so I knew for a fact I had to be awake and then – and then you looked up and saw me.

Sweetheart, I said as patiently and carefully as I could, it was in your dream that I did that. Even then, you were, you were dreaming.

You saw me. I saw you come up the path. There was a bit of snow. You had on your pink coat.

Dreams can feel entirely real, you know? There's a name for it, I forget what it's called – the kind of dreams you have when you really really think you are awake – Daddy would know.

Fin's voice began to crack.

But I saw you come home –

I did come home late that night but, you see, because you knew I was coming, because you knew I was out and you were expecting me back, you started to dream it.

He looked at me as if I was mad.

It happens, I said. I've done it too. My darling, I promise you, dreams like this happen.

Where did you go? Where were you?

I had dinner – with a friend.

What friend?

Just a man I knew long ago when I was much younger.

Dad said it was your old boyfriend.

Oh did he? Well, it wasn't. I mean, it was an old friend who was a boy, but not a boyfriend, no, that's entirely different.

Tom stared at me with cold, astonished eyes.

You're going out? Again?

Yes, yes I am. Why not?

Two nights in a row?

It's his last night in the country. It's the last time I'll see him for a very long time. Maybe ever.

259

So?

So – I want to spend one more evening with him. What's wrong with that?

The boys were downstairs watching TV. Tom got up and pushed the bedroom door shut.

Is he married? he said, and his voice was hard and sharp.

No. Not any more. Why?

Because you talk as though he's your lover.

Oh Tom, for goodness sake –

Nicole, I mean it – can't you hear yourself?

I felt as if my mind was crowding me and then I realised that what I really had was a headache. I went into the bathroom and looked for painkillers among the bottles and boxes of medicines. A pink bottle of Calpol for babies was still at the back of the cupboard, I couldn't remember having seen it in a long time. It looked sticky and old and it made my heart burst just to look at it. I knew I should throw it away but instead I shut the cupboard door.

Tom, I said as I came back in the bedroom with a glass of water and swallowed the painkillers, he's a very nice man and I admit it, I do like him a lot. But not in that way, obviously. And two dinners out with a man I knew from long ago doesn't exactly amount to anything.

I listened to my voice say all of this and I almost believed it and I was shocked. I couldn't remember when I'd tipped over the edge from truth into lies. Had it happened slowly, or had there been a single cold moment when I'd taken the choice? I was even more shocked to realise I didn't care.

Then don't go, Tom said quietly.

What?

If it means so little, don't go.

I looked at him and felt panicky.

You really mean that? You really want to stop me going?

His voice was slow – slow and cold.

I don't know. Maybe. If it means as little as you say then prove it.

I stared at him in an injured way and I realised that I did in fact feel injured.

Is that our relationship, then? I said. One where it's my job to prove things to you?

He shrugged and looked at me.

You're jealous?

Maybe, he said. Am I allowed to be?

I looked straight in his face and felt my heart cool so fast it hurt.

I don't know, I said. I'm not married either, remember?

What the fuck's that supposed to mean?

Just – leave me alone, that's all.

Well, fuck you, said Tom quite loudly.

Fuck you too, I said even louder and then I flinched in case, despite the closed door, the boys could possibly have heard.

I don't know exactly – it's very hard for me to say – when the story of you and me begins to unravel. It's harder still for me to recount that night – the night that follows, our last night, the night of grief and love, of pearls and snow – in a calm way. It's hard for me to tell it as it is, as it was – there are so many other things that keep on getting in the way.

It begins with snow, of course it does, it has to begin that way. There's snow falling hard through the cold air of

261

that dark and final night, all around your hotel. Downstairs the bar is full of music, jagged notes that barely seem to fit at all, and people saying things to each other through the fog of cigar breath and cheap scent. You're waiting for me in the same corner as before and this time you're not even pretending not to smoke a cigarette, and you suddenly look immensely tired, wrapped up in tiredness, all wrapped up for the day – for the first time, my darling, you really look your age.

It's all this sex, you joke. It's getting to me.

I say I wish I didn't have to always see you in bars and hotels. I wish I could take you to a proper place, a home with lights and wine and blinds pulled down. A home with a bed and our own ordinary things. I wish I could make you comfortable with me.

You don't say anything to that.

I put my arms around you and warm the coolness of my wrists on your neck and ears. You plant kisses on the insides of my elbows.

Beautiful girl, why don't you ever look tired? You never seem to eat or sleep and yet you always look just exactly the same, why?

Because I love you, I say, and this time I find that the words hurt me that much more than they hurt before.

This time, we don't even think about eating. This time, when you take me up to your hotel room, when you undress me and put me between your sheets, I'm already crying, big soft tears, already tearing myself up inside – so that when you go in, it's no big deal, I'm ready, I'm in pieces, I'm there.

We come almost in stages, apart and also together, gasping and holding and giving it everything – two people who know they've used it all up, who know there's nowhere else for this to go.

You lie next to me and (of course) the snow goes on falling outside the window, the same window I'm beginning to feel I've been looking out of all of my life – big fat flakes against the darkness of the city. And there's the stickiness of you all over my stomach and the insides of my thighs, also on you, in the hair around your sweet tired cock, on the sheets, the wetness of us two, dark as tears. Now your hand is on my breast, my face is turned to you. You're breathing slowly, easily, like a man who's done all he has to do.

Why does it always snow for us? I ask you, and I already know you can't answer that question.

Why didn't I find you earlier? is your sad reply.

You shift yourself slightly on the bed so you can see my face, and I have no answer to that either. There seem to be no answers for what life does and doesn't see fit to do to us.

I smile and pick your hand up off my breast and kiss it. Your fingers smell metallic, of me, of the metallic taste of insanity.

I said that, you tell me then.

Said what?

The metallic taste of insanity. That was my phrase.

It was, I agree, though I know that I neither spoke nor thought it. All the same, somehow it's yours, it's all yours.

You look in my face and you push a strand of hair out of my eyes.

What's falling in love? I ask you then. I mean, as opposed

to normal love. I mean, is it useful? Tell me why it never felt like this with Tom, not even at the beginning.

Tom's a good man, you say quietly. He doesn't hide any part of himself from you.

I say nothing when I hear this. I hold my breath.

He's good, you say again. I know it, Rosy. He loves you. He's got a big heart.

What are you saying? I ask you then as my heart caves in.

I'm saying you have a future together, you and Tom. You two and your kids.

I tell you this isn't really what I want to hear.

What, foolish girl, what do you want to hear?

I want to hear about love! Our love.

OK, then, listen up. Passion, what we call falling in love, it's an illusion. It's created entirely by you, don't you see – by the lover. Love is just how we choose to fill the gaps, the way we colour the blank bits, with our imaginations. You have a big imagination, Rosy. But then you know that.

Is it not a good thing, then, I ask you, a big imagination?

I don't know, you say. Maybe. Not always, perhaps. Depends I guess on what you do with it.

I take a breath. I'm trying not to listen to you. I'm afraid of the next thing you might say.

I don't want this to end, I tell you.

Neither do I, you reply.

There's so much I don't know about you, I hear myself say.

There's nothing more, you say. I told you already. You've filled the gaps, Rosy.

No, I say, and my eyes are filling up with tears because once again this isn't what I want to be told. No, that's not it, you're wrong. Think of all those words we wrote to each other –

I do, you say. All the time, I do.

You'll keep them?

Always. They're very precious to me.

What time is it? I ask you, and I'm really starting to cry now.

Baby, you say to me. Baby, please – don't start saying goodbye already. I don't think I can take it just now.

I don't want to, but tonight time doesn't stand still, tonight it's bad, it moves quite fast, it trips us up, it knows we feel unsteady and unsafe.

And suddenly it's eleven and I start to get up off the bed but you put out a hand to stop me.

No, you say. No. Rosy, I mean it, no. I don't do well on my own, you say.

You don't have to be on your own, I tell you.

I do, you say, I'm so alone. You've no idea how alone I am.

And you take me in your arms and look right into my eyes and with your hand you do what you did that first time – you start by making me a little sore and I protest that I don't need it, that I don't actually think I want it this time – I know that everything's sticky and slow and anyway my mind's on other things such as how to stop myself losing you, my love. But then – then something happens inside me, right where the muscle and wetness meet the bone and there's a click and my whole body starts to jump and slide up the slope.

When I come I almost take you with me.

You're laughing but you're crying too.

Mrs Rosy.

Yes? Yes?

You have a good soul. If I could, I'd take your soul. I would, you know. I'd steal it and put it in my pocket and take it back with me and keep it all for myself.

You would?

Yeah. And I'd tell no one but I'd take it out now and then to make me feel better.

Time passes and we no longer care. I sleep for a few moments in your arms.

What I haven't told you is, I went a little crazy, after Mary, I say.

Hush. I know that.

You don't know it. You can't. Hardly anyone knows it. How can you know it?

Shh. I do. Believe me, I just do.

You worked it out?

That's right.

Tom had a lot to deal with. He had to deal with everything. It was no joke, I tell you. Poor Tom. I was no fucking use at all.

A little more time goes by. It's moving more slowly now, its slowness pulling us closer.

You already have my soul anyway, I tell you then. You have it already, don't you realise that?

Do I?

You do. You know you do.

OK. Good. I'll take good care of it, then.

Promise me one thing. If they ever come after you and accuse you of taking it and demand to have it back, just deny it, OK?

OK.

Because they'll just be saying it. They don't need it, not really.

They don't? Who's they?

I don't know. All I know is that they don't.

OK.

I'd rather you had it.

You're too kind.

I am, aren't I? I am. I'm kind.

Three hours later, in the dark and frozen middle of the night, you put me into a cab. You hold me only for a second and then you kiss me and as you kiss me, you hand me a white paper package done up with ribbon, small and slightly, teasingly heavy.

Don't open it till I'm gone, you say. Promise me now. Don't open it till tomorrow.

I can't promise, I say, because I am now a girl without a soul, remember. I'm afraid I can't promise you anything.

Tears are falling down my face and all my breaths are coming in the wrong order.

Fine, don't promise me then, don't promise anything. But Mrs Rosy, I'm asking you nicely. Just keep it until –

Your hands – much colder now – are closing around mine, which are on the package, and I think you meant to say something like tomorrow but you could not get the word out because you were crying too, great shuddering sobs. It hurt me to hear them. And then you were shutting the door of the cab and it didn't quite close properly so you were having to do it all over again.

I began to say your name out loud but before I could pull down the window to call out to you, the cab had moved off and the snowy street was racing past the window and all I could see was the side of your face – pale and set and showing me nothing – as you turned, you turned, you turned.

You turned to go, but before I saw you even get close to the hotel, you'd dissolved to the exact same colour as the frozen air and all I saw was snow.

The driver slid open the glass and asked me to repeat the name of my street and I did and he nodded and shut the glass.

My heart was bumping hard as I unwrapped the package, undid the ribbon and pulled back the layers of tissue. The gift lying in my hand was exactly what I knew it would be – a necklace of pearls, real pearls, heavy and solid, creamy, glossy. I held them for a moment in my fingers and then I put them to my lips and then, like a baby, I tasted their coldness and hardness on my teeth and tongue.

When we wake that morning in each other's arms, it's cold and strange. The gas has finally run out, our night of the pearl necklace has run out and now in the worn-out morning light of the room we're too shy with each other, unnerved and wary.

I have on my dungarees, both straps undone. You still have on your tattered cords and sweater. I am nineteen, you are twenty. Your hair is mussed. My make-up has smudged around my eyes. You yawn and stretch and sort of smile at me and I gaze back at you and though your smile makes me go tight inside, I am a very stupid girl back then and I don't think I smile back, instead I'm cold with you.

I am so afraid of losing you that a part of me has already begun to say goodbye.

STILL LONDON

Tom did not say a word to me in the morning but his face was more afraid than angry. I couldn't bear that face, it ate me up – the long line of the mouth and nose, the heaviness of the eyes. He pulled on a thick sweater and packed his papers in his case and left the house while I was still getting the boys' breakfast. As I stacked the dirty plates in the dishwasher, I heard him say a brief goodbye to Jack and Fin but he left without even looking at me. All I heard was the squeak of his bike on the path.

Why is everyone in such a crap mood today? Fin remarked to no one in particular except maybe Lex 2 who was lying on her back with her big round belly in the air and batting an elastic band around. I pretended not to hear him because I had no answers I could give, not now. I gave Jack a hug he did not want, but let him leave without his piece of fruit. I wasn't even going to try to stop Fin taking a ball to school.

He told me he'd already found three people in his class who wanted a kitten when Lex 2 had her litter.

Fine, I heard my voice say. Just as long as their parents agree.

They do, he said. I told them they had to check with their parents and all that and it's OK, I promise you they have.

Well, great, I said.

You're not interested are you?

Fin, I am, of course I am.

He bit on a finger and glanced at me.

I just wish she'd hurry up and have them, he said. Look how fat she's getting – Mum, if you had to guess, how many would you say she's having?

I really really don't know, my darling, I said, and I sat down on a chair and looked at the cat who looked straight back at me in an accusing way as if she could see right inside my head.

Yes, I know, but guess.

Oh – three or four I expect.

Not five?

I doubt it. Now go, darling. You're going to be late.

After he and Jack had gone, I sat for a while in the kitchen. I thought about making some coffee but I knew that just the small effort of loading up the pot, of lighting the gas, would have felt like too much. I sat so still that I could hear the silent shudder of the fridge and the sound of snow melting and dripping on the roof outside.

It took a great effort to move myself out of the chair, but in the end I did and somehow got myself back upstairs where I lay on the bed and watched the frozen sky through the gap in the blinds of the bedroom window. It took me a while to understand what I felt and when I did I knew it was fear. I felt very afraid.

Finally I did it. I got up and went to my desk which had begun to feel like a war zone – the screen, the wall, the chair – and I turned on my computer. I opened my emails. I could hardly bear the noise of them opening and had to leave the room for a moment then go back in. Just as I'd dreaded, there was nothing, not a flicker or a word. No new messages. So I started one.

Baby? I wrote. Are you still there? Please tell me you're still there –

I sent it but nothing came back. Again, No new messages.

Then I waited a moment or two and pressed Send & Receive again. This time my email came bouncing straight back to me and my heart thudded. Quickly, I wrote another – Baby, what's going on? Please reply if you're there – and I sent it. It came straight back with an explanation from the server saying the communication had failed because the addressee was unknown.

I sat with my head in my hands and I started to shake.

I went back to bed. It was the only place. I put my cold limbs under the duvet and I looked at the wall for a while. Sun slid through the opening in the blinds and for a few seconds light flooded the room. But all around me the air had deepened and chasms were opening, I could tell. Right there in our bedroom. I could feel them. The sun might have been shining and people might have been saying there was going to be a thaw out there in the world but I was no part of it. I was somewhere else, shivering on an icy ledge and about to fall.

I felt cold, so very cold, but strangely alert and comfortable too.

It was after a few more moments of watching the light edge its slow way across the wall that I finally understood what had happened, what was happening. I realised I wasn't alone in the room any more.

She was standing on the carpet just a few feet away from me. At first the unexpected sight of her made me jump, but once I could see her clearly, I realised I'd known this would happen, I'd known she'd be there, in fact I'd been waiting for this moment all along. I think I'd even worked out exactly how it would feel – to see her there on that patch of blue bedroom carpet, lit up and haloed by the chilly sunshine. It was a bright, elastic moment all right. Every detail was perfect, just exactly as I'd have hoped. I smiled to myself, I couldn't help it. Someone's got this absolutely right, I thought.

Her feet, the feet whose shape and smallness always made my heart flinch, were bare just as they should have been – toes slightly curled as she rocked her weight back and forward. She had on just a nappy, ever so slightly heavy with damp at the back, and a T-shirt that she wore a lot in her last summer – pale yellow with a pinkish stain down the front. I knew what the stain was. Tinned raspberries. She'd gone through a phase of tipping bowls of food down her front. In the end, because it was summer, Tom took to stripping her for meals. He'd put her in her high chair in just a nappy, with newspaper laid out on the floor all around.

All we have to do is hose her down afterwards, he'd announced with some satisfaction as he left her to it and got on with something else.

Now I waited – hush – because here she was, my sweet, stained baby, come back to me.

The air in the room had gone very still and I was afraid even to breathe in case I disturbed something. I didn't want this to be over, didn't want to change a thing about it or be the one to stop it happening. I was happily addicted and adoring. I just wanted to keep it going on, exactly as it was.

So I watched her very closely, kept my eyes on her pale round face. In her small left hand was a drinking beaker with a lid, one of the old pale blue and green ones that I hadn't seen in a while. There may have been water in it, or, I don't know, milk. It wouldn't have been juice, I didn't give her juice. I saw that she was shaking it a little to see what happened, but fortunately nothing was coming out.

It was funny but it was the sight of the old stained T-shirt which hurt me the most. Because it somehow brought the exact taste of her with it, the long-ago flavour of my baby girl. I could tell from the slightly tired nap of it, its floppiness, the way it drooped against her shoulders, that it wasn't fresh out of the wash either, that it would smell delectably of her – of her furious small warmth and her creases. How I wished I could gulp it in, that smell. It was hard sometimes to believe that love could be so physical, that it could wipe you up like that, turn all your senses to liquid.

I heard myself catch my breath then, because she was looking at me, straight at me, her mum. Her face – those wide-apart black eyes, the flattish nose, the upper lip that curls up off the bottom one like a cartoon duckling's beak – I hadn't drunk in those details in so long. You think you remember, but you forget so much, so much. My whole body felt loose with hunger.

Ma!

She was holding her arms up and out now. She wanted me to pick her up.

Ma! She said it again, more insistently this time, as a shadow fell on her face and she reached out so intently towards me that I held my breath. I wanted so very much to go to her but – what exactly were the rules? – I was afraid that if I moved too much this time I'd shift things somehow, break the spell and the one thing I could not possibly do was let go of this moment, the one I'd longed for and dreamed of for so long. So I gazed at my baby hungrily. Please don't make me let go of this moment, I breathed, please don't make me let it go.

Ma!

Then, almost against my will, I heard my breath come sliding out in a whisper. Baby! Come here to Mummy.

For a single second she froze and seemed to listen, her head very slightly inclined, face baffled. It was as if she couldn't see me at all after all, as if she was listening from another place entirely and had just caught a snatch of my voice and it had knocked her a little off balance.

Tears were running down my face, are running down it – because all she can do now is listen and keep on holding out her arms, and now her lip wobbles a little as if she's about to cry and she takes the small rushed breath I know so well, that one that's normally a prelude to tears.

But in the end it's my fault that the bed creaks and the duvet is pushed to one side as I just can't leave her there, I have to get myself over to where she is. And right there on the carpet I hold her against me and breathe her in for three or maybe four seconds before the light is sucked from the room and my hands are empty and, dizzy with sorrow and loss, I feel her go.

That's when I did it. In that moment of darkness, that was when I finally called Tom's mobile.

It's me, I said.

Hey, he said, and though he didn't exactly sound surprised, still I could hear the sharp snatch of his breath. Are you OK?

No, I said. No, Tom, no, sorry but I'm not OK.

He lay on the bed, on our bed, and he held me. In the poor, cold light of day, just like that, with you gone, with Baby gone, with the kids at school, with the last of the snow melting on the ground outside. All of it, about to be gone.

He held me and I let him do it and his clothes smelled of coldness and of outdoors, and his chin was against me and that, too, was cold, his face was cold. I looked down at his hands which were around me – slim, pale hands with long fingers. I looked at them and wondered why I'd never looked at them properly before – such slim hands he had, for a man – just as I hadn't noticed until now how many shadows his face held.

I couldn't look at his face.

I told him as much as I could. Nearly everything in fact. All about you and me, the whole story. There was no other choice, finally, there was nothing else to do – and I heard it all come falling out of me – Paris, London, you and me, the whole lot. The only parts I held back were the ones I could not explain, not even to myself – the strangeness and the magic. I told myself that this was because Tom might think them stupid and crazy and anyway I didn't want to hurt him. And though I didn't, still I'm not sure that was the truthful reason. I think the reason I held back was greed on my part, wanting somehow to keep those parts for myself. I think I wanted them saved so I could make sense of them later, because I hadn't yet decided what I thought about any of this, not really.

I didn't tell him about the pearls.

Tom listened to all I had to say and I felt his grip on me tighten and I was glad I couldn't see his face.

I knew you'd do this, he said quietly, when I'd finished speaking. I could see it coming, you know. I knew you'd have an affair.

An affair? I echoed, wondering at the word.

That's what it is, isn't it? You've had an affair.

I said nothing. I tried to think about this.

You – knew – I'd do it? I said, only just catching up with this idea. I could feel his body shaking against mine. I could feel the tightness of his breath in his chest and the way it made his voice wobble.

It's been haunting me, the idea of it, the sense I had of – Christ, I've been so fucking stupid. I should have done something, why didn't I?

What could you have done? I asked him quietly.

He looked at me.

Well what? I said.

I know you, Nicole, you forget – all these years, what do you think? What are you expecting? What exactly are they supposed to amount to, those years? No one knows you better than I do.

But – what exactly is it you should have done? I asked him again, a little more coldly now.

I felt him shake his head.

I don't know. I just don't know. I should have stopped you.

Stopped me?

Yes, stopped you.

How would you have done that?

I don't know. You wouldn't have liked it. You'd have hated me.

What about you? I asked him. Wouldn't you have hated yourself?

He took my hand in his and he sighed heavily.

What about me? It's never about me, not really, is it, Nicole?

Minutes went by and we said nothing. He let go of my hand, let it lie among the creases on the duvet where it fell. The phone rang and we did nothing about it; we left it and eventually it stopped. In the street, a dog barked loudly for a few seconds, then a car door slammed.

You think it's all about me, I told him finally, but you never speak to me, Tom. I mean it, you've no idea – I've been so lonely.

He looked at me without emotion.

Now, for instance, I told him. What are you thinking right now?

If you really want to know, I'm wondering why I can't be angrier with you. I'm wondering why I can't hate you.

You want to hate me?

I'm thinking it might perhaps be better for me if I could.

You should. You should hate me and be furious. I'd understand if you did.

You'd have more respect for me if I did, is that it?

I don't know. No, I don't think so. I doubt it. But at least – I'd understand.

Tom turned to look at me carefully.

I can't be angry with you, Nicole. I can't hate you either.

I've hated you, I told him, but I began to know as I heard the words come out that they weren't quite true.

I know, he said, I know you have.

Tom –

I've been so worried about you, he said, though his voice was still hard and cold. I had no idea – I literally didn't have a clue what you were up to, what you were doing.

Neither did I, I said truthfully.

Great, he said. That's a nice responsible thing to say.

I'm sorry, I told him, and I wondered whether I was.

You don't love this man, he said then, I don't believe for a moment that you love him. You can't.

You know that, do you?

I think I know it, yes.

But – Tom, I'm sorry, but how can you say that, when you know nothing about it?

279

You've just told me quite a lot. And I know it's not real, none of it's real.

What I experienced – the feelings I experienced – they were real, I told him then.

I can't imagine what you experienced, he said coldly.

But, I said, thinking of you, and my mind suddenly lit up and grew warm at the thought, anyway, you're wrong, Tom, love isn't like that. It isn't real or unreal – it's real to the person who feels it and that's all that matters. You can't choose whether or not to feel it, you just feel it or you don't – the love – it just is. It's as simple as that.

Tom tried to laugh.

You sound like a teenager, do you know that, Nicole? You sound less mature than Jack.

I was silent. I thought of you and me as teenagers, pearls in our mouths, and I held the thought close to me, hoping for some comfort.

Tom took a breath.

How could you do this to me, Nicole? he said. I mean it. How could you make such a cold and calculated choice?

I stared at him.

It wasn't – a choice, I told him.

Oh for god's sake, he said.

No, I said, you don't choose to fall in love or not fall in love, Tom. I'm sorry but I told you, it just happens – you just fall.

He laughed again, a sad, cross laugh.

No it doesn't, that's a myth, I don't believe it. At our age, it's deliberate, it is, it's a choice made. You decide to do it – you decide to trip. Sure, once you've decided, then it's easy, the thing I am sure has its own momentum, it all unrolls. But you have to do it – you have to take your eyes off the ground, you have to walk near a chasm, you have to ignore the warnings and then, you know, you have to decide to let yourself drop in.

I said nothing.

Anyone can do it, he added. Any fool can lose their fucking balance in that fucking stupid irresponsible way. Fine, call it falling if you want. But don't tell me it's real. It's not real. In fact nothing could be more dangerously unreal.

And I'll tell you what is real, he said, if you want to know. Our children. What we've all been through together. Jack, Finlay and Mary – yes, even Mary, even that.

It sounded so strange to hear him say her name like that, so easily, and I shut my eyes for a second.

I wish it wasn't real, he said, that part of it, but it was.

It was then, I said slowly, that I began to fall.

I know, he said, I know, and I felt his grip on me tighten. But Nicole, the boys are still here and they're real – and our family and all of our shared history together, all the love we've had, don't you also think that's real?

I thought about this and we were both silent for a while. He'd moved away from me and his hands were folded behind his head. He was looking up at the ceiling, the same ceiling where the sun was still moving, making its crazy shadows and patterns, shadows and patterns I knew it would continue to make long after we all were gone. The room felt almost warm.

The snow is gone, I thought then. It won't come back now.

Do you love me? I asked him after about ten minutes.

I think so.

You're not sure?

I don't know if it's real love, do I, what I feel? I think – I can't imagine not loving you, Nic.

But you don't like me?

I don't know. I find it hard to respect someone who's lied to me.

I can understand that. That was the worst part, lying to you. I never would have thought I could do that.

But you did.

I did.

I'll have to think about whether I still like you, he said. But I'll tell you something, I envy you, Nicole, I really do. I envy you your certainty.

My certainty? I said, surprised because I thought of myself as the least certain person in the whole world.

Yes, he said, I envy you for the way you wake up in the morning and you look at the sky and the clouds and birds and trees, and you drink it all in and you're absolutely certain of your place in the world.

I smiled.

That sounds kind of funny, I said.

But you know what I mean.

I suppose so. Maybe, I said, a little uncertainly. But it makes me sound, well, a little mad.

You are a little mad, he said, so quickly that I laughed.

You are. That's why everyone loves you, you know, he said and his voice was deadly serious, almost bitter now. Why no one can resist you. Because of that certainty which verges on madness. Because of the way you always look like you belong.

Belong in the world? I said, trying to listen, trying to understand.

No, not in the world, not in this one. In a world of your own making. You have a bubble around you, Nicole, but you fit it. It fits you perfectly.

Sounds like you don't necessarily think it makes me a very nice person, I observed.

No, it doesn't, I don't. And I'm not sure it always makes you happy either, but it makes you –

What?

Tom thought for a moment.

It makes you dazzling, he said. You dazzle.

Tears came into my eyes for a moment.

Sometimes, Tom said, and his voice was bitter, I can hardly look at you, you dazzle so much.

It's not a good thing?

I'm not sure it is, no.

I pushed the tears away with my fingers and thumb. Because I didn't know what I felt about what Tom was saying, because we'd never had a conversation like this – not one that dug right deep inside us to the nub of what we were – not really, not ever. And I looked at the place on the carpet where Mary had been and I knew I could also still feel the places all over me where you'd been, where you'd touched me.

You never speak to me like this, I told Tom. Never.

I know.

I wish you would. I wish you'd spoken like this earlier.

I know that too.

Will you leave me? I asked him then.

I don't know. I might. Do you think I should?

I don't know.

I'm going to have to think about it, aren't I? But you're right, maybe I deserve something more than this. But the thing is, Nicole, I can't imagine loving anyone but you. Everything I've ever had, everything I've got, I've put into this family.

Lex 2 must have been a little more pregnant than we realised because very late that night I was woken by Fin at our bedroom door.

Mum, come quick! I think there's something wrong with Lex.

Dazed with sleep, I grabbed the nearest cardigan and followed him upstairs. His room was freezing and his bedside light was on. Football magazines were strewn all over the floor and the curtain was only half drawn across the window, so that a patch of black night sky and a cold white moon were visible outside.

Fin was shivering and his hair was sticking up stiffly on one side of his head.

Where is she? I asked him, and he pointed to the top bunk.

Up there.

Goodness. How did she get up there?

She always goes up there. Something woke me up, he said, his teeth chattering, I don't know what. And then I looked on the top bunk and it was Lex and she was making this funny noise and I got up and suddenly I saw it's all wet and Mum it's weird, I think she's peed or something.

I reached up and tried to look at Lex who was moving

and turning round and round on the bed. Every so often she let her haunches drop down and then pulled them up again. Her mouth was open in a silent mew.

Is she going to be OK? Fin asked anxiously, trying to grab the side of the bed and pull himself up to look.

Wait, I told him, and I saw that the duvet – an old spare one we kept for sleepovers and visiting kids – was soaked with something dark. She's OK, but you know what? I think she's started to have her kittens.

Fin gasped.

Already!

Tom called softly from the landing and asked what was going on, as Fin hastily shoved school books onto the floor and pulled his desk chair over to stand on so he could get a better view.

I think she's in labour, I told Tom as he came in.

Who's in labour?

The cat, of course.

Already? he echoed Fin, but before he could say anything else, Fin pulled on my hand and pointed to where a brown shape was bulging under Lex 2's tail.

She's having one! Dad, quick, look, come and see, one's actually coming out!

Tom was just in time to see Lex shudder a couple of times and give a strange rasping miaow, before she calmly turned around and started licking the slick wet shape that had just slipped out of her.

It took Lex 2 almost two hours to have all four of her kittens. The first was tabby, just like her, the second two were black and white, mostly white. We watched the colours develop slowly as, between deliveries, she licked each one clean with her tongue.

Such care, I told Fin, as we watched her careful pink mouth deal with every single tuft of wet dark fur. Just look at that, how thorough she is.

Fin crouched near the cat on the old duvet and I wondered if he was too near, but she didn't seem to mind at all. All you could hear in the room was his mouth breathing and the slow rasp of her licking.

She knows exactly what to do, said Tom. Even though she's never done it before.

He was lying on Fin's bed, watching and yawning. We'd moved the duvet down from the top bunk onto Fin's floor so we could all watch more easily.

It's in her genes, said Fin. Like how they know to go to her nipple for the milk and all that. Did we come out all covered in gunk and stuff like that?

Pretty much, I said, remembering the swoosh of relief at the end of labour when the baby slithers out in a slick of blood.

Except your mother didn't have to lick you, said Tom. Instead the midwives wiped you clean.

Hmm, Fin said, thinking about it. Sounds pretty disgusting.

Not at all, I told him, and suddenly I couldn't look at Tom. You were the most beautiful things I'd ever seen, all of you were, you smelled and tasted wonderful. I could easily have licked you all over.

Christ, Mum, growled Jack, who'd been woken in time for the second birth but was now almost asleep again on Fin's floor. Do you have to be so detailed about everything?

I saw Tom laugh to himself and for a moment his face was his old face and it squeezed at my heart.

Star! Fin said then, noticing a splodge of white on the third-born's forehead. I'm calling that one Star.

Huh, great, very original, said Jack.

They look like rats, Tom observed a few moments later. Don't they? Tiny wet rats.

Fin giggled.

Remember the rat? he said.

The rat?

Yeah, the one a long time ago when we were having tea and — and, well, Baby saw it first —

For a second Tom looked at me.

Ah, he said, the famous disappearing rat.

It was just a small one, a baby probably. Lex, the original Lex, had brought it in in the night and set it down on the landing with a terrible excited wailing noise. The noise the rat made had been worse though — a frantic rhythmic squeak, almost electronic. Tom and I — half-asleep and terrified — had shoved and poked it with a cricket bat and a broom, till we'd been able to drive it back downstairs and lock it in the kitchen. We thought we'd wait till morning and deal with it then.

But morning came and — though we opened the kitchen door very carefully and then flung open the garden doors and held the broom and waited nervously for the creature to show itself — nothing happened, no rat appeared. We searched everywhere — under the sink, behind cupboards, but found nothing. In the end, mystified but relieved, we gave up on it.

You had to wear wellingtons to look for it, Fin reminded me, In case it scampered over your toes.

Ugh, I said, remembering, you're right, I couldn't bear the idea of it –

You thought it had gone out of the cat flap, Jack said now, laughing along with Fin. But – no!

Ha! said Fin. But it was Baby who found it, remember?

I did. I did remember. A whole eight or nine hours later, I'd been giving the children their tea, all of them around the kitchen table, Baby in her little screw-on chair – and Fin had been telling me some kind of long involved story about school. Baby, who'd been going la, la, la and nodding her head and pretending to listen, had suddenly lifted a spoonful of baked beans to her mouth and frozen with the spoonful right there. Then her whole face had creased into a smile.

Ca! she shrieked with astonished delight, and she threw down the spoon which bounced, spattering tomato sauce across the table, and pointed. Ca! Ca!

Oh look! shouted Jack as he turned around.

Because there, under the tall canvas bag where we kept clean washing that was waiting to be ironed, a thick ringed tail poked out. It lay against the floor, curved and waiting.

Ca! Baby said again, and banged her hands on the table and gave a little whoop of delight.

Oh my god, I said to Jack, and I couldn't help it, I shuddered, That's it, it's there, it must have been there all along.

What, said Jack, you mean – all day?

Fin, like Baby, thought it was very funny.

Not Ca, Baby, he told her, passing her spoon back to her. Not Ca but Ra! It's a Rat! Say it – Rat!

Ra! Said Baby, and banged her spoon on the edge of the table.

No, said Fin, Ra – t!

Mummy had to call me and get me home, Tom said, laughing. She was in such a panic. You weren't even allowed to finish your tea.

She evacuated the room, Jack said, she was so fucking terrified.

But if Baby hadn't seen it, Fin pointed out then, none of us might have and then we'd have all just had to live with it in the house, perhaps for ever.

What crap, Jack said. Of course we wouldn't –

But I was looking at Fin. It was the first time in a long time that I'd heard him say her name like that, so easily.

It was pretty cool of her though, Fin said, still gazing at the new kittens. Wasn't it, Mum?

It was, I said. It was very clever of her, to see that tail poking out. She was – she was very observant.

She was, said Tom. But then babies see the world differently. I mean, they notice different things, don't they?

And I looked at him and didn't know whether he was thinking what I was thinking – that this was another of our family's stories, one of the stories that we told ourselves and would go on telling ourselves over and over for years and years. And though the memory of Baby pointing and smiling and throwing her tea on the table was for now as raw and hard as a punch in the solar plexus, still I was comforted by the fact that her name was so much a part of the story.

I hadn't thought about the rat in ages, Fin said then. I think part of me had forgotten and part of me hadn't.

Me too, I said.

It will be the same when we talk about tonight, I thought. We'll look back and we'll say, do you remember the night when we thought Lex was only a little bit pregnant – and then suddenly the kittens were born? Only this story won't include Baby, nor the one after. I thought this thought and then I looked at Tom and felt tears beginning to come, so I turned my head quickly so that no one would see.

By the time the last kitten emerged – Ginger! Look! whispered Fin – Jack had given up and gone back to bed, Tom was almost asleep in Fin's bed and I was in the armchair.

It's almost three in the morning, I muttered to Tom. That has to be the last one, surely?

Only Fin was still lively, though his eyes were huge with tiredness. He watched as Lex fed her kittens on the stained duvet, purring loudly, eyes tight shut, belly exposed.

You know what I just thought? he said.

No, I yawned, what did you just think?

After all that, she never even used the box we made.

By the time we actually got back into bed, it was three fifteen. Our house was full of cats and the world outside was black and cold. I thought Tom would turn away from me to go to sleep, but he didn't, instead he pulled me to him, kissed my head and neck, pulled up my nightie and brushed my nipples with his fingers.

I love you, he said, as if it was a thing out of his control.

I love you too.

You're a crazy woman, you know that?

I said nothing.

But you made some nice kids.

You like them?

They'll do for now.

I tried to settle against him, but he turned and kissed me again, long, on the mouth. He tasted nice. I'd forgotten how nice he tasted.

There's too many cats in this house, he told me as he touched me between the legs.

I know, I whispered as I moved my thighs slightly apart to let him. I know and I'm sorry.

All those hearts, he said, all beating away upstairs.

Six, I said, no, seven.

That's right, he said, seven beating hearts.

Animal hearts, I said, thinking of our boys deep in sleep, surrendered, in their beds.

He slid his fingers into me and I took a breath.

Don't hate me, he said, as if it was him who needed to be forgiven.

I don't hate you, I told him, confused. How could you ever think that?

He didn't answer and after all, I thought, why should he?

We made love slowly and carefully, as if there was a thing between us made of a substance so fragile it could have crumbled at any moment. Which, in a way, there was. I didn't know if it was our lost baby girl, or just the complicated structure of our lives and pasts, but it was there between us all the time, hopeless, unmoveable, brittle as glass.

At first I didn't think I could be even slightly aroused, but it seemed to me also that this didn't especially matter, that what mattered now was to go along with Tom, to go to wherever he wanted to go, to follow him in the warmth of our old sad bed and see what happened. The feelings were no different, really, from the old feelings – the years and years of using our bodies to please and comfort each other – but it was nice that he went a little more slowly this time and I supposed it was also nice that when he went inside me I discovered I did want him there a little more urgently than I'd thought I did.

I gasped as I widened to let him inside.

That's right, he said, and he smoothed the hair off my face and I felt him looking right in my eyes, something he never used to do.

As I started to come, it took me by surprise – a long, low ache that began in my feet and shuddered its zigzag way through the centre of me, through the centre of my body. My calm centre. My calm center.

Quickly I banish you from my head, I push all thoughts of anything else away and as I come it feels like I scatter parts of myself all over the room, the bed, everywhere. I don't cry, I don't feel anything bad at all. For the first time in a long time, too, I don't think of Mary.

We lie breathing in each other's arms and I hear the strange electric whirr of the milk van far away down the street.

Already? I say. He starts early.

Shh, says Tom, blindly patting my hair with his hand as if he could make me go to sleep that way.

It's funny, I whisper, what orgasm does.

Tom says nothing. I hear his breath on the pillow.

Don't you think? I say.

He makes a low noise and his half-asleep hand pats my head again.

I mean, I say, when I've come it's like instead of life being vertical and jagged, suddenly instead it's smooth and horizontal. I'm just moving along on this fast horizontal line . . .

I hear Tom's breath deepen.

And the line is so smooth and straight and long that really it should be easy to drop straight off to sleep, right off, just like that. But the problem –

I shift my weight a little against Tom.

The problem is, I'm moving so fast along this line that it's quite easy to just slip off, kind of at an angle, up or down. And that's when I tend to wake myself up – do you get that too?

Tom is silent and his breathing has changed again.

I wish I could do what you do, I whisper. Just disappear after sex.

His mouth opens a little as he breathes harder. I put my lips close to his. His breath smells clean and sweet like a child's breath.

I don't expect you have a clue about what I'm saying, do you? I say to him. It means nothing, what I've just said?

I kiss his shoulder and I listen to the milk van come closer and eventually I hear it – the clink of three glass bottles put down on the step.

PARIS AGAIN

This time we do everything differently. This time it's not our anniversary and we don't take the Eurostar, this time we fly. I don't like flying much, but to take my mind off it, I have my expensive French copy of *Elle*, bought at the airport.

Tom likes to tease me about my magazines, but he also likes to watch me read them.

You won't improve your French by looking at the pictures, he says now, swiping it from my hands as I flick through its shiny pages.

I have more French than you, I tell him, grabbing it back, and it's true, I do. There are plenty of things I do better than Tom and one of the worst things I ever did to us was to pretend there weren't.

Tom does a mock sigh and, as the tone of the engine

changes and the interior of the plane starts to creak and I glance anxiously out at the long white gleam of its wing, he puts his chin on my shoulder and looks at the fashion pictures. An impossibly young woman in a white broderie anglaise pinafore-style sun dress is sitting in bright sunshine and spooning raspberries into the mouths of two beautiful toddlers.

No way are those her children, Tom says. I mean, how old would you say she is – fifteen? Sixteen?

She could be twenty, I say. She could have had them at eighteen. Or she might be the nanny. Or their older sister?

OK, he says, but whoever she is, she's not going to stand a chance dressed like that. There's going to be one almighty mess down that frock in a minute.

Mary's stained T-shirt flashes through my mind. The juice of berries – the way it pales a little in the wash but remains there for ever.

Tears before bedtime, I agree, quickly turning the page.

Yeah, he says idly, as the equally impossibly young stewardesses strap themselves into their seats for take-off. Tears before bedtime, definitely.

I tug quickly at my belt to check it's fastened. The plane starts to move along and the sound changes. Tom squeezes my hand and I squeeze back.

You're fine, he says.

I know, I say, and I try to smile.

Before I met Tom, when I was young, when I wore dungarees and plastic jewellery, I flew without a single thought for what I was doing. Willingly, I put myself in other people's hands. I let my body be pulled up through the skies, through the clouds, above this fat dark earth, and I just shut my eyes and slept and dreamed of the places I would go. My life rolled out before me and I knew I needed to cover a lot of ground fast if I was going to see it all.

Then when I had Jack, it all changed. The first time I flew away from him – for what was supposed to be a long and romantic weekend in Dublin with Tom – it suddenly dawned on me what I was doing: standing in a metal box, balanced in thin air, my baby left far behind me, a small dark speck swallowed up by distance on the cold earth below.

I panicked. The world tilted and so did the plane. I dropped to my hands and knees on the floor and clung on. I smelled brown carpet and saw the crumbs dropped under people's seats. Tom – startled and worried – begged me to get back in my seat and fasten my belt. I begged any god who was listening to take me back down to earth.

The stewardess had to give me brandy. Other passengers gazed at me with sympathetic but embarrassed eyes.

For a year or so after that I didn't fly at all. But when Fin was small, Tom persuaded me that staying at ground level for ever and ever wasn't an option, not really, and for the sake of our kids more than anything, I started again. So we all got on a plane together and flew through the frozen blue air to Greece – and I discovered that with my children on board, I could be brave. If my heart beat fast, I just smiled harder and spoke more slowly and brightly. I even managed to eat the airline food. We flew to Italy, all five of us, when Mary was about four months old. They gave us a special pull-out cot for her and she slept the whole journey. I almost enjoyed it. I began to think we might all be safe up there in the sky. As it turned out, in the sky, we were.

Once the plane is airborne and I've stopped clenching so hard onto his hand, Tom closes his eyes and reclines his seat a little. It's cold, the air-conditioned chill you only get on planes, the soft bland coldness that seems to come from all around you but never gets right inside your bones.

I shiver and try to read my magazine, but now and then I snatch glances at Tom. With his smooth skin and dark lashes, he too looks impossibly young – he could almost be Jack asleep. His faded navy holiday T-shirt is clean but not ironed and his arms are covered in goose pimples, a mass of tiny bumps, each small hair on his forearms sticking up.

He sighs deeply and his mouth relaxes. I can see the wetness begin on his lower lip. I can't imagine how anyone could possibly sleep on a plane, but the sight of him like this – asleep and goose-pimpled and oblivious – fills me with tenderness.

I watch him for a long time.

This time the hotel we stay in couldn't be more different from the blush-pink techno sophistication of the first one. It's a small white old-fashioned place which we found in the *Charming and Affordable Small Hotels in Paris* guide – chipped blue-and-brown tiled floors, simple worn rugs, an old fat lady eating something behind the desk. But it's clean and sweet and everything works. Tom thanks god for the lack of gadgets, while I hang my three dresses up in the old walnut wardrobe.

He flops down on the clean white bed which is quite small, barely even a double, while I walk across the room and throw open the shutters. Light spills in. It's almost warm outside – early April, cold one day, hot the next, everything shrill and green and sappy, determined to burst into bud. On a branch outside, a solitary bird is singing, a city bird. If I lean right out, I can just see him, yellow feet curled around the branch, brown head cocked.

Tell him to please for fuck's sake sing something else, Tom says, but his voice is loose and happy and I notice that he hasn't zapped on the TV for once. Then I realise there isn't a TV.

I look at the bird and the bird looks back at me.

It's the only one he knows, I say, and I know Tom will be smiling, and I realise it's the fact I can rely on it that's nice.

Come here, he says, and I do, I go and lie on the bed with him and we don't do sex or kissing, we don't do anything really, we just lie there together, my head in the crook of his arm, my hand on his belly, and we watch the whitewashed walls with the cracked plaster in the corner and the picture of the Virgin and Child on them, and I don't know what Tom's thinking, I've no idea, but I know that I'm trying not to think. I'm trying hard to forget how very far we've come.

Sometimes now, sometimes still, I am afraid to be alone because of exactly that, because of how much I am inclined to think. I don't want, any more, to wander these streets alone, for fear that I'll suddenly be forced too close up to my thoughts or, worse, that I'll run right into them – or you – that I'll collide with whatever lies out there, beyond the newly quiet safety of this life of mine.

Tom suggests I go out and look at the shops. He's feeling

lazy, happy. I stand on the threadbare carpet of the small bedroom and hesitate and look across at him. Can he really have forgotten the last time he suggested this?

I'd far rather go with you, I say quickly.

He yawns and looks at his watch. I can see he's torn.

I need a bath.

Have one. I'll wait. Let's go together. Please, Tom. It's no fun shopping alone.

So I lie on the bed and try to decipher an article about shoes in French *Elle* while he lies in the large but old-fashioned bath with claw feet and talks to me through the open door. Now and then I read a difficult word out to him and we try to remember what it means. I usually let Tom get it first. It means a lot to him, to know things. When he gets out and dries himself, I watch with pleasure as he chooses a fresh shirt, as he buttons it, as he pulls on socks and ties the laces on his shoes.

You look like Jack, I tell him.

Like Jack?

Yeah. When he first learnt to do laces, he used to make a mouth just like that.

He grabs my hair and pulls me to him and I feel his lips on my forehead.

I'm glad, he begins, and then he looks at me and stops.

Glad?

That – you wanted to wait, so I could go with you.

I give him a steady look. I think how much I love his face.

It's important, I tell him, and for once I know it's the truth. It just – suddenly felt important.

It is, he says. It's the right thing. For you and me –

299

To be together?

And he smiles as if I've said an obvious thing, but it doesn't matter because the smile says yes.

And I want to say it back to him – I want to say yes, my love, yes it is. But I don't – probably because it's all there already, all the unspoken things are lodged there waiting in the gaps between the things we say and the things we don't. I don't have to tell him what I'm afraid of because he already knows. And if there are gaps, then fine. It's just I'm not sure I want to have to fill them without Tom.

And so we go together, we wander down the busy, blossomy streets and we look in windows, we buy various little presents for the boys – a tiny black radio with earphones for Jack, a green and yellow nylon football shirt for Fin, chocolate pastilles for both of them and – best of all – a bright pink fake-fur cat bed. Tom says he's never seen anything quite so hideous.

We bought you a present, I tell Fin on the phone as we sit in a crowded afternoon café and Tom sips a café au lait and I take stabs at his cream cake with his fork. Well it's not for you personally, it's for Star. Something she'll like a lot. You have to guess what it is.

Fin gasps and I scoop some cream off the doily and onto the fork. Tom grabs my wrist and forces the fork into his own mouth.

For – Star?

Yes, I say as I give Tom back his fork. Yes, for Star.

Does that mean – I hear Fin catch his breath and whisper something to Jack – is that your way of saying I can – keep her?

I laugh and tell him yes, that we've talked about it

seriously, Tom and me, and though we'd meant it when we said we should find homes for all the kittens, we know he and Star have a special thing going, so he should probably keep her.

I swear I'll do everything, says Fin. All the feeding and the grooming and all of it, I swear.

You'll live to regret that, Tom tells me as he forks the last of his cake into my mouth. And he's right of course, which is why it's funny. This is what I think as the final blob of cream melts on my tongue.

Later, in a cranky old-fashioned red-velvet restaurant in the Marais, we eat lemon sole and drink champagne. Tom has half a dozen oysters to start, and wants me to try one but I won't. I just can't bear the way they breathe and crinkle, wet and grey in their shells.

I should have made you have the ravioli stuffed with snails, says Tom.

The waitress puts an old grease-spattered candlestick on the table and I slide my wrap from my shoulders and feel a little sigh of pleasure all over. Shadows creep up the walls. You can smell French cooking – blackened pots and warm red wine and something cooked in goose fat.

Mmm, I like this place, I say as Tom squeezes lemon juice on one of the poor creatures and I have to look quickly away.

Apart from the food, he says.

Don't be silly, I like the food. I like it all.

Well – and you're famously hard to please, he agrees, and looks up for a second, oyster in hand, and smiles at me and I think how much I like the look of his face doing that, liking me, approving of me.

No, I tell him, I like it because it's slightly shabby but it's real. Look, you can see they're all French in here, no tourists, no Japanese or Americans, not a single one, and –

Immediately, a shadow crosses his face.

And?

Nothing. Just – you know, the touristy places. Even the ones that are just a little bit touristy. I can't bear them.

Yeah, he says flatly, and I try to smile and forget I said that word. American.

We did well, I tell him, or you did well – to find us this one.

He looks down at his plate.

I just looked in the guide, he says.

I remind him of the holiday with the kids when they were small – was it Crete or was it Rome? – where all the restaurants had menus with full-colour photographs of English food. We were nearly going crazy, just trying to find a restaurant that served local food.

He makes a face.

Oh my god, he says. Full English breakfast.

And though he tries to laugh and I reach across to touch his hand and he lifts mine and kisses it, presses his lips on the tips of my fingers, still he won't look at me, he can't. It will always be like this, I think. There will always be things I cannot, should not, say. I will always, all my life with him, have to be on guard about – the words I use. And it's me, I did this to us. This is the endless residue of it, the thing that I did.

Later that night, in the middle of the warmish April

night, when the sex and chat are done and Tom is asleep, I try so hard not to be awake, really I do. All I want is to be able to do it, to go where he has gone, but I can't, it doesn't seem to work like that for me.

So I gaze at the grey moonlit wall for a while and soon, sure enough, my eyes are closing, but as I drift back to sleep, my thoughts do as they often do these days. They snap back into a pattern they remember. They arrange themselves, despite everything, around the shape of you.

Three weeks or maybe a month ago, I finally had an email from our mutual, distant friend, Simon Riley. He'd been asked to let me know, he said, about a reunion of our old university year that was going to be happening in a London pub. He wasn't organising it himself, he said, but he'd been asked to pass on the message.

He said there was supposed to be one every year but there hadn't been one last year as no one had got around to organising it. However, as the years passed, more and more people seemed to want to meet up. A middle-aged thing, he said. So he gave me the address and date and time and said I must please try and come, that he would love to see me again and have a chance to catch up, as would many others, he was sure.

He named some of the names that he knew had said for a fact would be turning up and I recognised one or two, though none of them were people who I'd been particular friends with.

I emailed back and thanked him and said I'd try and make it, though I already knew I was unlikely to want to when the time came. And then, to be polite and because I remembered he was a nice enough guy, I asked him how things were with him, and he said good – that his photography business was doing OK and he'd just got married for the second time, to a nurse, and a baby was on the way, his first.

I'm enjoying the last gasp of freedom before the sleepless nights kick in, he wrote. He asked me how my kids were – last time we'd corresponded, I think Fin had been about three.

Fine, I wrote. Teenagers now. Huge, loud, difficult, poisonous.

I hesitated, then I realised there was really no need to tell him about Mary.

Well Rosy, I envy you, he wrote back a day later. You had yours young. That's the way to do it. Get all the baby stuff over with so you can be free. You wouldn't believe how many people I'm in touch with from our year – mostly the blokes, admittedly – who are only just on their first kid, like me, would you believe it? Early forties and we're all just beginning.

Who, for instance? I asked him – and he mentioned a couple of names I thought I vaguely remembered, though however hard I thought about it, I couldn't quite bring their faces to mind. I'd heard that one had gone into advertising and another had made video films for a while. The most surprising was the one who'd always been completely out of it and had more or less failed his degree – a friend of yours I think – who'd made a lot of money in the City, retired at forty, and set up a school for kids in Mozambique.

Because we were on the subject, I asked him then, as casually as I could, if he'd heard from you lately.

The reply came straight back within seconds.

Oh fuck, I don't believe it. I thought – so that means you haven't heard? About what happened to him?

In a way, it wasn't a surprise or a shock, not at all. In a way, baby, I did know, I knew, I think a part of me had always known.

So when I read the next few lines of Simon's email – the lines that told me about the crash that had taken place somewhere outside Oregon, about the drunken driver (just a kid, no older than your son) who'd also died, about how the car had burst into flames and burned for so long that it had taken them a while to identify you and to let your poor boy and your ex know – well, I didn't weep or shake or go dizzy with shock, no, I just went very still inside. Still and quiet. My head felt like a blade had just passed through it, a clean sharp blade dividing my head in two, but my body was calm, I swear that my body was still.

Christ, but I'm sorry Rosy, Simon wrote. To be the one to tell you. What I mean is, I really thought you'd have heard, I thought you knew.

When? I wrote back. Please. I'm sorry. Just, if you can, tell me when?

January, Simon wrote back. Mid or late January, in fact the last week of January I know it was because – and I hope this doesn't make it worse for you Rosy – but you see I only got to know about all of this because he had plans to come over. He'd written to me just a week or so before and said he'd often wondered what happened to you, so I'd given him your email address just – well, but that was literally a day or so before so – I doubt he ever had a chance to get in touch?

I sat for a long time after I read this. I just gazed and gazed at my screen, at its squareness and its dumbness. I sat there and I could hear the boiler clicking noisily on and off and some builders working in a house down the street with a too loud radio that played stupid disco songs. Three or four gardens away, I could hear a child calling and calling even though it was clear the parent was not going to answer.

And I thought about you – your hands on me – the bright warmth and surprising urgency of a connection that I'd taken for granted so long ago, only to discover that it was after all unique, that such a feeling was unique and would not come again, not in this life anyway.

And I thought about the pearls, the ones you gave me, safe in their wrapper in my desk drawer – a place where no one would ever think to look and where, even if they ever did, such a small strange item would not necessarily need to be explained – and I wondered if I should check to see if they were still there, if they'd ever been there.

I decided not to. I decided I'd wait and do it another time, when I felt stronger and when it might matter less. And then I thought of the other pearls, the plastic ones, scattered on a carpet in a freezing January that belonged in another world long ago. They were real, I told myself, those ones were real – and the certainty I felt about that almost made me smile.

I almost wrote you an email then, just to see what would happen – just to see if I could somehow make it reach you, just to see whether it would at least do me the favour of settling somewhere in the great wide unknown of cyberspace and time, instead of coming bouncing back again to hurt me. I nearly did it, but in the end I didn't, I decided to spare myself.

But you know, baby, I lied when I said I didn't gasp or cry. I did, I did. I wasn't still or calm at all. I was in pieces. I wept and sobbed for about half an hour, and then I wiped my face and held myself, I hugged myself hard to make me stop.

Hush, stop, wait.

Then I sat at my desk and looked at my old poems, the sad and flimsy and ridiculous things I'd written in the last year or so, and I wondered if I'd ever go back to any of them and I thought probably not.

Then I drew a line under everything I'd written so far, and under that, I wrote **THE STORY OF YOU.**

LONDON

Spring turns to summer and the weather is bright and warm. Fin is glad. He loves it. It's boy weather. No coat weather, he calls it, and he stays out even on school nights, till the dusk falls, playing football on the Common with his friends. He comes home tired, sweaty, hectic-cheeked and glittery-eyed and does his homework with some reluctance and with Star curled upside down on his lap.

Jack is so big he towers over me. His voice is so deep that I sometimes jump when he comes into the room. He still doesn't have a girlfriend but there's a girl down the street who rings him up all the time.

Why does she always phone when she could so easily just drop round? I ask him, and he looks at me as if I'd just walked off another planet.

Phoning's what you do, Tom says. That or text or email.

Don't you realise, Nic? You can reinvent yourself that way –
be anyone you want to be. It's far too much of a challenge
to start relationships off face to face.

And Jack rolls his eyes because he thinks this is just
another of Tom's regular criticisms of his generation, but
I know better, I know it's really a gentle criticism of me.

I think that Tom and I are happy now – our family feels
happy – most days I am perfectly happy, as long as I don't
try to stop and question that happiness too much. Too
much thinking. It took me a long time to understand how
hard and deeply I loved and needed Tom, but I did, I do.
In the end it's entirely in your own hands – it's what you
decide to let yourself feel that matters. It's how much love
you decide to give, not what you spend time imagining
you ought to get back. I think I believe this, certainly I
try to. I do believe I hurt him deeply and, though I don't
think I could have done otherwise, not at the time, still
I'm so very sorry for that, I'm sorry it has to be a hard
fact lodged between us for ever like that in our mutual
past.

He asked me the other day whether, if his vasectomy
could be reversed, I'd like to try for another baby.

I was incredibly shocked that he was even having the
thought.

But – I'm way too old, I told him straightaway, and he
looked at me with surprise.

Don't be silly, he said, and he reached over and tweaked
my ponytail. It's nothing. Plenty of women have babies at
your age or even older.

I thought about it for a few moments – seconds really

– and I realised that the feelings that washed over me were not quite what I expected or wanted to feel.

I don't want another baby, I told him as gently as I could. I don't think we do. But thank you for saying it.

He looked almost disappointed and maybe I should have continued the conversation a little further. Maybe I should have tried to be more surprised and tender, or told him how much I loved him, but I didn't, I couldn't, not then. Just at that moment it wasn't what I felt I wanted to do.

Because some days I can almost believe she is still here among us, her spirit or her soul or whatever you want to call it. The part of her that lasts, that will go on for ever. I swear I'm not morbid, I don't spend too much time thinking of her, but now and then I catch myself relaxing, softening, and it's as if I've forgotten for a perfect little second that her death ever happened, as if I've papered over the actual cracks of the loss and it's that cold Sunday morning all over again and the snow is still falling and all is quiet and all is well and none of it has happened yet.

Second chances.

It always takes me by surprise, when I feel that, when that happens.

And now and then, just occasionally, you too, you still take me by surprise. I'll be going along fine, or at least I'll think I am, and then something will happen to change it – it could be anything, a sweet blur of song, a snatch of unlikely colour, the clean sharpness of a peeled apple, the back of a stranger's head, the way the sky bends over itself on a freezing afternoon – and I'll be pulled straight back to another time, to the feeling of your arms around me, your hands and your face close to mine, and I'll stand frozen for a moment, paralysed, unable to go forwards or back.

Smiles, kiddo.

I wish I could weep at these moments, but mostly I can't. Mostly I just have to wait for them to pass. They always have, they always do.

I like to imagine things that may never happen. I like to imagine that I might get a chance one day to ask you, baby, why it had to be like this, why you had to come and find me and make me love you so very hard and then why you had to hurt us both, why you had to go?

I like to tell myself I'll have you sitting there, right there in front of me, and you'll have no choice now but to give me all the answers, that you won't be allowed to go until you've made it all come clear for me.

And I like to think that it will go like this: that you'll touch my hair or my lips or the place on my cheek where the hot sad tears are already falling, and you'll say, Rosy, don't you know that hearts are the last wild bits of us? – as if that explains it, as if that is all a person ever needs to know.

And I like to think that I'll perhaps nod wisely as if I know what you mean, as if I understand you perfectly, even though I don't, not at all, not really. I like to think that I'll at least give you the impression that all is well, that it is good, that nothing was wasted, that – though I'm melting and grieving inside – still, the wildness and the sadness make some sense to me.

*   *   *

Am I still in love with you? Was I ever? Was it real? Is it still?

The answer isn't simple. I love Tom, I love my children, I love this family we made. But there's a thread, a fine, elastic thread, that holds me to you somehow. And right now it's pretty slack and that's just fine, I hope it stays that way. But tug on it even a very little and I'm afraid that I could fall again, over and over, would fall and keep on falling, down, down, down, would always fall, if you let me.

Because it's not the story, it's the way that I tell it, the way I'll keep on telling it for as long as I want to. But then you know that really don't you, baby? Even though you're not here any more, even though you seem to be gone, still you know the shape of the story. It's the story of you and it stretches both ways, into past and future, and it begins right here and now, with snow.